GH00832346

THE
GARDEN OF
THE PEACOCKS

THE
GARDEN OF
THE PEACOCKS

Anthony Weller

MARLOWE & COMPANY
NEW YORK

First Edition

Published by
Marlowe & Company
632 Broadway, Seventh Floor
New York, NY 10012

Grateful acknowlegment is made to The Jargon Society, Inc. for permission to reprint an excerpt from "San Vitale: 1970" by Peyton Houston. Copyright © 1980 by Peyton Houston.

Manufactured in the United States of America.

Library of Congress Cataloguing-in Publication Data

Weller, Anthony, 1957-
    The garden of the peacocks / by Anthony Weller. — 1st ed.
        p.   cm.
    ISBN 1-56924-763-3 (alk. paper)
    I. Title.
PS3573.E4569G37 1996
813'.54—dc20   963087
                                                                    CIP

In loving memory

Julián Orbón
(1925–1991)

Rey de la Torre
(1917–1994)

Rod Marriott
(1938–1990)

strong hands I was privileged to grasp

What shape and color is this
That we so impossibly dream?
Soul, that perceiver within,
Must work in the things that seem:
Once they saw it a peacock—
Ravenna has that wall...
Built when the world was falling,
It is an illusion, of course.
The peacocks make a design,
It stretches from world to heaven,
And all the feathers have eyes.

Peyton Houston,
from "San Vitale: 1970"

THE
GARDEN OF
THE PEACOCKS

1

A BREEZE BLEW THE SCENT OF WILD limes across the island and out to sea. Along the coast another wind, fresh with morning, shifted landward to stir the palms. A flock of man-o'-war birds went scattering above the beach and were soon lost among the trees. The tide was on its way out, and the castaway seaweed at the high-water mark lay gaunt from an hour in the swarming heat. A mile offshore, white water settled heavily within the great arms of the reef.

Two mating swallows broke in a commotion, traversed the open sand, and were gone in beaten silence behind the palms.

From the water's edge a tiny land crab scuttled along inspecting the abandoned debris of high tide—the usual array of shells, and bits of bottle-glass smoothed by the ocean, and a lensless pair of rusted wire spectacles. Beside them, already bleaching in the sun, lay the battered skeleton of a large fish that would disintegrate with the next tide.

Also, nearby, the body of a man. Sprawled face-down, toes toward the sea. As if he had been running from it and collapsed in the first instant of safety.

The crab approached the body cautiously. It wandered slowly alongside, gently brushing the worn khaki on the man's thighs and the softer cotton on his back before finally

1

daring to climb up his wrist and onto the bare flesh of one splayed arm. At the elbow the crab paused, searching for something to eat. The body didn't budge. The crab clambered over the folds of the old T-shirt and tentatively up the neck. It lingered a moment, measuring the pulse, then fussily ventured the white tangle of hair. Several strands got tugged out by the pincers as the crab descended along one ear to the beach.

From the island's interior the air was pierced with a cry that was answered by another, severely keening, then by many more. They came in long squalls of frustration and rage, shattering the morning.

A black man came down a path through the palms. He walked with a mild limp, as if there were a pebble in one of his tattered sneakers. He had lean, knotted arms and a slightly protuberant belly, and he wore a fisherman's big-billed cap. At the edge of the palms, beneath an arch of ruined stone, he hitched up his black shorts, dotted with paint speckles and fish-blood stains, and tucked in his red T-shirt. He pulled the cap lower against the sun and furrowed his gaze, scanning the beach. When he lit upon the sprawled figure of the old man—not so much older than he—he let out an emphatic bark, shook his head and loped back into the palms.

Gradually the steady murmurs of the awakening island roused the old man. His head burned inside and his back felt as if someone had been pounding it. He raised his chin off the sand and let his eyes take in the beach. The palms looked like ruffled parrots spreading green feathers in the breeze.

Dazed from the effort of lifting his head, he put his chin back on the sand and closed his eyes. Small blotched figures squirmed across his vision; their frenzied movements startled him. He managed to roll painfully onto his back and look up. The sun blazed harshly down on him like the incandescent eye of God. He tried to prop himself on his elbows.

Reluctantly he squinted at the ocean, its pale surface chattering with quick light. On the bluer horizon the smudge of a tiny cay shimmered like a mirage.

One more, he thought.

He got gingerly to his feet. The wet sand sucked at his bare toes. With irritation he brushed the grit from his face, winced and licked his lips. In the heat of the morning, encumbered by sleep, his body felt dehydrated and weary.

He staggered slowly into the water. When it came to the edge of his shorts he bent down and splashed his face and neck. The sting, the saline tang, fully awakened him.

One more day. One more day and it will all be over.

His body stiffened as the air was battered by a catastrophe of screams from somewhere in the palms. He saw himself suddenly from above, an old man made absurd by the easy beauty of this deserted beach, standing knee-deep in this miraculous water. He was tanned to animal hide, his face broad and his forehead high beneath wild white hair, white eyebrows like clouds spanning green territorial eyes, his ears undulant as banana leaves, his jaw bluntly leonine. He had been sleeping out here for a week, but other mornings he'd awakened earlier, soon after dawn—the sea gentle, the sky a delicate pink and amber. Silken daybreaks: to him they conjured lost princesses.

The black man came out of the palms again, carrying a rusted thermos. He regarded the old man's back sourly.

"You have coffee with you, I can smell it."

The black man snorted. "Ain't you the Einstein with the nose."

He watched the old man come out of the water like a wading bird, contemplating where to put each foot. The black man stayed where he was, in shade. He opened the thermos, and when the old man came up the beach, he said amiably, "You look terrible."

"Good."

"Ridiculous how you behave. Sleeping out here like some old fool. Pretending some stupid Robinson Crusoe thing. Birds shitting all over your back."

"Why shouldn't they?"

"All over the top you head as well. Looks like eggs frying."

"Pour the coffee, Scully."

The black man kept talking. "Weather report smooth out of Nassau, in case you interested. Clear right through Christmas. Wouldn't mind being there myself. Still, can't leave old Einstein in the lurch, fend for himself. Old fool get carried out by the tide and next thing you know he back in Cuba, eh? Causing trouble and whatnot. No way, man."

The old man gave a little laugh. He drained the cup and held it out to be refilled.

"You laugh all you want, man. Still ridiculous how you behave."

"Probably you're right."

The old man thought: Soon she will be touching down in Nassau. The plane giving up its tourists. She among them. Soon.

He imagined her changed after three years, her beauty charged, more defined at twenty-eight. She would still have her mother's straight gaze, her decisive mouth. In her brown hair and green eyes a curious reminder of himself when young. And in her body's long shape an exact echo of her mother. Voice he kept imagining he would hear again.

The weather report was unalloyed good news. The Caribbean played unpredictable this time of year, storms like pent-up bursts of ill temper. Three clear days could be read as a good omen, a promise. For an instant he felt a faint prick of ice around his heart, felt it dissolve as he swallowed coffee.

Look at this outcast light, he thought. All these years I gloried in it, let it bring me back to life, while you remained immune. If only you had let its direct gaze convince you.

Scully said, "No way to treat a daughter. You think I don't know what's in these daft letters you sending? Think I can't read between the lines, man? Lie to she, make she do what you want? Man like you, Einstein. Some kind of disgrace."

With the cast of his eyes and mouth he spurned the old man, the beach, the generous ocean and all mendacious correspondence.

"You read my mail?"

"Read you mind, man."

"In what way have I lied to her?"

Scully spat at the tidemark. "Telling she you dying practically tomorrow."

Tomorrow, when she's rested, I'll show Esther all I have done here. What I have finished. And if that doesn't reach her, nothing will. Not a week's growth of beard nor sleeping on this beach like a shipwrecked sailor. Scully's right. I am ridiculous.

He said, "You know she wouldn't be coming out here if she thought I had another ten, fifteen years to go. She would say: Let him wait on his island."

If only I had not had to lie to reach this morning.

"She got to already know you can't wait here forever, man. Not even God content to hang around, eh? He got all eternity and He still ain't got the time."

A quarter-mile down the beach an old wooden boat, white paint peeling, leaned between two palms, her deck partly covered by a green tarpaulin. Dismasted, her spars lay in the sand, bound with stray lines. At her bow was painted in black letters MISS LINDA.

The old man said, "Pinder will bring her right away, yes?"

Before his unlimited eye the Caribbean flashed and danced.

"Maybe I take myself a vacation while she with you. Fix

that old sloop and see what doing up San Salvador way. This ain't a calm profession, man. Come down here every morning to find out if you float out to sea."

"She expects me to look like I'm at death's door."

"You better step back, Einstein. One day it going to slam you in the face."

Bring her here from half a world away. Bring her to me and six years on this island will be justified. Give her a more sympathetic glance than the last time, give me a body which has not been nurtured by pure light and petalled water but damned, and needs her blessing. And bring her mother's gaze with her.

He set off down the beach, to where the palms broke. A breeze followed.

"Why you don't get cleaned up, eh? She here before you know it."

By now she is retrieving her bags, showing her passport, being met. Stepping into a smaller private plane. Its propellers begin to hum. Now Nassau is dwindling.

He heard Scully call but that didn't matter. The sky was widening. Soon there would be the drone of a dragonfly in it.

Now she is searching the crinkled ocean, expecting this island to appear.

He waited for all the angels inhabiting his dream to come to life, to descend from the sky and claim him.

2

WHEN THE FIRST ISLANDS CAME OVER the hazed rim of the blue world, the nagging of inner voices grew stronger. Her father was somewhere down there, waiting. Far below her, mists hung over tracts of wrinkled sea. The emerald shallows lay milky across sand bars, the sun dazzled the turning water.

I can't possibly face him again, she thought. It feels suicidal to have come even this far.

The interminable transatlantic flight to Nassau had been broken by near-waking, near-dreaming patches of listless sleep. Over the years she had proven too many times to herself that a visit would help neither of them, would only harm the uneasy truce, the healthy distance and silence that lay between them. Her father was dangerous: even from thousands of miles of ocean away, he had successfully pulled her in.

He had written her that he was dying.

Now memories that had eluded her for so long were returning. A Havana evening when she was six, a house where her mother went for a few yoga lessons with a strange man whose ancestors had come in a boat from India. (The words were her mother's.) Through the jalousies the waning light threw the bodies' hand-shadow patterns on the walls as Esther sat cross-legged, watching in absolute silence. An intimate breeze rustled the branches of palm and plum trees in the garden and whispered to her, a child hypnotized by the changing human shapes, until the house and its dreaming shadows became a secret power emanating across all Cuba and she drifted into a sleep, wondering where her father was.

Then her mother's lifting arms had awakened her.

She awakened as the plane descended over the ugly middle of the tourist island, all scrub brush, dirt, and tin roofs. Outside the plane the blast of heat singed her skin and squeezed her. She felt it burn away all the dry ambivalence of the last week. By the time she was through Nassau customs, her mind was made up.

The supply pilot, Henry Pinder, greeted her with a horsey grin. Three years earlier, he'd flown her out to Desirada and a few days later brought her back to Nassau when abruptly she decided to leave. Three years had made him bulkier.

"All ready for a vacation, missy? Look like you desperate for a tan."

Was she that pale? "I'm sorry you had to wait so long, Mr. Pinder."

"These Europe flights always late. We get there quick enough."

He was looking her over as if she were lunch.

"How long since you've seen my father?"

"Just last week, I guess."

As long as his illness existed only by mail it was not entirely real.

"How's his health?"

"Well, seem to me like he lose all his pep," said Pinder gravely. "Still, you never know. Maybe too much celebrating." He favored her with a wink. "On account his lovely daughter fly all the way over from Switzerland to visit, eh?"

He reached for her bags. Around them the shabby airport muttered and stirred with Bahamian chaos.

"You go on without me," she said.

"I can wait, no trouble. You want the ladies' room?"

"I've changed my mind."

He stared at her curiously, waiting for more.

She said, "I've decided I'm not going to see him."

"You not serious, missy."

"I'd appreciate it if you just said I wasn't on the plane."

He said incredulously, "You don't mean you come ten thousand miles and turn back the last ten steps. What you want me to tell your father, eh?"

"You can say my reservation was canceled back in Geneva. At the last minute."

Pinder snorted. "I can't tell the man that. I already radio out that your name on the passenger list. Buddy of mine check it for me here last night."

"Tell him I got off in London. I said I didn't feel well. That's all you know."

"Missy, I'm not going out today if you don't. I got to make a supply run in three days anyway."

"Then radio that neither one of us is coming."

He said with exasperation, "How you want me to explain that?"

"Tell him I'm ill."

"You want to tell him yourself, there's a radio here."

"If I wanted to talk to him I'd be going with you."

In the clamminess of the airport she really did feel ill.

"Missy, he expecting you for months."

She said, "He'll understand."

She was trembling, exhausted by her rudeness to Pinder, by his insistence. This was the moment to walk away, book a flight home for the afternoon, get her ticket altered. To leave as soon as possible—but that required a far greater will than she could marshal. Better to get a night's sleep and fly back overseas tomorrow.

"Can you help me find a taxi, Mr. Pinder?"

"I can probably find you a submarine, you want one bad enough. You got the right idea, missy. Find yourself a nice hotel, maybe get a little tan, we fly you out to the man tomorrow."

"I'm sorry to have wasted your time, Mr. Pinder."

"Okay, okay." Pinder shook his head. "What we going to do about your father?"

"Just say I wasn't on the plane. I'll write him from Geneva. He doesn't have to know I made it this far."

He fidgeted. "I can't stand there and lie to the man. After he tell me for two months now you arriving for Christmas. You think he won't know I seen you face to face?"

I promised nothing, she thought, only that I'd try to come. She said wearily, "Look, I'll write him a letter tonight. I'll get it to you tomorrow. I'll tell him you did your best. You won't have to explain anything."

How does he win so much loyalty from people? she thought.

Pinder grunted. "Your father a busy man, writing you all the time. Don't write no one else, you know."

They're loyal only because they don't know him. They're people with nothing to lose from knowing him.

"He's always been a very busy man," she said.

Blinded by the glare outside, watching her bags bundled into the back of a taxi, shaking hands automatically with Pinder, she felt the tropical heat stir more glimpses of Havana from twenty-two years ago, her sole visit to her father's birthplace. The drowsy tedium of afternoon on a breezeless balcony; all around her the florid geometry of baroque streets, and mingled scents of unknown plants, coffee, boiling sugar, urine. She had stored the memories away like seashells in a drawer, shells whose fragility she hadn't understood at the time, thinking she could keep them intact forever. And now that all the colors had been sipped out by the covetous air, the years had left her with dried-out and faded trinkets from the ocean crumbling in her hand.

What startled her was that in every image of Cuba she could retrieve she was alone, or watching her mother as if in some darkened theater. She was never with her father in those memories, and it had been his island. The first of the invaluable possessions he'd lost.

The Nassau taxi took her to hotel after hotel along the coast, past spindly casuarina pines, spread fans of palmettos, and blue sea. Her taxi driver was content to wait, the meter clicking, while at the reception desks she received the same air-conditioned headshake and saw, through great windows, people bustling about on white sand with the hard glitter of ocean beyond.

In the end the taxi driver suggested a small hotel in town if she didn't mind walking to the beach. She didn't care about a beach. The afternoon was blazing, but her watch read eight P.M., Switzerland time. (A concert would be beginning back home; her favorite restaurant—the owner and his wife Sephardic Jews from Córdoba—would just be starting to fill. It was drizzling, with the faintest hint of snow to follow tomorrow.) She wanted only to sleep and then wake, remade, knowing she could leave.

The hotel was shaded and pink, a stucco seashell. She paid the driver and went up some stairs, past two plaster lions. Echoes of her father's marble gate, from years ago. The small lobby had cane chairs, a single cane table and sofa. As she was filling in the registration card, using her mother's maiden name as on her passport, a man came into the lobby from the street and asked for his key.

American, she thought.

He was in torn-up sneakers, loose trousers, and a blue shirt, and he had the kind of height that only Americans car-

ANTHONY WELLER

ried without self-consciousness. He looked too independent to be a tourist. His face was sunburned and rather angular, with some humor in it, but his eyes were gray, his stare guarded. His dark hair was pushed every which way, as if he hadn't slept well—nor had he shaved. But he had a careful mouth and the measured movements of someone who economized on effort. She noticed that he wore an expensive camera over his shoulder; one hand hid it automatically.

He gave her a slight smile. "Want a hand with those bags?"

"I think they're putting me just down the hall. But thank you."

"They can give you a better room than that. At least one with a view of the carnival." To the receptionist he said, "Don't you have a room higher up?"

"All those rooms taken."

"What about the room I looked at earlier? On the second floor."

"We expecting people all day long." The girl eyed the list of reservations dubiously. She frowned. She realized the man was still waiting. She sighed, unhooked a key and handed it over with reluctance. "I got to change everyone all around now."

Esther thought: He'll ask me to have dinner with him.

He picked up her bags, his camera shielded by one arm. "After you."

Halfway up the stairs, leading the way but with no sense of where she was going, she asked idly, "When's the carnival?"

"In two days," he said. "It'll start Christmas night, and go till morning. You'll get a good view."

"I'll be leaving tomorrow."

He set her bags down, one door in from the landing. "Too bad. It's a big celebration."

12

"I'm supposed to spend Christmas somewhere else."

He gave her a pardon-me smile and handed over her key. He said, "Well, have a good holiday."

He was headed up the stairs before she could thank him.

In her room the afternoon light came fiercely slitted through the blinds. She looked down the narrow street and watched the white people stroll along in sunglasses and the Bahamians slide anxiously past them, as if the two races were moving to different musics. In the bathroom mirror she looked pallid and worn. She ran a bath and lay in the steaming water, sweating the flight from her pores.

Is this how much your father's life is worth? Not even a visit every three years? Not even one last visit, after the labor of a lifetime?

She hated the imagined tenor of his voice.

From the terrace below her open window floated the voluptuous scent of a cigar—it triggered an image from childhood, of a humid bar and an enormous man encased in a dark suit, staring at her, a cigar clamped in one pudgy hand. The man's head was immense, black eyes stolid and penetrating, his mustachioed face Buddha-like with weird ancient wisdom. She remembered the enormous man joking with her, remembered his silken necktie; her feelings toward him were warm, not fearful, but she couldn't think who he was, place herself in the scene—a café in Havana perhaps. She tried to reason with the memory, but it was too far away, as strange as a borrowed photograph.

And the fellow on the terrace below had put out the cigar.

She shifted in the bath, trying to wash the tobacco scent from her body, her hair billowing behind her in the water. She felt waves of drowsiness approach and pass. She hauled herself out and toweled herself dry.

Even with the blinds closed the bedroom was bright. Sunlight flared at the edges of her brain. She lay down naked on the bed, the sheets cool on her skin. Her fatigue and the bath, the sense of real heat outside, had aroused her—as if a dense liqueur had invaded her bloodstream and was keeping her awake. All she wanted was to slip between those sheets and be pressed languorously down into a dreamless sleep.

She turned over and put her face in the pillow. Why not get up, pull open the desk for writing paper, write the letter? Leave on the next plane, be back in Geneva in her own apartment, her own bed tomorrow night—it would be snowing on the stone courtyard of her building, a wet wind off the lake howling at her balcony. She would lie awake hearing the prewar elevator trundle up and down with a clatter as people came back early from Christmas parties; the Swiss did not believe in staying out late. Surrounded by her books, the large portrait of her mother staring at her, she would wonder if she'd done the right thing and be too tired to consider the question until morning, when the ordinary scents of coffee and newspapers would assure her she had. That was all.

I'd better make the reservation now, she thought. I should've made it back at the airport.

She could not will herself to do anything. Did it matter if she wrote the letter? Her father would simply wait a suitable month, let her worry that she had struck him deeply, then write her once again, another letter as accusatory in its good humor as the last.

You will be interested to know I had one of the best Nassau lung specialists out here, under the strictest secrecy of course. A cancerous excuse for upping his fee. I diagnosed him right away as a drinker: a portly pink puffing man. He spoke knowledgeably of certain Havana blends while he examined your cigarillo of a father—from the butt upwards. Told me with the usual bedside manner that I am ready to go up in smoke. Holy smoke? I asked. When? Soon, he said.

Of course he can't know.

Still, if you could slip over for Christmas I would be grateful. Naturally I await your visit at any time but, it would seem, the sooner the better. There is much I should probably tell you before my coughs (like my devils and my humors) get the better of me. You know you are really in every sense the only person left in my life— you have always been the darling of my heart's hope. I count myself lucky to have finished my work with time to spare. It took longer than I imagined, but you really must see it to believe it. It's yours, after all.

They'd come for years now, the same imploring letters full of corny promises of secrets to be imparted, the same studied high spirits, the same gestures of fatherly affection, begging a visit but really demanding forgiveness—when it was her mother, years too late, he should have been begging.

She remembered the thunderous light along the coast from her only visit to Desirada. From the air the unfurling scrolls of surf on his beach of palms had seemed a fitting place for a journey's end. And she'd said to herself: Yes, this island is the right place for him to die, to give all that is left of himself. He'll be remembered for this place, for whatever it is he is making here.

She'd left early, after only a few days and many arguments. That was three years ago, and nothing in her life had moved as she expected it to move. She'd vowed never to come out here again, to stay completely out of her father's shadow; years before she'd even dropped his surname in favor of her mother's. She'd sworn she would not be pressured by him, not be fettered by the limited future he'd made for himself on that little island. Writing letters in silence was his future, and he'd chosen it deliberately.

ANTHONY WELLER

But he had written her that he was dying.

She felt something crumple within her as she realized what she'd wanted all those years was her father's death, and though she thought she had prepared herself for it, garnered enough bitterness to accept it in return for her mother's death over two decades ago, now she was not prepared to face it, to see him even one last time.

Easier to pretend that he was already gone. Easier to pretend there was nothing more to wait for.

She felt inadequate tears knife up inside her. She was sweating heavily and shivering. She needed to get out of the room, into a breeze outside. By now her father would've received the message that she wasn't coming. She swung her legs off the bed. Her bare toes stammered on the hard floor.

Somewhere miles to the south, she thought, he is walking angrily across acquiescent sand to where his ocean is still gathering sunlight. Swimming as he has swum every afternoon for six years and will swim for some little time more, perhaps. But not another afternoon with me, ever.

3

Earlier that day, for Thomas
Simmons the morning sea had lost all color, awash with
ultraviolet glare. At least he could finally make out the pink
houses of Nassau against the settled confusion of the coast.

He stood on the deck of the mail boat, feeling it crawl across
the sluggish water like an insect struggling through deep-piled
carpet. Beneath his feet the aged engines gargled and shook in
the rust-stained hull. They'd broken down five times in three
days, sending the Costa Rican mechanic diving frantically
below while the Bahamian mail boat crew made noises of
boredom, picked their teeth, and started drinking early.

Success has really spoiled these guys, thought Thomas. If
she breaks down now, we'll be lucky to drift into Nassau
next week. No wonder no one writes letters anymore.

Several nights ago on Inagua—a wild and barren island
hundreds of miles to the south—the moon had been so bright
above the vast salt lakes that he sat awake in his tent, watching the silhouettes of flamingos skim the shallow waters. He
tried some very long exposures by moonlight, the tripod
wedged into the mud. Eventually cloud banks like fantastic
wigs came out of the west and hid the moon. Without light
he could put the camera away, his work for *The Geographer*
virtually finished.

Early the next morning he hiked to the Inagua International Airport—a brief landing strip tufted with weeds, a concrete bunker at one end. Inside were a barking dog and an immense Bahamian woman reading a Bible, and a sign that read: WILL THE LAST PERSON TO LEAVE THE ISLAND PLEASE TURN OUT THE LIGHTS? A black telephone rang and rang, and by noon it was over a hundred degrees and the bunker was full of flies. Every few minutes the woman licked her thumb and methodically rustled on to the next page. Thomas took her portrait with the sign eloquent over her shoulder.

The plane from Nassau was delayed: a teenage boy materialized and said it would arrive at noon exactly. At five-thirty, when it was too dark for the plane to land, Thomas shouldered his bags. The woman assured him the plane would be there first thing in the morning.

"We got a new man in the Nassau Parley-ment," she said. "He see to it."

Thomas stumbled along a broken road toward the small settlement. Clouds swamped the moon. In a four-room hotel he ate badly and spent the night on a cot. At breakfast the girl who brought him coffee told him the plane was officially canceled that week, but the mail boat back to Nassau was due that afternoon. At the wharf he could see it still several hours away, a child's sketch on the horizon, spewing squiggly pipe-puffs of smoke.

Having done all he could and about to spend a good part of his Christmas vacation simply trying to leave Inagua, he could accept the situation with equanimity. What disturbed him was that this sort of thing was beginning to seem, at thirty-eight, a completely normal life, as inevitable as the solitude that went with it.

He was still troubled by his night in Nassau en route. The in-between places on the way to a magazine assignment always drained him; his nervousness about what lay ahead left him too anxious to enjoy the time. Not knowing Nassau, he'd put up in a once-fancy hotel, now on its last legs and attracting package tourists. He found himself at the bar with a couple of young secretaries from Minnesota. One woman, slightly frayed at the edges, sniffed a lot and didn't say much. He didn't catch her name.

The other attracted him, since he knew he was safely leaving for Inagua the following morning. A redhead, in five years she'd probably be plump, but at twenty-two she looked packed and strong, with a pleasant unpleasantness that reminded him of a Toulouse-Lautrec. Her name was Adele— an absurd spinsterish name, he thought. They drank and finally went for a walk on the beach; he was surprised when she swarmed all over him. After some grappling on the sand he suggested she come to his room. She refused modestly, then invited him to hers.

It'd been years since he'd gone to bed with someone so directly, so baldly, so briefly—especially someone with whom he wouldn't ever spend a single evening if there were the threat of a second. Once in her room her sheer aggressiveness, the brute force that took over her, made him feel out of his depth and no longer young. He'd never seen a woman strip herself like someone tearing off wallpaper. Even her body was curious, like the lumpen firm body of a woman from a nineteenth-century photograph. She wanted to be thrown from wall to wall, bulldozed and then paved over. Did her boyfriend demolish her like this every night?

At dawn, not having slept, aware he had to fly to Inagua and start work on the flamingos in a few hours, he'd staggered back to his room. Climbing into his own bed he could still smell her cheesy odor, as if her flesh had left a crust all over his body.

He'd arrived in Inagua exhausted, unprepared for the barren solitude of the place. It looked like somewhere left after the rest of the world had conveniently ended. Alone on the salt lakes—wading muckily through shallow and putrid water too hot to swim in, tugging his equipment behind him in an inflatable rubber raft, surrounded by thousands of birds whose flamboyance was like red fire on his mind after staring through a camera all day—he'd been assaulted by a sense that it was too late. Too late to stop traveling. Too late to achieve any work he'd feel like looking at a year afterward. Too late to make room for someone in his life.

And after a week of nothing but flamingos he felt too worn down to take the very photographs here that interested him—the half-deserted places, the Inaguas of the world, where no one was arriving and anyone with sense was trying to leave. There was unusual beauty on this hot road, this empty harbor waiting for the salamander time to pass, that ruin of a boat splashed with aquamarine light providing shade for someone's donkey on a beach of snow. It was an unadorned beauty, without pose or self-consciousness, a beauty that went its own way. There was less and less of it in the world.

It was always like this. He ended up in a place where a project of his own was possible, yet since he was living on someone else's time, all his energy got spent serving up their view of the world, arguably no less truthful than his own but simply not his own. He could nearly pinpoint the moment when his private work had ceased to exist; it hadn't been long after his brief marriage had gone awry. He'd become obsessed with moving from assignment to assignment, taking any offer that came his way. He hadn't said no to any work for years. Yes to this corporate propaganda, yes to that fashion propaganda, hallelujah to all travel propaganda. And the work that mattered never got done, seemed farther away; after so many years, almost alien to him.

Once he'd felt the whole world his subject—now it drew back more with each assignment, reducing itself out of range. He'd started young and gotten old very quickly. It was no coincidence that his best work had been done in his first seven or eight years at it. Something about photography restricted a more mature wisdom. It was a young man's art, too spontaneous to age well as a vision.

I am as dried out as a cactus, he thought.

In the full heat of noon the mail boat was plodding into Nassau. There was something ironic about it actually arriving. Tomorrow was Christmas Eve. Naturally there was another picture to be taken here to complete the story for the magazine. That would have to wait until the morning. At the wharf he thanked the taciturn captain and collected his bags.

Well, that ate three and a half days of life.

At least he could give himself a vacation here, if he didn't run into that secretary. And there was the carnival the day after Christmas. He would force himself to put his distrust aside for a week. He'd made reservations at a small hotel, right in town, that lay along the Junkanoo's route, where the dancers in loud, gigantic papier-mâché costumes would collect to light their torches. A better situation for photographs than the main avenue, which would surely be all crowd.

The hotel, of ageless pink stucco, had the staid, leisurely air of a boardinghouse. Two white plaster lions guarded the steps. Across the little street was a park set off by royal palms whose high fronds moved rhythmically. There was a terrace restaurant and behind the bar a pretty Bahamian girl, all pouting mouth and almond eyes, lolled on her elbows and sucked a slice of orange. Above her fans whirred dreamily.

The receptionist showed him rooms on the first two floors before he was satisfied with a room on the third, whose windows had an unobstructed view of the street and the little green park. Filled with Junkanoo purpose, he cranked up the air-conditioning, washed his face, loaded the camera, and went downstairs.

He wandered along Bay Street, breezeless and busy with fleshy sightseers at lunch hour. In enormous straw hats they were a kind of carnival unto themselves, and their presence gave Nassau a cut-rate phoniness. An army of local straw-hat women was encamped, sewing away, shouting, "Can I sell you something, darling?" Every third store sold T-shirts with foolish slogans, there couldn't possibly be enough cruise ships or airplanes bearing enough tourists, ever, to buy half those T-shirts and straw hats.

No surprising photographs here, he thought. I should've stayed on Inagua.

In a large store where he stopped to buy a postcard, he was dismayed to find upstairs in the book department a copy of his own book. It lay among the other expensive gift books, its price double what it went for in the States. *Earth's Returns: A Portrait of the Fading South.* It'd been published in the spring; this was the British edition, bound from the same printing. The publisher had agreed to let him supervise the final corrected pull in Japan, and a month afterward told him it was too late, already done. Fifteen years' wait to put out this travesty, while the real work was still sitting in the massive safe at his studio, growing old.

To his eye the thing looked terrible. He could no longer see any quality in the photographs, only a layout by turns too crowded or too empty, a second-rate color separation, and a mawkish text that the writer had fattened out of the original magazine article. The paper was expensive, at least.

He browsed through it, trying to see it afresh, like someone coming across it unexpectedly. *Ah,* they might say, *at last. A photo essay on the rural South.* Did anyone ever say that? Opening spread: twilight fields rheumy with mist, at their edge a wrecked barn with a ghostly white horse aglow.

Not a shred of intuition in that photograph, only technique. Then portraits of descendants of slaves and slave owners. Ruined plantations, their fields ruled by collapsing stone walls. "A broken past, fast vanishing." Text by a famous self-appointed pundit to the world. If you didn't look too hard the pictures held up, even the text held up if you didn't compare it to good writing.

At twenty-three he'd undertaken the same subject in black-and-white: the South of the last carpetbaggers, the ever-wandering dispossessed, the casual labor, the hobos. Two years' concentrated work as a young man: those pictures had made his name. Portfolios appeared in magazines everywhere, prints were in the permanent collections of forty museums, two galleries in Paris and London regularly sold for him overseas. No book had ever been published. One was always being planned, laid out, talked about over expensive lunches. Something always went wrong. The lethargic divorce five years ago, Barbara having written an accompanying text during the short time they were together, had wrapped the thing in legal red tape for far longer than their marriage.

Most oppressive of all, he felt those pictures still cluttering his imagination, as if his mental desk couldn't be cleared until they were published. At this point it was almost as if they'd been done by someone else, yet every personal project he attempted got filtered through their fate, measured against the purity of their vision. Coming across this book done to contract, this impostor, he saw how much the original vision had been sugarcoated by color, made suitably appetizing as he tried to copy himself.

He put the book down ruefully and was glancing through the British paperbacks on the wall when some instinct made him turn. A man older than he, with an indolent face, glamorously dressed for the tropics—probably one of Nassau's resident millionaires—was looking through the gift books.

He already had three cradled in his arms. He flipped through a book of fashion shots from the thirties and forties, then came to Thomas's book.

He set the others down and gave the masterpiece the attention it deserved. He flipped through the pages as rapidly as someone moving through a phone book. He paused here and there, but it took him perhaps half a minute. So much for the ruined South. He put the book back, grabbed the others, and headed for the cash register.

"Christmas emergency," he said to the clerk.

That's right, thought Thomas. Sensible man. Wait till mine's been remaindered and you can get them by the pound in Miami.

He remembered to buy a stamp for his postcard on the way out. Standing in the sunlight, sweating, his head was full of bees. He couldn't think of anyone he wanted to write to, only what he wanted to say. He scribbled *I quit*. How could he quit when he worked for himself? Freelancers couldn't quit. He addressed the card to his apartment in New York and dropped it in an old British Empire letter box on the corner.

And a Happy New Year, he thought.

Back at his hotel a taxi was just driving off. When he went up the stairs to the little lobby, the first thing he noticed in the spartan light was a pair of overnight bags. Then the young woman registering turned to glance at him, and it was all he could do to resist the impulse to lift his camera.

4

FIFTY YARDS FROM HIS BALCONY, drenched in palm shadows, a young Bahamian girl in a red frock was reading on the steps of the domed colonial library at the edge of the park. Just above her head green shutters were open. All the colors were delicate in afternoon light. Thomas took the picture and an instant later the woman he'd met downstairs an hour earlier strode into the eye of his camera lens.

She was in white now. Brown hair—still wet from a shower?—fell restlessly down her back. Via his long lens her look went through him, a stray indecision in her green eyes. But her face was resonant with defiance; as she turned he saw again the strength in her profile, pride in how she held her head.

She glanced toward the little girl, then pushed back her hair and let her hand linger, as if doubtful where she should go. There was warmth in her body's shape through the skirt and blouse, but the long line of her was strung tight as a bow. In their distracted conversation he'd sensed a buried desperation in her; now he felt it coming through the lens at him.

She reached a decision, for she strode purposefully out of his view. He swung the camera round to follow her like a telescope as she passed the old library. It was less her beauty tugging him than the nakedness in her face, the sense of someone at the quick curling crest of a wave.

He watched her walk and wondered where she'd decided to go. She carried herself with the self-possession of someone completely alone. She was walking away from him, if he didn't follow her now he wouldn't get another chance. Hadn't she said she was leaving the next day? A woman like this was always walking deliberately away—her back told as much as her face. There was no chance.

He grabbed the camera bag and hurried downstairs.

In the park there was no sign of her. The library was closing, so she wasn't in there, or among the surrounding palms. The modest stream of stalled day-end traffic brayed impatiently. Where was she? Across the street was a stone wall and steps and profusely spilling foliage. On the stone wall was a tiled emblem of a queen's gold crown against a green leaf, and in blue letters the inscription ROYAL VICTORIA HOTEL.

She's changing hotels already, he thought. Or meeting someone for a drink.

He darted through the hooting cars and went up the steps, into a tropical forest.

All around him trees rose like pillars in a cathedral, blocking sunlight. Nearby were squat sapodilla, monstrous breadfruit hung with pendulous blooms, lemon and almond trees, a soursop weighed down with green prickly hearts.

He stood on a path that sloped gently upward. It parted for a gigantic silk-cotton tree that raised great sagging arms high above the enveloping jungle. Beyond, the trees opened to a colonial mansion of creamy yellow wood with white trim, a huge decayed hotel in sprawling disrepair with windows smashed or boarded over and balconies collapsed, hanging forlornly. Like something out of his book, majestic in abandonment. Before the sad ruin obsequious palms bowed and soared. He imagined small tables among the trees, calypso bands, white-suited Bahamian waiters moving like chameleons among the guests. Where once there must've been pools of goldfish, weeds grew around rusted pipes.

The gardens were still half-tended, for among the dismal concrete paths burst hibiscus in exploding purples and pinks, poinciana, scarlet frangipani, and climbing the great central tree, flaming bougainvillea.

He saw her. She was farther up the path, down some steps by a separate wing of the hotel, peering into a derelict doorway faintly marked *Café Royal*. The stone entrance was mottled and overgrown and from the darkness within came the steady sound of dripping.

Against the dankness and decay everywhere, the graceful line of her back in the white blouse and the tight curve of her white skirt seemed outrageous. Her slip-on shoes made her look barefoot.

He knew if he came too close in this shadowy place it might appear too obvious. He lifted his camera and, looking past her, took in the old hotel. Very, very slow speed.

She said suddenly, without turning, "Am I in the way? I can move if you want."

The shutter clicked as she spoke. He said, "The light's impossible. What's in the café?"

She turned and stepped back onto the path. "Just broken glass and garbage."

Her voice was low, a blur of accents.

He said, "I wonder if you can see into the hotel."

From a nearby branch a lizard watched them in a state of petrified alertness.

"I haven't looked," she said.

"Do you want to try?"

He saw she sensed how much he wanted to take her photograph, but the unmistakable message of her body was: Don't.

"All right," she said.

Slowly they started up the path.

He said, "We didn't really meet. My name's Thomas Simmons."

"Esther Gautier." She pronounced it *Es-tair*. She didn't put out her hand. "Thank you for helping at the hotel. You were right, it's a much better room."

"I made them show me everything but the basement," he said.

French? Spanish? He was still unable to place her accent. They proceeded up the path in silence. Her skin looked lightly tanned, but he couldn't tell if that was from time in the islands or her natural color.

He was about to ask where she'd flown in from when she said, "Are you in Nassau for long?"

Her tone was only polite—she was still thanking him for having carried her bags.

"I haven't decided. I have to photograph some flamingos tomorrow morning. Then I'm a free man."

"You photograph birds."

"If I get asked to. Not usually."

"What do you usually photograph?"

"Anything I get offered," he said.

"What does that mean?"

"Woolen socks. Business executives. The ruins of Baghdad."

She had a gesture of pushing her sheaf of hair back behind her ear with her whole hand and leaning forward as she listened.

She said, "And which is most difficult to photograph—the birds? Or Baghdad?"

"Socks are impossible."

Unexpectedly, she laughed. He thought: Why aren't you spending Christmas here?

He said, "I've been trying to decide where you could be from. I can hear a bit of French. And a bit of something else."

"A bit of Cuban."

"I've been to both places."

Around them birds clattered and bragged in the trees.

She said mildly, "So have I."

"Were you brought up in both?"

"In-between. I wasn't really brought up anywhere." He heard an impasse in her voice. He said, fumbling, "Are you here on vacation?"

"Family business." She didn't elaborate. "I fly home tomorrow."

"Where's home?"

For a moment she seemed to be considering whether it was safe to tell him. It would've been easier to take her picture.

"Geneva."

"Do you work in Geneva?"

"I'm a translator. In a bank." She glanced over at him as if assessing the impression this made. "I've finally begun doing other translating too. Books. It's very satisfying."

With nothing to lose at this point, he said, "Can you have dinner with me before you fly back?"

She didn't look at him. He wondered if she'd heard.

"Aren't you going to get a photograph of the hotel?" she said.

"The light's too flat in all these trees."

"You should've come a few minutes earlier. It was lovely."

As if that were indeed why they'd walked together up the path.

In unspoken assent they started back. Along Parliament Street a horse-drawn surrey with bell tinkling passed them. The sloping sunlight of late afternoon flooded the little park.

Walking down through the shade he asked, "So which of your parents was Cuban?"

He realized he'd adopted her past tense.

"My mother was French," she said.

"What kept your family traveling so much?"

"My father. He was a sculptor. And a painter, from time to time. So we journeyed a great deal."

Her tone suggested innumerable packings and unpackings.

"Perhaps I've heard of him?"

"I doubt you've ever heard of a painter called Gautier."

She spoke with amused certainty.

"I can't say I have." It struck him that Gautier was not a very Cuban name. "Are your parents still alive?"

She said gently, "You ask a lot of personal questions. My mother died when I was a little girl."

"I'm sorry."

"And then my father died a few years ago."

She glanced over at him and he thought she might say something else. But they had reached the hotel. She looked at once tired and very relieved.

He said, "Thank you for walking with me. Can we have dinner?"

"If you'd like." She gazed at him as if not sure why he was asking.

"Is eight all right?"

"Seven-thirty would be better," she murmured, going ahead of him up the steps. "I have an early plane to catch tomorrow."

And he had missed the photograph.

5

AN EVENING BREEZE WAS CLANKING THE lanterns in the vine-hung trees, but the breath of the day was still hot. The American Simmons sat across from her on the hotel terrace, pouring more wine as they waited for their dinners to come. Esther watched him glance at the street's idle passers-by and thought: He can't quite fathom what I'm doing here. So that's fair, neither can I.

Now that she'd revealed the barest edge of the truth—one vague remark about family business—the temptation to tell more was unbearable. He was safe because she knew she would never see him again. What if she were to say: Can you keep a secret?

She didn't know a more daring challenge, a greater risk than that sidling phrase. It was how her father had told her his intentions years ago, with the amused air of someone offering a poisoned candy to a child: *Can you keep a secret?*

What if she were to tell this total stranger everything? She'd stepped to the edge of the cliff with Thomas merely by speaking to him here. Suppose she told it all anonymously, without invoking her father's real name or her own? That wouldn't be breaking a promise. It wasn't a betrayal of her father if no one associated the story with him.

She'd not once given in to that temptation since her father

had gone out to his island six years earlier. For a long time she believed that all the stories she was forced to tell on his behalf showed on her face; in nightmares they even altered its shape, transformed her into someone unrecognizable to herself. But eventually the lie became automatic, with the flat untheatricality of fact. People no longer proffered their condolences over the tragic accident, journalists no longer asked probing questions. It was simply history now.

Can you keep a secret, Mr. Simmons? My father didn't drown.

And she'd come to fear there was no candor left in her face. She'd had several lovers during that time, two serious. One was a lawyer, the other a cellist; neither expressed much curiosity or ever questioned her father's demise. Unwittingly she made it a kind of test, and because they failed the test, because she revealed nothing to them, felt no need to tell them the truth, the relations ended. She protected her father as he demanded, and by his absence he planted himself all the more firmly between her and a lover.

For the first time, with this American stranger, the lie had come full circle, into a lie about who she was. She was surprised to find it preferable: there was liberation in this lie.

Their dinners arrived. She felt him watching her acutely. Beneath his ease she could sense a separate room within him where a committee was deciding exactly what to think of her. She knew how anxious she must seem. At this moment her father would be eating by torchlight with Scully Moses. Wondering what she was doing. Wondering where she was.

She didn't want her father invading her dinner. She wanted to change the tidal drift of her mind from his direction. She seized the first banal thing that offered itself. She said, "You must enjoy traveling so much as a photographer."

"I used to. Now I dream of staying in one place."

"That's hard to believe," she said. "You're lucky to have such freedom."

He said dryly, "A photographer's at everyone's mercy."

"In my experience it's always been the reverse."

He said, "Look, I'm at the mercy of the light, the mercy of airplane schedules, of film labs, of magazine editors from Mars. This week I was at the mercy of seventy thousand innocent flamingos who ought to be left alone. Not brought back in living color to attract every nature lover with a long lens and the price of a plane ticket."

"I thought you said flamingos are much easier than socks."

For an American he seemed to enjoy a gentle café argument.

"It's still hard to do pictures of birds that don't look like bird pictures. Like telling the same joke over and over again. I kept hoping I'd get lucky, and stumble on some cranky old hermit squatting out there with them."

She said, "I sometimes wonder what it's like to live on a remote island. It must be a healthy life, no?"

"That depends on the island. If there's plenty of rain."

"Can we say there is? Or a very small lake. So water is no difficulty."

"Better make it natural underground wells," he said, going along. "Otherwise you've got all kinds of interesting bugs. You're living there by yourself?"

"Absolutely alone."

"No local settlements up the coast?"

"Nothing," she said. "No one knows this island exists. No banks, no visitors, no telephone. One supply plane a month."

"Do you have electricity?"

"A generator."

"That'll keep you distracted, every time it breaks down.

What else are you doing to keep busy?"

Waiting for someone, she thought. Someone who never comes.

"Getting some sun."

"That's it?"

"Learning to fish."

"You call that busy?"

"Let's say I'm working on a new translation of *Robinson Crusoe*," she said. "Does it really matter?"

"Of course it matters. My first day on Inagua I was ready to move there for six months. After a few days I decided a month would be about right. After a week I couldn't wait to leave."

"What if I'm not able to leave?"

"You said there was a supply plane."

"Let's say I'm an important criminal. Or a dictator, exiled to the island for years and years. I'm there to stay."

"No one else to talk to?"

"Perhaps there's a Man Friday," she said, "but we don't get along."

"Then it's a prison. I give you a couple of weeks before you crack." He poured her more wine. "I cracked out on Inagua. Good place for it."

She couldn't tell how serious he was.

He said, "You're not going to experiment around here, are you?"

"Not for a moment. I'm trying to understand why anyone would. I heard people do it all the time."

"You never know, you might flourish," he said. "Whenever I go somewhere remote, I always consider moving there. Then I ask myself what I'll do when I run out of things to photograph. Or run out of curiosity. I multiply the local cooking by several years. And I decide to wait until the next place." He paused. "I hope I wasn't too nosy this afternoon."

"That sounds like an apology for more questions. Americans are famous for not asking any at all."

"We're just not sure we'll like the answers."

She wondered how he would react to being interrogated.

"I must say, you sound sick of your work," she said.

"Maybe I got too much sun. And the flamingos made me feel more of a fool than usual. Then I ended up taking this hulk of a mail boat back." His face was transfigured by the memory. "The crew slept on deck with the goats. The sea was beautiful, the goats were beautiful, the crew were such vagabonds even they were beautiful—" He made a gesture of exasperation. "I couldn't begin to take the pictures I saw in front of me. When that happens you know you're really on the skids."

"And the old hotel this afternoon?"

"That was different. There wasn't enough light. I was after your photograph, anyway."

His honesty about his intentions danced over her.

She said without thinking, "My father told me once that his favorite sculptures were the ones that went wrong. He said they were like disobedient children he never despaired of."

Abruptly she felt her father there, standing behind her. They might've been in a forest, with the trees and vines of the terrace and the lanterns cloaked like blinking owls. Her father had come stealing across the forest floor on bare feet and whispered something in her ear so faintly she couldn't make out the phrase. He drew away behind her and she felt him vanish into the shadows, but there was still the soft imprint of his mouth at her ear.

She saw Thomas watching her thought but, mercifully, he changed the subject. He said, "How long have you lived in Geneva?"

"Nearly three years. I've finally gotten some good work

outside the bank. Translating a couple of serious French novels for a Madrid publisher."

He didn't ask the titles and she wondered if he was a man who read. She was accustomed to men with whom the ardent discussion of literature actually mattered.

"And before Geneva?" he asked.

"I tried acting for a while. Like everyone else. This was when I was finishing up university, in Barcelona. I wasn't much good. So I went to study theater in Paris. The waiting all the time made me crazy, so I didn't last very long. Then I got talked into a little modeling." She laughed at his grimace. "That lasted even less."

"You were one of the lucky ones."

"I thought so," she said. "I decided I didn't want a crashing great city. I only wanted a calm job in an anonymous place. You know what they say about Switzerland being the right country to sit out a war. And I had some friends who made a long work permit possible. It's usually very difficult for a foreigner."

How refreshing to speak from behind an incomplete identity. Like traveling comfortably in disguise.

"Do you enjoy living with the Swiss?"

"The temperature's a little low sometimes. In Madrid everyone tells you absolutely everything that happens right away. In Paris you hear stories about yourself even from strangers. In Geneva they're still puzzling out the news from last year. But everyone comes through, sooner or later."

He said, "That's one place I've never been."

"You might like Geneva. The lake, anyway. I suppose it would depend upon the light."

It was easy to speak so glibly, so flirtatiously, if you were leaving in the morning.

He said, "Why don't you stay another day and see the flamingos with me? I only need one photograph, it won't take long. The beaches are empty at that end of the island."

So the committee had decided. At that moment the waitress came and broke the mood, clattering away the plates.

"What's the photograph you have to take?"

"Civilized flamingos. I've done barbarians in the wild all week. Now I have to show what a tourist can see. Work a child into the picture if possible."

He had a nonchalantly cynical way of talking, like someone who pretended his occupation mattered little to him in order to conceal the passion beneath it.

Their coffees arrived. She said, "I'd like to stay, but I really have to get home."

"It can't be warm in Geneva this time of year."

She realized that, having earlier told him part of the truth, she could not begin completely inventing now.

"I was only here to clean up some old family business. My father retired to one of the Out Islands. I've finally sold the property."

That made it sound as if so much had been accomplished.

"Lucky man," said Thomas. "Which island?"

"No one's heard of it," she answered quickly. "Anyway, I need to be back in my office on Monday."

She knew that every lie, every new admission with its kernel of truth, showed on her face. She felt ashen.

He said, "Wouldn't it make more sense to live in the tropics and spend Christmas in the Alps?"

His expression was so mild, his voice so calm, he could not see the hurt his simple words were encompassing.

"That depends what you want. My father didn't want to see anyone."

Her coffee cup had gone cold against her hand.

"Still," said Thomas, "living on a tropical island is a fate no New Yorker can argue with. Would you like more coffee?"

Her father had invaded her dinner again. She'd thought him driven out, but he was there all the time. She felt a quick shame at leaving Nassau like a traitor.

She said, "I should go up. I still have a letter to write this evening."

—

She did not write the letter, and by morning it was like an oncoming illness. She awoke early, still on European time, and called the airline office; it wasn't open yet. She prepared her bags and went downstairs for coffee. Back in her room two sheets of hotel stationery waited with blank accusation on the writing desk beside an envelope on which she'd already underlined the name of Henry Pinder. This time the airline office did answer: as on her return ticket for two weeks hence, the flight would leave early that evening. She'd have the whole day. She changed her reservation; and freed for a time from the imprisoning letter, she went walking.

She was too tired to feel anything but cold-blooded about yesterday's decision. The hours would slowly make their way and she would be gone. She tried not to think of her father, tried to avoid the inevitable fact that she would not, having come this close and turned back, ever come out here again. Her father was dying not very far away and she would never see him. It was as if, through an act of her will, he were already dead.

And why not? This was the lie he had perpetrated on the rest of the world. She could not take responsibility for it, he had to. It'd been his choice, he'd barely consulted her about it. Nothing she might've said or done then would've changed his mind, he listened to no one. And what had she known or imagined then about consequences, at twenty-two?

She told herself to concentrate on finding him a Christmas

gift, to send via Pinder and ease the pain of the letter—or at least her own guilt. In Geneva her imagination had failed her: what could you get for the man who'd given up practically everything? It occurred to her that she must've already decided not to see him before she left Switzerland. To come this far had been only a charade.

Around the corner of Parliament Street she stepped into a tobacconist's shop with a huge mahogany pipe suspended outside, and bought a large box of expensive Havana cigars. He hadn't smoked for years, but he'd enjoy having the humid fragrance at hand. She asked to have the box wrapped. And then it struck her that, with the whole day ahead of her, she could find a few seashells to ornament the box—an acknowledgment of the last six years of his life.

At a pharmacy she bought a tube of glue and headed back to the hotel. There was a note with Thomas's New York address and telephone number waiting in her box. The receptionist told her, without being asked, that Mr. Simmons had left to see the birds.

On impulse she changed quickly, khaki shorts and a green blouse over her swimsuit, and grabbed a towel. It was already nine-thirty. A taxi took her from town past cabana'd stretches of beach and, across the water, the white lighthouse set like a candle at the tip of Paradise Island.

When they came within sight of an old fort, gray ramparts and mossy cannon high on a greensward, the taxi took a road that wound inland. The day was already sultry.

The taxi let her off by a sign: ARDASTRA GARDENS, HOME OF THE FAMOUS MARCHING FLAMINGOS. She paid the admission fee—already this seemed as good a place as any to use up the morning—and headed down a path through the botanical gardens. From down the narrow way came voices, the idle chat of people waiting.

The foliage drew back around an arena of open ground

and several rows of seats, beyond it a small bridge, a pond, thick trees. Perhaps two dozen people were seated, some fiddling with cameras. Esther sat in the last row. She could not glimpse Thomas anywhere. She realized then that he'd been in back of her thoughts all morning, as if the interest of someone who had nothing to do with her father could be a balm, a repelling of dangerous illness.

A black man in a checked shirt came into the arena, glanced at his watch, and said, "Ladies and gentlemen, the world-famous—" She saw Thomas backing over the bridge and stopped listening to the litany. He ran off several photographs and reached into his bag to change lenses. As he did so he glanced over at the audience for a moment, the nervous gesture of someone covering his flank, and grinned when he saw her. She felt a little wave of embarrassment.

Then she heard loud bickering. A flock of flamingos, close together, came over the bridge as Thomas shot away and got himself into the front row of seats. The flamingos moved like ice-skaters gliding, wings folded, red as embers and burned black at the edges. Their heads were held high, as if to say: We expected more acolytes.

They assembled, clamoring anxiously. The trainer clapped his hands and the flamingos, on fragile skinny legs, scurried around the arena with a high-stepping chorus-girl gait. The hands clapped, the birds halted; the trainer strode around the flock, neatening it, encouraging a few children to come closer. He kept his face turned toward Thomas's camera. Another bark from his hands and the birds scurried again.

They must get bored, she thought, running through this act all day just to be fed.

When the show was done and the flamingos back at their pond, she went to where Thomas stood with the trainer. Two peacocks, their tails brushing the dirt, meandered in front of the men.

Thomas was saying, "Can't we get them to open their tails?"

The trainer said, "No way, man. Can't train they the way you train a fillymingo. These the most human of all the birds. Nothing but vanity. Can't get they to do nothing they don't want."

When the trainer walked away, she said, "Did you get the photograph you need?"

"I got a lot of pictures of this guy staring at the camera. I thought you'd be on a plane by now."

"I misread the ticket. Not until this evening."

They started back through the botanical gardens.

"Did you sleep well?" he asked.

"Strange dreams. And you?"

"Better than on the mail boat." He stopped. "Look at this giant thing. Soursop, they call it."

It was a huge green fruit in the shape of a spiny heart. He tugged it gingerly from the tree.

"I wonder how it tastes," she said.

"Not bad. Tart. They mix it with milk in the Antilles. Would you hold it? Against yourself with one hand."

"All right."

"Better move back a step or two." He got the camera out of its gray bag. "Don't worry," he said. "I'm not going to do a portrait. Just your throat and the green of your blouse and the green fruit against it. You'll be headless, do you mind?"

"Better that way."

She felt the points of the fruit against her breasts and flinched.

"That's very good, please don't move."

His voice had changed to the tones of a professional, used to giving orders when a camera was out.

"Is it ripe?" she asked. It satisfied her to move a little.

"I suppose it must be. It came away in my hand." He

clicked away. "That's it." He took the fruit back from her and laid it beside the tree.

She was ready for him to kiss her, but instead he rewound. These slow Americans, she thought.

They walked down the grassy hill past the old fort toward the shore. Farther up the coast stood the great casino-hotels like enormous air-conditioning units. Here the beach ran on for cove after cove of palms.

Their beach was hot and deserted in noon glare. Far out to sea gray thunderclouds were shifting like clouds of battle. Nearer, in the shallows, sunlight roared off the prism of water.

"We'll have rain before the afternoon's done," he said. "Better swim now."

"You go ahead. I want to look for some shells."

There was the slightly charged sensation of stripping, even to a bikini, for someone who had the possibility of becoming a lover. She felt their sole afternoon together, the mutual sense of limited time, standing inert between them. As he went wordlessly down to the water and waded in, she saw he had the fit body of a younger man.

She wandered among the tide wrack of braided seaweed and endless shells. There was no point in speculating: every passing minute confirmed her departure. She knelt and began sifting through shells. It didn't take long to have enough— cowries and cockles and razor shells and whirled miniature palaces of mollusks. That was what her father always said: Work with materials that lie naturally close at hand. And transform them.

Kneeling in the sand, brushing her hair out of her face, she had the uneasy sensation of knowing she had not performed these movements since she was a child. It was disconcerting to think that something as insubstantial as the passage of time turned the same act from idle play into a recapitulation of another life, an earlier person who could never be regained. Even if you tried to restore the years until all actions were simple as a child's, they would be robbed of the simple pleasures of a child. Therefore all meaning was out of one's hands: it fled like the creature in the shell, leaving something behind as empty and useless as memory.

Yet her father had spent these years—his last years—sifting how many thousands of shells on his beach.

She was finished by the time Thomas came out of the water.

"Take my towel," she called out. She noticed he had a slightly pigeon-toed walk.

Now the thunderheads of war-smoke were darkening the sea.

"Aren't you going in?" he said. "Those clouds mean business."

Rain here tomorrow for Christmas, she thought. Snow in Geneva.

In the silken water she swam under and traced her fingertips along the sandy bottom until her breath gave out. She imagined Pinder delivering the cigar box and the letter in two or three days' time; she could see him handing them to her father, she could not see the expression on her father's face. Fury? Surprise, and sadness? Or perhaps he would not be surprised by any of it, her cowardice or her gift.

The strength of his presence startled her, even an hour's flight distant by small plane. It was as if he lurked one cove away, barely out of sight.

Time to get back to the hotel, she thought. Time to get on with that letter and then leave.

Walking back up the beach, she saw that Thomas was already dressed. It had been a good idea to pass the morning distracted by this man. He seemed impervious to nuisances like rain and plane schedules and, whether this was so or not, his calm was contagious.

43

He was looking through her shells. He said, "Are you starting a collection?"

"They're a gift."

He handed her back the hotel towel.

"For my boss," she added.

She felt his eyes toweling her body. She said, "Will it take long to glue them on a cigar box?"

"It won't be quick."

After one now. She'd have to leave for the airport by five. And the letter.

She pulled on her clothes. Fat raindrops were plopping singly in the sand. Forget the shells, she thought.

But she scooped them up.

"We'd better go," she murmured.

"You say that like someone who doesn't want to miss her plane. I think you should. I miss at least one plane every week, it's good for the soul."

They threaded their way through the palms to the road.

She said, "All I've done since I came here is miss planes. It hasn't done my soul any good at all."

"Stay another few days. This rain won't last. You're in a wonderful spot to see the Junkanoo. It's freezing in Geneva. I paid three dollars to read that in the *Herald Trib* this morning. There's no one else on our beach. We can have a picnic and swim tomorrow for Christmas."

It began to rain in earnest.

She said, "What do you know? Sometimes it rains for a week here this time of year."

Just then a taxi honked angrily and swerved over in the rain. They ran to get in and the taxi was off again before Thomas had the door shut.

If I stay on here, she thought, I can write the letter properly and still leave the day before Pinder flies out. And do a careful job with the shells.

In her mind an artificial connection had solidified between her own departure and Pinder's—that she must not stay long enough to refuse, for the second time, a ride to Desirada. The longer she spent so near to her father without going to see him, the greater the destruction would be, to herself and to him.

"All right," she said. "I'll call my bank."

Not to leave was a relief.

He said, "I'll find us a different restaurant. It's Christmas Eve, we have to celebrate." They were stitching their way through anxious Bay Street traffic. "I'm going to get out here, I need a few things and the stores will close early." He smiled. "My rule is never leave anywhere during a local holiday. Very unlucky."

He handed some money to the driver and was out of the taxi so quickly, hurrying under an awning to get his camera bag out of the pelting rain, that she felt a stab of worry she'd made the wrong decision.

But back at the hotel, this time when she stripped and lay down she knew she would fall asleep. Around the hotel rain had taken command of the little park, the faded library, the narrow streets and all those expectant gardens. Rain would be busily dripping in the ruined hotel just up the hill. There would be no photographs of it today. Perhaps tomorrow. The light would be different, softer after the rain; and she and Thomas Simmons would be lovers. She wondered now not if but when. It was as if they were conspirators who alone knew a secret revolution was brewing in the streets. They didn't have much time.

The more she turned that prospect over in her mind, her body imagining how his might feel, the more she could put aside the responsibility of the letter, the idea of her father. Nassau had come to life: she had met this man here. It could, unexpectedly, be an end in itself. This time lying naked on the bed she slipped down through waves of oblivion until sleep closed over her.

6

IT WAS RAINING THROUGH THE AFTER-
noon, a din on the hotel roof, and on the floor below a work-
man was banging with determination on an irreparable pipe.
Each noise encouraged the other, and they drove all ideas for
a suitable dedication out of Thomas's head.

It annoyed him that he couldn't decide what to write in his
own book. He sat with pen poised over the title page of the
copy he'd just purchased for Esther at an exorbitant price on
Bay Street. He could feel his attraction to her turning in his
mind as though, from another angle, it might be revealed as
something simple. It'd been so long since he'd felt someone
quicken his life, galvanize him—since he'd met someone he
wanted to win—that the unexpected event left him darkly
suspicious. He hunted his own motivations and, because he
barely knew the woman, came back clueless and clouded.

Don't write anything, he thought. Anything you write will
be wrong.

He invented a past for her out of the bits and pieces he
knew. She seemed to walk in the perpetual solitude of an only
child; he imagined a shy girlhood, a succession of schools in
different countries. Probably a late blooming physically:
there was still a touch of the good student in her. In a black
bikini there was nothing shy in her body, nor how frankly she

moved. The room was sultry enough in the rain, even with the air-conditioner slaving away, to help him imagine tasting the salt tang of the morning's beach on her skin.

Better if desire were all that was at stake.

The rain was untiring. At this rate, no beach for Christmas tomorrow, no Junkanoo tomorrow night. Having persuaded her to stay, he felt responsible for the weather.

He sat down on the bed and began unloading his camera bag, setting apart the black plastic containers of exposed film. Six this morning, that made seventy-three flamingos in all. Hopefully enough. Another eighty-odd rolls of fresh film left. Use them on Esther.

He tossed the day's work into a plastic carrier bag in the closet along with the rest. One slide of her already in there, that would come out underexposed. Blind optimism.

She had that gesture of impatience and real concentration, of pushing back her sheaf of hair and leaning in to listen. To see her do this excited him because it seemed all her personality in one movement, her momentary way of letting the world in wholly, and he yearned to take a picture of it.

He went back to the bed and got to work cleaning the camera and lenses.

The jolting restlessness he felt toward Esther troubled him. In his analytical way he could not find its wilder source. Not the ten-year difference in their ages, nor a longing to break the brooding of her body. He couldn't explain his desperation and he found himself imagining what the men in her life must be like. Solitary, she seemed to have an enormous need of someone and yet she would clearly be quickly bored. Easier to imagine her in the independent role of a mistress who came and went as she pleased and was finally alone.

Anyway, it was clear what the outcome would be: in a matter of two or three days, they'd each leave. Esther would leave first. Probably they'd be lovers by then—surely she'd not have stayed otherwise. To stay meant nearly yes. The curtness of the time, for him, did not lend passion to whatever might take place. They might as well be mosquitoes in some swamp.

For him it was too easy to see the ending. This was supposed to heighten desire—desire for someone about to slip away. But that was a separate desire nurtured and fed every day by the act of taking photographs, a desire he was sick of, the need to capture what would soon be lost. It bothered him to remember the young secretary on the way to Inagua: he'd seen that ending the instant she started talking. Yet he'd gone ahead anyway.

He held the polarizing filter up to the light to see if it was smudged.

What was so troubling was that Esther seemed full of possibility, a woman with the world in her, not a person to be met and forgotten conveniently, and she was already about to vanish an entire hemisphere away. He couldn't get her look, nor the warm line of her body, out of his imagination. At twenty-eight there was a depth of emotional experience in her green eyes, the secret edge of knowing, that she was barely aware of herself. One rarely saw it in the eyes of young women: he'd photographed too many to have any illusions about that. No light meter had been invented that could measure the narcissism in most young women's eyes. In Esther's steady gaze was the sense of someone listening, trying to echo herself back into the world. And the occasional look of having tried already and failed: there was no echo out there.

No echo indeed. The pipe man had given up clanking. The reprieve made Thomas feel abruptly alone. Probably Esther was in her room directly below, perhaps asleep to the diligent hum of the rain. The image of her body on the bed bothered him so much he went to take a tepid shower and ended up nodding off, standing there with the water pouring across him.

They ate dinner at a balconied mansion set in trees on a hill above Nassau, a restaurant with the candlelit humor of an elegant home of a century before. A breeze blew through the steady drizzle this high over the town and made the life below seem drowsy and purposeless. Even though church bells occasionally went off like guns in the darkness the air smelled of jasmine and honeysuckle spring, not Christmas Eve. Up here he felt centuries distant from his other, professional life, with this woman across from him and the ordered Victorian streets spreading like vines to the harbor far below. He had arrived somewhere, complete at last.

In a square-necklined dress of red silk she looked lightly tanned and at ease. The change in the weather and now the rain's slackening gave them both the impression of having been on the island, having known each other, longer than they had.

She was full of questions: his studio, his travels, how he'd started. It struck him that she was using them to fend off any questions about herself. In retrospect it all sounded less aimless and encumbered, more purposeful, than he'd felt at the time—he'd left college in Boston at twenty and gone impatiently down to New York to assist different photographers before finally getting up the nerve to go out on his own. It was hard to conceive or convey, that determination almost like quiet rage, as if photography had attacked him and he had to attack back. He mentioned his year of marriage in passing and thankfully she let it go by.

In the airless taxi drawing them back down the hill through the rain he felt her pressing against him and once, when the car lurched around a slick corner, she caught at him to keep from falling. Her reaction seemed so natural that he thought then of putting his arm around her. But the taxi was too warm and not right.

And yet going up the stairs of the little hotel, after an effortless evening together with the sense of something decided behind it, he sensed her withdrawing slightly. His talk rang small and unnecessary. The weather, the island.

At her door he said, "It's hard to believe it's Christmas tomorrow."

She was already inside her room, smiling with blithe attendant satisfaction at him outside. She said, "I don't mind swimming in the rain, do you?" When he answered, "Not a bit," she thanked him for dinner, wished him good night, and closed the door on his echo.

He walked away slowly, feeling eighteen and stymied by the conviction that he belonged on the other side of her door. Amazing how you lost your nerve with women as you got older—once upon a time he'd have charged right in there. What he needed, now that the moment had passed, was an excuse to go back.

He was already fitting the key into his own door a floor above. The disappointing room was frigid: he'd left the air-conditioner on. He shivered and shut the thing off, heard it whine down and then, in a lightning flash of inspiration, noticed the uninscribed copy of his book lying open on the table.

He took up his pen and wrote: *The only copy in Nassau.* His signature and the date. He surveyed it an instant to see if it annoyed him, then headed back downstairs, book in hand.

At her door he paused, trying to hear sounds of her moving about inside. Could she already be asleep? He knocked.

Silence.

Serves you right for being so slow, he thought.

He knocked again, last try, heard a door open within the room, a tap running. The water was shut off and he heard her come to the door. "Yes?"

"It's Thomas."

It's Quasimodo, he thought, with a book of his etchings.

She opened the door and stood there, still in her red dress, barefoot. Why did barefoot women always seem half-naked?

He could not read the expression on her face.

"I meant to give this to you earlier."

He handed over the fading South.

She took it with some surprise. "It won't be Christmas for a few minutes."

He thought she was about to close the door again.

She said, "Perhaps you'd better stay."

He caught her arm lightly across the threshold and pulled her to him. She came easily and at once everything changed, everything was understood. He kissed her hesitantly, and again, and then the kiss became languorous as her body gave in.

Someone was coming. He drew away for a moment and simply held her; her eyes were amused at the pretense of innocence. Another guest came up the stairs in flip-flops, must have noticed them, moved on.

She drew him inside, leaned against the doorway. He kissed her offered throat. Silk along the upper swell of her breasts, while his hands began to roam her, slowly. Slowly. The book would be heavy, held behind her. Slowly. He felt for it and she let it go from her hands to his. As he bent to let it drop to the carpet he kissed the inward country below her waist. His hands cradled her, pressing her to his face. Her eyes were closed and two fingers in her mouth.

Beside them the door shut slowly by itself. She leaned against the wall, her toes digging into the carpet. Their bodies' shadows played across the wall, joining and rejoining, and it struck him that in one's shadow lay a shapely self more fluid, more reconcilable to others, more easily shared than the desperate being that cast it. As if by making love bodies were trying to become for a time as easily translatable as their shadows. And it seemed right that his posture, pressed against Esther, made the shadow of a man praying.

He stood up, lifting the edges of her red dress; she put her arms over her head and he pulled it off. She was wearing nothing underneath, and she shook out her hair.

He laid the dress across an armchair. There was a strange force in being clothed, in being the one still hidden. When he turned back she was already on the bed. In the dim light of the single lamp on the bedside table her nakedness blazed at him.

There was a curious moment, as he tugged off his clothes, when he saw on the writing desk beneath the window a color photograph, much faded, in a silver frame. A couple stood holding hands with a little girl in a park. He could not make out the faces, only that the woman was tall, with black hair, and she wore a red dress.

He was not prepared for the sudden candor he felt in Esther's arms, the sense of no phantoms in the way, the percussive gestures of their bodies that seemed to go on of their own energy and singing inspiration against the simple tune of tropical rain. Nor was he prepared for the quiet unfolding into sleep much later, her head in the crook of his shoulder, her hair spread across his chest, their feet oddly intertwined beneath a single sheet. His last thought was that they had not spoken for hours.

⬤

She awoke before him: the light through the window was gray, ambivalent. The rain had stopped in the night. Thomas lay asleep on the other side of the bed. The sunburned skin on his back had begun to peel. He did not stir as she slipped quietly out of bed. Hastily she took down the family photograph and slid it into her small carry-on bag, zipped the bag shut.

She stepped into the shower. With water streaming down her body, her skin awakened to bring back the night before. She was accustomed to lovers trying either to impress her or to impress themselves; their self-flattering passion was so far from any erotic possibility she felt in herself, so little being said by one body to another, that going to bed with them was like taking an aspirin. But last night she'd felt herself asking questions and Thomas trying to find the answers, with her. She wondered how long, given a chance, that sensation might last. Until they ran out of questions?

In any case they would not have that chance, since she was leaving tomorrow.

She knew it with the alabaster logic of morning. Making love had calmed her and she saw there was no way around her father were she to stay. To be in the same climate, the same latitude, the same archipelago as he brought on all the gravitational pull of his dark, weighty star. This close to her father, there was a limit to how long she would be able to lie to Thomas: the temptation to entrust him with the truth was too great.

It would be different once she was safely back in her life. Surely Thomas came to Europe from time to time. She knew she wanted to see him again. She would explain then who her father had been, that she hadn't wished to draw attention to the property changing hands. People made excuses like this all the time. And if he didn't come, if she didn't see him again, it was no tragedy. Not as if she had told him anything she had-n't told anyone else, anything she couldn't take back.

As she shut off the water she heard the bed sigh. When she came out of the bathroom, wrapped in a towel, patting her head dry with one end, he was sitting modestly in his trousers in the corner armchair, looking rumpled and uncomfortable. She said, "Merry Christmas."

He's not sure who I am, she thought.

"Merry Christmas," he said. "Did you sleep well?"

"Very well. No dreams at all."

It was never natural, that first morning with a new someone. She saw him glance around the room, noticed his eyes light momentarily on the bare writing desk where the photograph had been. She felt her own unease and she kissed him to disguise it.

He said, "I'm going upstairs. Shall we go to the beach later?"

"If you'd like," she said. "We could bring a picnic lunch."

After the door shut and she heard the stairs creak she rang several airline offices at the airport—in town they were all closed for the holiday—and found a morning flight out in a day's time, to London, via another airline. She booked it gratefully; there was even an easy connection to Geneva. She phoned downstairs for coffee, then lay down and began to look through the defeated South.

The book startled her. He had given it to her so casually she had been ready to look through it casually. Instead it was the work of someone who had gone his own way. She'd spent part of her childhood surrounded by people like this, her parents' friends, and she saw immediately in the photographs the grip, the sustained risk of a private vision. It came through in every picture, a pressure of the imagination, and she felt his pictures embedding themselves in her memory. Beneath the quiet violence of how very difficult life was for these wandering poor, and the sense of things fraying—the old mansions like sorry mementos, simply collapsing—there was beauty, the beauty of decay.

What was most extraordinary was how the people in the portraits stood before her, with nothing in the way; Thomas wasn't present in the tone of any of the photographs. It was difficult to connect the man who must've taken them and the man she'd gone to bed with. The personal man wasn't entirely sure of himself, not sure at all of his life; she knew this because the vast uncertainty in her responded as if to an ally. But the eye, the seeing hand, was calm and unwavering in him. He was a monster, like her father.

Another reason for her to move on, tomorrow. The sole question was whether to tell him.

—

Just before noon a small jitney dropped them near the cove of beach they'd found the day before. The day had continued opening to glazed blue sky, Christmas parodied by heat. Out to sea two distant cruise ships were gently underway, like bits of blanched coral in the noon light.

In the full heat of the day they had the cove to themselves. All that had passed between them since being at this little beach made it more vivid and memorable to her eye. Among the palms the light was directionless and hard.

They swam and ate lunch and fell asleep in the palm shadows. When they awoke the shank of the afternoon was upon them, the light beginning to relax, the pure line separating sea and sky blotted like an amateur watercolor.

They swam again briefly and by the time they were dressed it was dusk, the taxis already racing toward the lights of town and the tourist casinos. At the hotel they decided to eat at the terrace restaurant again, for in the streets barricades were being erected for the Junkanoo. An electrified silence hung over the low town, like a child being kept strictly waiting. The carnival would not begin officially until three in the morning, and the nonchalance of the waiters seemed forced. They knew they were in for a long night. The strains of a scratched calypso record being played over and over floated through the terrace tables.

At dinner she felt herself short of breath, smothered at the thought of tomorrow. She'd told Thomas nothing and he hadn't asked. Her flight, on Boxing Day—only the British could think up a name like this for the day after Christmas—left at eleven. She'd have to be at the airport well before ten.

It only now crossed her mind that she might possibly run into Pinder at the airport.

She thought: It was a terrible mistake to stay on, even for a day. To get involved with someone I barely know, who keeps asking ordinary questions I can't answer. Except with lies that double back.

Surely he too must be aware how their talk was circular, around everything but the singular fact of what had happened between them. It was like an enormous abyss in their conversation, and somewhere within was the further question of how much longer they would each be here—though she already knew.

Fifteen hours from now she'd be airborne. She'd have to call Pinder. There'd be no letter. What could she tell her father? She couldn't even bring herself to tell Thomas she was leaving.

After dinner they went up to his room. A breeze full with the sea-scent came in, carrying haphazard rattles and shouts and drums rumbling across the rooftops, as if the carnival were being barely kept at bay until the darkness was at its height and the torches could be lit with exhalations of fiery breath and the insistent call of group to group, drum to drum could begin.

He said, "We can try to sleep for a few hours or we can stay awake. I don't want to miss the beginning and it'll take me a little while to set up the camera."

"Let's try to stay awake."

This time their love-making was troubled and slightly false, as if they were trying to re-create what had already passed. It's my fault, she thought, I can't even leave him with something honest of myself. It was better last night, when nothing was at stake.

They were lying on the sheets, in the weak light of one bedside lamp. He was stroking her back. The room was close even with the breeze.

"I noticed your family photograph last night," he said.

She swallowed. She was grateful for the shadows. "Sometimes it bothers me to have it out. It was taken in Paris. We lived there several years. Off and on."

"Was that your mother's dress you wore?"

What sharp eyes you've got, she thought. "It was her favorite. I don't wear it very often." And then, by accident—she was distracted by the first noises of the Junkanoo—more slipped out. "I'd planned to wear it tonight."

"For the Junkanoo."

She felt embattled. Should she turn back? Her ears were roaring. Staring resolutely at the wall, she said, "For my father."

His silence told her he wasn't sure he'd heard correctly. He said hesitantly, "In his memory?"

"In his presence."

"I must've misunderstood," he said quickly. "I thought he was dead."

"He was dead. He's had a speedy recovery." She glanced over at Thomas from many miles away, feeling a little heady with the surge of what she was saying. "He's very alive. Out on his island."

What have I done, she thought. She reached across him and switched on the other bedside lamp. Behind his steady gaze she could see him swinging through great arcs of uncertainty.

"You never said which island."

"The island we invented. The island we didn't invent." She pulled the sheet close. "I was supposed to spend Christmas with him."

She couldn't read anything in his expression.

She said, "I felt ridiculous yesterday, lying to you."

A false note there. Even she heard it.

"No, you didn't," he said easily. "It wasn't any of my business, why should you feel ridiculous? It's my fault for being rude and asking too many questions. I'm not very subtle."

"Bringing me your book last night was pretty subtle."

He actually blushed. To cover himself, he said, "I'm glad to hear he's alive, anyway."

What did he mean by that? She tried not to sound nervous. "Did you get a good look at my mother?"

She meant: Did you recognize my father?

"Not really. All I could see was the red of the dress. You should get a new print made, if you've got the negative."

"Why's that?"

Better to keep him off the subject.

He started to explain something chemical, then broke off. "Trust me, those old color negatives fade very unevenly unless they're stored properly. I'd make several prints, to be safe."

What a peculiar relief it was to have told a little bit of the truth, even when she saw the damage it had done.

He said, "Is the cigar box with shells for your father?"

"I know it's absurd. The things people do to ease their consciences."

"Don't be so hard on yourself. I'm sure he'll be glad to get it. Even by mail."

"He doesn't get mail," she said, and felt assailed by having told too much.

They could hear steady drumming now, like muted cannon-fire from the hill above the hotel, and shouts in the street.

"He's not out there alone, surely."

"There's an old Bahamian who looks after him. They argue constantly. I'm sure it's awful for both of them. I doubt either one understands half what the other says."

More damage.

"It doesn't sound very sociable. What does he do all day? Paint?"

She'd forgotten what she'd told Thomas in the park. It took her a moment to recover.

"Oh, he stopped painting years ago," she said offhandedly. "He writes me letters. Asking me to stay out there with him. Not to visit, to stay. He's been asking since he got there. Six years! 'Dear Esther, please give up your life and come keep me company until I die.'"

She was wide awake with the danger now, skirting the edge of the unsayable. It was thrilling, almost a kind of arousal.

"Would it satisfy him if you visited more often?"

"He's happiest talking only to himself. He stopped listening to other people when my mother died, and he hasn't changed. For a long time I wanted him there to talk to, but he was always away."

"And where were you?"

"I got sent to live with a great-aunt in Barcelona. A warm, billowy old woman. She still spoke about an early edition of Cervantes she'd lost in the Civil War. Along with her husband. To make me feel better, I suppose. She was sympathetic to my moods and silences and could usually pretend nothing was wrong. Then my auntie died after a few years, so I was packed off to a good Swiss boarding school. The kind where half the children have movie-star parents and know how to ski and order wine at the age of twelve." She was nearly breathless. "At first I dreamed about traveling with him while he was working. That was the life we'd had as a family. I couldn't understand why he wasn't around. He'd always been busy, but we were always with him. Or if he had to be away he was still in the atmosphere. I guess he finally evaporated completely."

"He must've thought you'd be better looked after by your aunt."

"Better looked after!" she said. "A child of seven or eight doesn't want to be looked after. By that time it's companionship you want. Instead he sent postcards. He'd go somewhere to work, and then I'd get a whole series. He was in Southeast Asia for a time, during the Vietnam War, sketching. You should've seen the old postcards I got. Or else he'd go on some trip with a mistress, and I'd get a card of an elephant in Africa or a lake somewhere."

"He sounds like a painter I should've heard of. Gautier? What's his first name?"

She froze for an instant. "Christophe. I don't see why. He wasn't much of a painter." That's true, too, she thought. "This is why I never send postcards. A postcard is like calling someone up from the other side of the world and saying, 'Hello, we must have dinner sometime,' then hanging up. I used to think: If he loves me so much why doesn't he come see me?" She made a dismissive noise. "Why bother to write him? If he wants an explanation let him think back. Better—I'll send him a postcard of the Junkanoo. I saw one yesterday."

Outside, the shouts and the clanging gossip of cowbells had become insistent. They heard the low mutter of people gathered expectantly in the street, awaiting the slow surge of the hordes of dancers. The Junkanoo was approaching as steadily as a thunderstorm, bringing chants like bursts of thunder and always the many-voiced call and response of the drums. It gathered strength and quickness and filled the night like a hurricane.

But he's dying, she thought. He really is going to evaporate. Like smoke that will hang low for an instant and be gone forever.

She realized sharply that she had chosen. It was too late to take back what she'd said, too late to cover herself. Abruptly Thomas Simmons had become the only man who knew this much about her, knew her father was alive and roughly where he lived. If Thomas ever found out who she really was, it was over for her father.

That meant: if Thomas ever saw her again.

He said, "How old were you when your mother died?"

Shall I tell you the whole story? she thought. My God, how I would love to tell someone every inch of it.

She said quietly, "She committed suicide two weeks before my seventh birthday."

He winced.

"It used to shock me, too. But the past acquires a deeper logic the farther away it recedes. The older I got the more I'd think about how they were together, just before. And I could see all the tension between them. He barely spoke to her near the end of her life. For the last few months I don't suppose he said a hundred words to her. I didn't know what was happening. There was always a strangeness about him, but it never seemed to bother her, she knew how to take the strangeness away. Then suddenly she seemed to need his approval and he wouldn't give it to her. They even stopped sleeping in the same room."

She heard how flat her voice sounded, as if she were describing someone else's life.

She said, "I remember feeling, but not being able to articulate, that it was all right, she still had me. And afterward for a long time I even accused myself of not having done what I could to save her."

"What could you have done?" he said. "You were six."

"I don't know. Hug her more? Perhaps seem more worth staying alive for? Sometimes I imagine sitting down with her as an adult and trying to talk her out of it. I don't blame her. For years I was angry at her for abandoning me to him. Then I realized she'd not have killed herself unless there was an unbearable amount of pain. It's the time leading up to it, all that pain, that makes me sad now. And it was my father who rejected me, the living person, not the dead."

He said, "I'm so sorry, Esther."

She felt light-headed. Everything was clear now. At this

time tomorrow night she would be changing planes in London for Geneva.

She gave a rueful relieving laugh. "I certainly didn't mean to tell you all this. It happened a long time ago."

In the street the Junkanoo had taken command: a steadily rising *tam tam tam! tam tam te-tam!* repeated by hundreds of drums while the horde thundered along to cowbells and shrilling whistles. It was like a pulse in the blood, stronger with every breath.

I should tell him, now, what I've decided, she thought. I can't just sneak away in the morning.

And if I were to tell him he would ask for my address. How could I refuse? Invent one? He knows my name, anyway. He can find me easily if he ever comes to Geneva. Then he'll learn who my father was quickly enough. Who my father is.

Unless he were convinced I don't want to see him again.

She felt buffeted by a sense of impossible responsibility to someone who disgusted her, who knew nothing really of her life, who could not imagine how he had blasted it by his absence, by the falseness of his death.

Naked, she went to the window. Great papier-mâché masks in red and white and yellow and black were passing, crepe paper giants on stilts, and alongside them flames leaping into the night to the triumphant rumble of the drums.

He came over to stand beside her. He said, "I think the view's better from your room, after all. We're too high up here, I'll only get the tops of their heads. Your balcony should be right at the level of the masks."

She felt a chill go through her. But she said, "We can go downstairs if you want."

She shivered. He kissed her slowly and she was aware of his body again, moving against her.

He said, "It will go on all night."

That was when she heard, faintly as some distant music played beyond silence, her mother's voice, in French.

—*Is this how much your father's life is worth? He is dying, Esther. Is this how you want to say good-bye to him? With nothing? Because when he is gone that is your last good-bye to anything of me,* ma petite.

———

She went down ahead of him, saying she wanted a shower, promising to leave her door unlocked. In his eagerness not to miss the passing commotion he pulled on some clothes, gathered up the camera and tripod, and headed downstairs hurriedly. Outside was rhythmic pandemonium. He let himself into her room; she was still in the shower. He was setting up the tripod at the balcony's edge when he noticed her carry-on bag hidden in the corner behind her dresser. It crossed his mind that her passport might be in there. He wondered vaguely what nationality she carried and then realized it was only the beginning of what he wondered. The shower was still going strong.

He went to the bag and unzipped it silently. There was the silver-framed photograph, taken in a park with classical statues. Esther as a little girl, holding hands with her parents before a fountain with jets of water playing. Her father, solidly built, looking down at her. Her mother, dark-haired, luminous in the dress of red silk.

And a leather passport wallet. He pulled out her passport hastily, guiltily. Spanish. He flipped it open. *Esther Lucía Gautier.* Good picture of her. Hadn't lied about her age, though she'd be twenty-nine in a month. Geneva address. Folded into the passport was a photocopy of her Madrid birth certificate. Her mother French, maiden name *Thérèse Gautier.* That was curious. Father—

She was out of her mind.

He stiffened as he heard the shower suddenly stop. She called out, "Thomas, are you there?"

He couldn't find a voice to answer. He thrust the passport back into the bag. In the old photograph her father's face was indistinct. He called out something to mollify her.

The shower started up. Trembling, he slid the passport out again, laid it open, gazed at her face in the photo and compared it to his memory of the famous Cartier-Bresson of her father. As a precaution he quickly snapped on the flash attachment and photographed her passport, his fingers holding it down, then her birth certificate. The flash blinded him in the mirror of the shut bathroom door. No wonder she'd hidden the family photo, no wonder he'd sensed she was never quite telling the truth. Her father's name was listed as *Cristóbal de la Torre*—the great Cuban sculptor. And he had drowned off Key West several years ago.

7

LIKE ANY OTHER MAN NOW, HE STOPPED on the wild path through the island to his shrine, the refuge he had built with his years, hearing his daughter's imagined voice echo through him.

—Father, I won't be coming. Not today, not ever.

As if from a lifetime ago a tired following wind blew down the path and made him limp with memory. The wind carried away the health that had suffused him here for years, leaving behind an old defeated body standing among dense shadows of swarming palms while a half-mile away, where he'd expected that first glimpse of his daughter's plane, the last light of afternoon trumpeted off the sea and the shut lip of horizon.

Give me back my daughter!

From afar, devastated by time, he heard the honks of automobiles.

He looked out the hotel window, worried. Thérèse wasn't back yet, it was after midnight, she didn't know Charleston, what could have happened? Twelve-seventeen: the pristine watchface taunted him. In the next room Esther lay asleep, small legs tucked beneath her, made a single shape by the white cotton bedspread. She was motionless; for an instant he had a premonition that she'd ceased breathing and he started into her shadowy room but then she stirred and adjusted her hands beneath her head.

Beside her pillow, on the bedside table next to the plaited sisal fan she'd paid for with her pocket money, was the long-stemmed pink rose he'd brought her. Despite the pale halo of the night light the rose was beginning to furl its petals.

Where could Thérèse be? She'd left no message. Presumably she'd gone out after putting their daughter to sleep; Esther felt comfortable enough in the hotel to be left alone. There'd been no calls all evening. This was just like Thérèse—to eat up his concentration when she knew how little he had left. He thought of summoning the hotel manager but his every movement since arriving in Charleston five days before had been reported in such detail by the local newspapers that he was scared to do anything that might be fodder for the journalists.

And this evening, tardy on the heels of Dutch and Spanish television crews, a large American television company had flown down a reporter to do an interview for one of those incessant morning talk shows that coupled a polished ignorance with grinning enthusiasm. Tomorrow morning there'd be a formal ceremony in front of his unveiled white marble gate of lions; then the planes to Miami, to Mexico City, and finally to a Havana irrevocably changed, for the first time in ten years.

Twelve thirty-one.

He felt his chest tighten. His parents were long buried in the country cemetery of Bejucal, the tiny village just south of Havana where they'd spent so many weekends. Could there be a gratitude sufficient for the entwined smells of pastures and coal smoke, for horseback rides behind his father or lantern-lit nights in that rough stone house with its nearby creek? That weekend he would see it all again, would apologize to them for—for what? His absence? Surely they'd have understood why he'd stayed away so long.

Through luck he'd returned briefly, just after the revolution, as if some instinct had whispered to him, "Fix it all clearly in your mind, Cristóbal. As if you were trying to memorize the lines of a poem you must recall for the rest of your life and will never be able to consult again. The poem is irretrievably lost and all the poets are in jail or dead or disgraced. And it is a poem you must pass on to your wife and child as if they too had read it."

Tomorrow at this time Thérèse and Esther would be on the island of his birth, would meet Lezama—and this would almost certainly be their only chance. He had prepared himself for the hurt of actually watching Cubans standing in line to buy rations of coffee or bananas, or coming to a gracious house of marble columns amid palms and saying, "You see the Russian Embassy? That was Victor's house, where I played as a child…"

The structure of the poem might remain, even if most of the natural music of its strophes was gone.

Too late. He took off his wristwatch and put it in his trousers pocket, so its ticking would not grow any more annoying. Around him the empty white armchairs and sofa gaped at him, the golden fleur-de-lis on the wallpaper watched him with many eyes. The breeze that apparently pervaded Charleston had deserted him here on the eighth floor. The television studio had been frigid with air-conditioning—an extreme of the hemisphere, as he pointed out. In the old days in Havana, the air-conditioning at the Floridita was strong enough to blow out cigarette lighters and hence most helpful if you were with a lady: it gave you an excuse to lean in. He understood that most of the air-conditioners in Havana weren't working so well these days.

He stepped onto the balcony. Earlier there'd been fireworks, exploded into falling shards above the blue-black sea.

Then the moon rose, an ancient coin flipped upward. Now it was gone in clouds, and the night was slow and thick. He could not stay out here, waiting for the moon to reappear, and he came in from the balcony, wary.

Then as he paced the sitting room he heard her key scrape and rasp as it was fitted into the lock. He hurried over and pulled the door open before she could get the key out. Her blue eyes met his with astonishment, a doll with its mouth clicked open. She wore the long dress of red silk he'd given her for her birthday, and for once she looked momentarily clumsy.

Why so surprised? he thought. Surely you knew I'd be here by now.

For an instant he saw her as if it were the first time, a younger woman sailing into a busy room and tumbling the lesser boats in her wake. He'd wondered what it would be like to be around such beauty every day: that long flag of black hair, her unexplored blue eyes with their jungles of hidden meaning; her high cheekbones a hint of the Manouche gypsy strain three generations back. A generous mouth that a former suitor, an overly enthusiastic poet, had called "red lips that are the poison of ancient houses." Difficult to tumble himself back to the innocence of not knowing her, not having made a life, a truce, a daughter with her.

She went wordlessly ahead of him into the suite. He retrieved her key from the door and followed her.

"I've been so worried. Why didn't you leave word downstairs?"

She was busily putting down her bag, checking something in it. "You know they can't keep order here. I called to say I wouldn't be in until midnight. You shouldn't have worried."

He saw a shadow cross her face and felt something knock against a corner of his heart. She swept into the master bedroom of the suite as he asked, "Did you have a good time?"

Maybe she's a little drunk, he thought.

"Delightful," she answered, over her shoulder.

Delightful?

He went to the doorway and looked in. She sat taking off her turquoise earrings, inspecting herself in the dressing-table mirror. Her Spanish had a French lilt even though her accent was Castilian; it was an effect that still charmed him.

Before he could ask, she said, "I had dinner with that family we met at the party the first night. The Sanders, you remember."

"No."

"The judge with the distinguished beard."

What did she talk about with these people? He never could imagine how she sounded when she was not with him.

"I don't remember."

"They called to invite us both."

"I see."

The front desk had said there'd been no calls.

"Don't you remember? You said his wife looks like a wax-works."

"Ah, yes." But he didn't remember.

"She was more animated tonight," said Thérèse. "I think you paralyze people sometimes, without realizing it."

"I can't believe that."

Her eyes hadn't left her reflection in the mirror. "When that lady asked what you thought of Picasso's pottery, because she had a signed plate."

"I said *bon appétit*."

"You told her Picasso was a terrible cook, it would be better to have a signed bedsheet."

"Did I say that?" He chuckled. That was pretty funny.

"People don't know how to talk to you."

"The only protection I have."

"You intimidate them."

"No," he said irritably. "Their idea of me intimidates them."

"You intimidate me sometimes," she said, and glanced at him over her shoulder again—as if to make sure that he was not just a reflection before her.

Since when don't you know how to paralyze me? he thought.

"What could possibly intimidate you, after all these years?"

"I don't know," she said, with the assurance of someone holding a list. "Your concentration, I suppose. I never know how to hold it. Or break it."

"You know very well how to hold it," he said. "I simply don't concentrate enough. That's my fault. My days are a stampede of distractions."

"I hope you weren't waiting long," she said. "You weren't sure earlier how long the interview would take."

"Not long." He crossed the room to the gigantic bed—North Americans fashioned their hotel beds to the scale of their continent—and sat on its end, so his reflection was over her shoulder in the mirror. "Esther ate with you?"

"I let her try a cheeseburger. She felt sleepy so we came back. Then those people telephoned."

"Those people."

"They wondered if you knew of a Danish photographer called Jacobsen. The judge saw an exhibit of his pictures in Paris last summer. He said quite a few were of your work."

"You know Jacobsen. That parasite can make anything look minimalist. Even something the size of a house." He added with annoyance, "The revenge of a tiny mind."

"Don't be angry with me," she said. "I didn't mean to be late."

She put the second earring on the dressing table and stood up before the mirror, watching his reflection, then came over to him and put out both her hands. He took them gently and ran his thumbs over their backs.

"How was the interview?" she said quietly.

"My bicycle of an accent ran amok." The twin lamps on the dressing table threw her face into shadow and limned her tall body in the red silk. The gold on one finger glinted at him.

"You look exasperated," she said.

He let her hands go and she placed them on his shoulders and kissed him softly.

"Did you talk about Cuba?"

"Enough. Enough to let them know who's coming to visit whom."

Mr. de la Torre, you have not lived in Cuba for many years. Where do you consider home?

—I'm an exile, so home is wherever my family is. Since we're usually together, I'm usually at home. My work keeps us traveling, but we keep an apartment in Paris and a house at Nerja, in Andalucía.

Where will your next project take you?

—To the coast near Boston, Massachusetts, after a couple of months in Paris. But next week I'll be returning to Havana for the first time in many years. A ten-day arts festival. I'm to be one of the guests of honor. We'll see.

You knew Castro a long time ago, didn't you? Weren't you friends?

—You make me remember a remark by Oscar Levant, the pianist and raconteur. He said, "I knew Doris Day before she was a virgin." I knew Fidel before he was a freedom fighter and a torturer of poets, homosexuals, and former colleagues. I used to see him moping around the university. We were hardly friends. I promise you, in the end history may overlook a record of systematic cruelty and murder, but it doesn't forgive eight-hour speeches.

Castro himself has said that as a young man he always had

several books with him, he read incessantly.

—All revolutionaries when they grow up want to become intellectuals, and vice-versa. A gangster with a book is still a gangster. Too bad! If only baseball had worked out.

I beg your pardon?

—Fidel was a very good third baseman. He had a tryout for the Minnesota Twins and they offered him a contract for their second team—what do you call it? Farm team. He refused. He didn't want to work on a farm like ordinary Cubans, he wanted to go directly to the Major Leagues. And he did, unfortunately for Cuba. This is why, unlike some of my compatriots, I cannot blame Kennedy or Eisenhower or the CIA or the United Fruit Company for the Cuban revolution. I blame the Minnesota Twins. If they'd offered him a better contract, history might have been different.

"You know," she said, "as much as we've talked about Lezama I almost feel I know him. What will he think, seeing you with a family?"

"He used to say I should never get married again." She was playing with the tips of his ears. "He'll take me aside and say, in that resounding voice, 'I see, Cristóbal, you are like a knight in a fifteenth-century French romance. Returning at last from a deep forest to the castle of your birth, with a vital damsel at your side.'"

"You did find me in a forest. A forest of people." She touched his cheek and he felt her hand tremble. She turned around. "Will you unzip me, please?"

His mouth was dry with folded questions. He said, "With pleasure."

As he fumbled at the top of her dress for the zipper he reached around with his free hand and rubbed it against her flat stomach. She captured his hand and pulled it up. He felt her nipple swell suddenly against the pressure of his inquiring hand.

The sway of her haunches, as she shifted her weight from one foot to the other so she was doing a little trot in place, a circular dance, brought a moan from him. Her hair swept around his face; he kissed her neck through it.

Your work has been called religious. Are there any other religious artists you particularly admire?

—Lots and lots. You want names? Among the dead, Michelangelo. Among the living, Charlie Chaplin.

As he inhaled the perfume from her hair, their fluid shadows on the ceiling reminded him of their first shadows together. They'd met in Paris at a party given to raise money for a friend of his, an elderly Cuban painter. She was twenty-five. She'd come on the arm of an impeccably dressed lawyer who was showing her off, and she'd seemed bored—an impoverished graduate student who couldn't afford to look bored. They talked for only a few minutes, but with naturalness even through his uncomfortable French; he got her telephone number and wondered if he'd transcribed it correctly. At that time she didn't speak a word of Spanish.

Several days later, from New York, he called her—it took several permutations of the number before he succeeded—and suggested she fly over at his expense. At thirty-six he was already having a major retrospective of his work at the Modern. She had virtually no money, but she paid her own way over. That gesture of independence (calculated, he saw) impressed him: she would have to be won.

In New York he was staying in a townhouse borrowed from a friend for a month. Rain clouds the night she arrived—her plane several hours late—veiled the lights of the city in the darkened guest bedroom with high studio windows. She seemed tired and tentative after the protracted journey. Still more or less a Cuban gentleman, he brought her bags up there to the top floor and left her, hoping for much but expecting little. He took his time locking up below, turned off the lamps. Then he went upstairs to wish her good night.

The lights were off on the top landing, but her door was open. She lay on her stomach on the bed, a slim landscape of flesh, scant moonlight draped from twin rounded hills all the way up to her rumpled black hair. Her long legs were in shadow; he'd watched them carefully at that party in Paris the week before, in a black silk dress that taunted him by being short but not short enough. Legs that even when demurely crossed appeared to establish their own law.

As she lay there awaiting him, her body gave off a slow rhythm of its own, a counterpoint to his own quickening heartbeat. She seemed charged with an energy that fed on the splashed darkness and emanated from her body on the bed as if from undersea, rising slowly to burst on contact with the air. Through the high windows the shadows shifting in the sky with the movements of passing clouds were like the shadows cast on submarine reefs by undulant coral fans.

He navigated his way to her body. He placed his hand on the bedspread between the backs of her knees. Involuntarily her legs moved an inch or so together. He did absolutely nothing. He waited. He heard her breathing become dusky; he felt he could almost reach down and brush away the shadows that lay across her ankles. She moaned softly, a curse.

Even this close, darkness lay like an enigmatic path up her legs, eventually merging with the tangled forest whose lushness would never fail to intrigue him. He eased his hand across the taut sheet, stroking it rather than her, until he felt the outskirts of forest, and then a shadowy river's dampness. Along the river, fever; the air unexpectedly humid here. Slowly her warm currents swallowed his fingers, and he felt their sliding eddies stir as she rolled onto her left side and looked over her shoulder at him through half-lidded eyes.

Now, standing up a decade later, with her haunches playing against the front of his trousers, she looked over her shoulder at him with the same bemused smile, the same look, half sleepy, half beckoning. He tugged the zipper steadily down and she slipped off her sandals and stepped easily out of the dress, graceful even in these ungainly movements. He put aside the thought of how awkward he would feel in a moment stepping out of his trousers.

In the lamplight the sluggish passing of mere seconds seemed unbearable. As she walked away from him in bare feet to drape the red silk over an armchair he swiftly crossed the room and shut off the two lamps that straddled the dressing-table mirror, banishing his and her reflections along with a moth that fluttered toward the window.

He undressed and turned. She stood beside the bed, still slim, only slightly heavier than ten years ago, but her face and bearing now held a nobility; he felt the girl in her gone and the power, the assurance of the woman standing a few feet away from him. He was no longer the stranger, the welcome invader of her countryside: a wheel of mutual possession revolved between them, resolved. As she fell backwards he sensed a sacred honey awaiting his tongue. Her hands grasped his forearms, his hands measured her hips and felt the first sweat of desire on her skin, shield-points beneath his palms.

We are falling, I am following. A rub of the magic lantern. We are two frogs.

A small shock went through her and shook him within her; he pulled suddenly out and she caught at his arms.

He lifted her all the way onto the bed. One of her legs lay stretched out, the other bent with abandon. Her hair a tumult of darkness across the pillow. He hovered backwards over her vining body, his legs straddling her face. Twirled beneath his tongue the warm berries, each in turn. Kissed his way down until he reached her salt curls, damp against his cheek. Not a woman, a cave. He licked insistently lower until he reached the narrow portal of a small shell, and as he plunged his tongue into her she pulled him down into her hot mouth, overwhelming him.

Mr. de la Torre, are you pleased to be in Charleston?

—Very. It devours many influences and still follows its own rules. This keeps it original.

Rather like your marble gate, unveiled here this weekend. Could you talk about your inspiration for it?

—I think many artists become so paralyzed by the idea of originality, of escaping every tradition they can think of, that they lose their way. I don't want to discard the past, I want to use as much of it as I can. This work doesn't speak Greek, it speaks my very limited language. But I've made a white marble gateway with lions, in homage to one standing for several thousand years at Mycenae.

Do you feel a particular kinship with Greek sculpture?

...massive palms swarm upward to the terrace, watch them move, watch them move, their fronds obscuring the black gate to the garden far below. Fragrance of hibiscus, scent of Mama sometimes, wafts upward. Smell, oh smell! And awful odor of unwashed Pepito, here comes the brown fur. Stay still, Pepito, good dog.

He tugs himself upright, tiny hands slipping. Looks up: overhead his grandmother's massive marble bust of Aristotle, gazing out toward the courtyard's jungle of palms, what does he see, what does he see...

—Let's say I try to be worthy of my former colleagues. The ones who have been dead for several centuries.

What's next on your agenda, Mr. de la Torre?

—The problem is by the time you approach fifty, you start to feel your life littered with the wreckage of unfinished work, or work you haven't started, or that's second-rate. You become obsessed with doing one piece which will justify all the rest. I have always dreamed of finally doing one work by which I will happily stand or fall.

Any ideas for it?

—Oh, a sculpture that would involve people in a more active way. Sculpture today is something big you walk past. This is pointless, eh? For this reason I made my gate here in Charleston. Either you walk through it, or not. At least you are involved. You see? The most flexible form for a work of art, for me the ideal, is a maze. In a symphony, a novel, a play or a film, you must start at the beginning and carry on to the end or else something vital is lost. In a maze there is not really that ironclad consecutivism, it is different every time. Everything is equally vital. It is all of paramount importance. You enter the maze, you get captured, you find your own way out. Along the way you make up your own plot, in a collaboration with whoever made the maze. And maybe you don't ever escape! So there is a kind of creative improvisation also.

Afterward in the hotel suite, many miles afterward, they lay apart, broken and separate sculptures. Her breathing was deep and even; he lay uneasily in darkness and wondered whether to wake her.

...warm and enchanted arms cradle him, so high up, so safe! His mother's arms rocking him in the garden to the rhythm of a *son*, he laughing, her voice pure like a bell, chanting:

> "*When the full moon rises I will go*
> *To Santiago de Cuba,*
> *I will go to Santiago*
> *In a coach of black water...*
> *The roofs of palm will sing*
> *I will go to Santiago.*"

His mother's voice, vague with many decades, came to him, speaking to him as a child, patiently explaining the truth.

"Yes, Cristóbal, you were born on a Wednesday. The middle day of the week. Not on a Tuesday or a Thursday. A Wednesday. Now what is it about Wednesday's child that makes him special?"

He had piped up confidently, then; he heard his child-voice now, seeking the answer.

"Has far to journey."

She smiled, a rather plain brown-haired woman with the bluest eyes he could imagine, twilight-blue eyes of utter devotion to him: mother's eyes. Eyes of Thérèse, as they once were.

"No, no, Cristóbal. Overcomes woe. You were born on a Wednesday, so you are very lucky. Can you tell me why? Try again."

And he, not having any sense what the words meant, complying to keep her happy.

"Yes, Mama. Wednesday's child—Wednesday's child—overcomes woe!"

And Mama clapping her hands and he trying to clap his too, and she lifting him and he laughing at the rush of air...

Overcomes woe.

Of all your works, which has given you the most pleasure, which the most pain? Or perhaps I should say the most difficulty.

—It has been so long since I felt that purely either way. The most pleasure, I suppose, apart from the professional pride of knowing one has done a good job, was when I was a boy in Havana, about three or four years old, at my grandmother's house. It had a gallery that looked out through palm trees to the garden below, and some days I played on the gallery, pretending it was the deck of a pirate ship, and some days I played in the garden...

Now in the garden was one very ugly toad that, when I was small, seemed gigantic, a monster, with warts that bulged and eyes that popped out of his head and hideous marks all over him. And when he made his noises they sounded as if they were coming out of the earth. One day after a heavy rain I was playing in a corner of the garden, and I found some wet clay, dark red, and I mixed some ferns into the clay and it looked a little greener. At first I didn't know what I wanted to do with it. Then I thought of the toad, so I made myself a toad out of clay, just like the real one, right before his eyes...

Of course I made an awful mess, and my nanny whipped me that afternoon for ruining my clothes, and kept me out of the garden for a week. But what did I care? I'd made a toad out of clay and ferns, that's all, nothing else. I can still remember how I felt when I finished, it was such a new and marvelous feeling, of having made something, and I thought: What will I make next? What will I make tomorrow? The real toad made his noises at my toad and I thought how beautiful they both were, especially the real one, so much a toad, and me like me, and this clay toad between us, part him, part me. It was wonderful. I don't think it can ever be that purely wonderful again. Being a man is too complicated.

And the works of pain, of difficulty?

—They are all difficult in different ways, so they have each given me different degrees of pain. Some births are more a struggle than others. But that sort of pain doesn't affect you as if, say, a friend or a beloved had hurt you. And when I look back on my work it is almost as if someone else did it. I have my life with my daughter, Esther, and my wife, Thérèse, but there is someone else inside me who has his own life, who is still trying to make his ugly clay toad as beautiful as the living one he sees before him, with all its warts and eyes. And if this is difficult, that is after all the point. The difficulties are here to be dealt with, not avoided. All joy comes out of risk.

How pointless it seemed now, to have waited for Esther to arrive on his island as he had awaited Thérèse's return that night in Charleston, a night that in retrospect seemed like the cracked door between two lifetimes. He remembered every detail of the next morning: watching himself on television after almost no sleep while Thérèse packed in the other room in silence, exhausted by their long night. Esther curled up on the sofa, bony legs tucked under her, loudly slurping down her second bowl of cereal. His legs stretched toward the television in the same charcoal trousers he'd worn for the interview. How different he looked there on the screen, he could barely recognize himself. He thought: That is someone else, I can never be him again.

Now, in the dwindling daylight on the path to his shrine, beneath his uncertain feet the sand cursed him. He began to run, hurrying through late afternoon shadows, feeling the sweat spring from his flesh and mingle with the dried salt water on his skin so he glistened as the toad had so many decades ago. Shards of sunlight flashed through the palms at him, burning the ridges of his eyelids.

Behind him from down the path came echoes of the sea chiding him, the blank horizon with its lame unfulfilled promise of peace. Ringing laughter barreled around the rim of the world and off the blue dome of sky. He felt dazed and shrunken. What could he do to lure her here now?

He sensed the old ache of arthritis, that he'd thought the sea had banished from his bones forever, return complaining. He felt himself running out of time on this path, squeezing his head with both hands, trying to squeeze out the images crowding his brain. His unearthly rage later that night in Charleston after Thérèse had made her pathetic speech and he had failed to understand or respond properly. The few strange months before Thérèse's suicide, first in Havana, then Paris, then Massachusetts, as she sank lower and lower into a darkness he refused to soak up for her, that (he still argued to himself) no one could have. The years since with nothing for him to do but continue working, an aging man waiting here to die and be rid of it all since Esther, an untouchable Esther lost to him, refused to face him or see what he'd made for her. Lurching aimlessly about this shrine he had built for Thérèse and to bring back their protected daughter and it had not, never would, it was useless, as useless as he—

Give me back my daughter!

—Father, I've decided not to come, I'm going back to Geneva. Happy holidays.

What? I can't believe it.

"Forget about she, man!" Scully had said, relaying Pinder's message. "Let she know she replaceable!"

He felt his chest tighten and he forced himself to stop running, heaving with breathlessness. In his mind's eye his ghost ran on ahead, careening up the path, caroming off an elephant-gray palm, staggering wildly into the deep pangola grass. From the direction of the shrine a peahen screamed. All the peacocks had been fed that afternoon, what did this one want? Now he was coming empty-handed. All his life empty-handed in the service of women.

Can't you talk to her, Thérèse? Sometimes I can almost feel you beside me but then I find myself alone, here alone. Yet somewhere our souls must be beside each other, still.

—Sorry, Father. I turned back in Nassau. This far and no farther.

I can't believe it, Esther, don't say this. You know I can't come visit you. Please. If you only knew how full of time you seem.

Against the blue Venus appeared, evening star high on his

left shoulder; below it the rim of the sun still hung, heavily contemplating the sea spread before it, etched like cut glass. As always in the tropics, Venus was the first star to steal attention from the sun and would steal it in memory, long after twilight descended. Yet Venus had no reflection anywhere in the aquamarine mirror.

Thérèse, how can I have come this far to end up alone?

Faces floated about him, real ghosts, voices. The face of Lezama, old friend dead now for nearly two decades, avuncular creator encouraging him from boyhood: that low voice with its curious upward inflection at the end of every muscular line, the sinews of the poet transforming every phrase. And after the revolution the two of them exiled from each other. He still had with him the letter Lezama had sent from Havana immediately after Thérèse's suicide, the brief statement of lifelong friendship in a sweeping hand. What letter of utter despair would Lezama have written him today?

—Look at the two of us, Lezama had said to him the first evening of his return to Cuba, back in Havana in the subdued tumult of one of the few bars as yet un-castrated. Lezama even bigger and fatter than he'd remembered, positively heroic that boiling afternoon in his usual meticulous suit.

—Look at us, Cristóbal. From our epitaphs no one will imagine we had ever crossed paths, let alone been friends. My epitaph you already know, it will be: He was born in Havana, he lived in Havana, he died in Havana.

And mine, Lezama?

Then had come that gaze, the stare of a solitary giant encircled by midget humanity, brown eyes transfixing him from beneath a shock of black hair edged white, inflated face in reproachful repose until the carefully modulated voice issued again, tinged with a slight asthmatic wheeze, accompanied by Lezama's gourmand hand squeezing his forearm gently.

—You, Cristóbal, your epitaph will be: He was born in Havana; he lived nowhere; he died somewhere. He left parts of himself everywhere.

Then the rumble of godlike laughter inducing the laughter of everyone present, including a subdued Thérèse and a wide-eyed Esther at six hanging on Lezama's every word—after that year only his spoken words were not banned—having whispered that he must be the biggest person in the world. For an instant Cristóbal had seen his own thought echoed in Lezama's eyes.

—Now Havana too is nowhere. You left in time, Cristóbal, and longer ago than it feels with you across the table from me again. But I am too heavy now to leave here, ever.

And ten days later, in front of the hotel just prior to their departure, Lezama had said to him softly: Shall we see each other again, old friend? Not in Havana. Not in this world. But when you arrive home, and you go slowly up the steps of your building in Paris that I will never see, I want you to notice that one particular step is friendlier to you than all the others.

How could Esther possibly imagine how it felt to have so little time left? How could she possibly know?

And before him suddenly, at the end of the path, the first self-portrait, a younger Cristóbal gazing out from the rock.

The false image of a man who did not give up. Better you than me waiting out time, waiting for my daughter to discover you. I cannot wait anymore. I might as well get on with it and prove the journalists correct.

In my dream, Esther, I wanted never to feel any of this, I wanted you only to let me love you. I did not want to possess you or claim your life or interfere, I did not want to explain, I did not need to be forgiven. I wanted only some time, a little time with you.

In my dream I would not live long enough to reach this point, I was going to die. I did not imagine what effect this reviving island would have, I did not imagine when building from the blueprint of my dream that afterward the final mark would be one of futility. I never imagined so green and vibrant an island could frighten you. I never imagined that after I had finished building Eden you wouldn't want to see it. The ability to hurt those closest to you is the beginning of real maturity.

In my dream I built this place for us at a time when the world was falling, it was to be our sanctuary, and when I died you would pass it on to the world. And you would be able to say that in at least one place at that dangerous time something was raised up, conceived and built to outlast any danger; to hurl its power outward and frighten men with its intelligence and beauty and then hold them in its arms afterward.

Consider a naked man. In my dream he was always a castaway, disgorged by violent seas of shipwreck, borne like a discarded spar, some human detritus here. Washed up on this beach utterly by accident, a survivor awakening as into a deeper, more penetrating daylight. Barely alive.

In my dream he sees the ruined arch of stone I built so deliberately on the beach and it leads him down the path, the trees waving their swishing skirts at him, the taller palms like great tropical islands levitating themselves in air. He wonders how long he can survive here, as I have wondered every night waiting for a letter of assurance from you, he meanders down that path through the jungle, not knowing he will find me waiting, and beyond me the angels of destruction and beyond them all the eyes of God. He will see all these things until the layers of hiding have been stripped from him like the skins of a snake, but will he ever know this was all built by a man for his lost wife, his lost daughter?

Around him darkness had settled, the familiar and enormous night of the tropics. Hanging constellations he had learned as a boy in Cuba. A full moon rising from a net of trees, floating through the dust of many stars. Bright holes that went clear through to the back of the universe, holes through which his solitude and his years were sieved every night to leave him able to sleep. Not tonight: tonight the stars were burning torches, real suns up there like ideas in the mind of heaven, blazing from the infinite blackness of God and staring down on him as if they knew he was watching, far from the jealous lights of cities.

Look at this night yawning around me. Difficult to believe that you are alive somewhere under this star-infested blackness too. It is day where you are: people are shaking their alarm clocks, making their coffee, hurrying to work to the loud shunting of trains. Watching their lives go by on television screens, turning them off at night. I wonder when you think of me, since think of me you must. On falling asleep? At the bank? Do people speak to you of me? Do the biographers still call? They doubtless will not let you forget. At least you have not become a whore with a famous last name, like the children of certain colleagues. Your mother is proud of that.

In my dream she watches you, she does not speak to me but I watch her eyes. Perhaps it is at her request you do not come here. Perhaps you await a gesture from her hand. If you only knew what I would give for the lilt of her voice once more, for the knowledgeable garden of her arms.

It was perhaps stupid and unrealistic of me to have this dream, of myself bringing an island from the sea-foam and building my shrine here: a dead man willing himself back to life simply to have his daughter come to him. Just to speak a little. I have your mother's blue scarf to give you yet. Your Christmas present.

In my dream there was never to be this much time here, I

was to have joined your mother long ago. I never imagined that one day I would be that naked man lying on the shore, stumbling down this path, and after seeing what some other more hopeful man had imagined and built and left behind, discover myself alone on this island, ready to believe myself dead, errant in the dark.

8

When Thomas awakened, soaked in sweat, his air-conditioner off, wrung out from having slept in great heat, it was early afternoon.

It had been eight that morning before the Junkanoo finally wound down. Esther seemed slightly jumpy, and suggested they go back to their own rooms. He hadn't mentioned what he'd learned.

After five hours' fitful sleep he felt he'd dreamed only of her passport. On the way downstairs he listened at her door and heard the hum of an air-conditioner. Let her sleep, he thought.

Post-Junkanoo, the waiters at the terrace restaurant were even more listless than usual.

For two days he'd questioned his initial contradictory sense of her. He saw now that he had been right, saw the source of the desperation he'd felt in her even through the camera lens. She talked as though her father were actually alive, out on some island. It was significant that she'd begun by admitting that he was dead. Perhaps the business with selling the family property was true. She'd come out only to sign some papers and leave. Staying here, she'd begun to feel more and more as if it were an earlier time. Perhaps Esther owed her father that visit from many years ago. She hadn't gone to see him, then he'd drowned and it was too late. Perhaps she was deliberately arguing out old regrets, using Thomas as an anvil to hammer the past against.

What if there were no property to be sold? What if she came here every year simply to repeat this theater? Could she be as unbalanced as that?

He was realist enough to know it was impossible to solve anyone's problems for them. It was difficult enough to solve your own—he held no expectations that another person would make his life open out, it was too late for that. Years ago, before the severe mistake of his marriage, he'd gotten involved with too many women who seemed wonderful but for this or that profound fissure that he thought he could glue together for them; no doubt they'd seen him the same way. As if a lover were like some plastic model kit that came unassembled and you had to put it together and paint it at home. This was a waste of time, to try this on anyone.

If Esther were as unassembled as she seemed, as in need of real professional help—if she believed her dead father was still somewhere in the Bahamas, hoping she'd join him for Christmas—what could he say to her? What was their next move together? Go spend the New Year with Cristóbal de la Torre, famous sculptor and equally famous corpse?

He didn't know how long he could keep up the pretense of not knowing what he knew now. He'd had no right to look at her passport, he couldn't very well pretend to have recognized her. What if he could push her to admit who her father was? In the light of day facts were facts. He could always plague her with more questions, but he felt retroactive guilt at having questioned her so much in the first place. She'd been ready to go back to Geneva when they met; it was he who'd pressured her to stay on. Who knew how much of this he was responsible for.

I'll ask point-blank, he thought.

At two his coffee was cold and she still hadn't come down. On the way upstairs he was tempted to knock, then wondered why he was in such a hurry to speak to her when he wasn't sure what to say. The day was very humid and the air in his room was dripping. The maid hadn't done the room yet. When he held the pillow to his face he could smell Esther.

He cleaned his lenses thoroughly and organized the film he'd shot the night before. Photos of her passport in there. At three he went down to her room and knocked. In the lobby the receptionist, a burly black woman with humane eyes, looked surprised at his inquiry.

"She check out. Long time ago."

"What?"

"This morning. Right after Junkanoo. Round about ten, I imagine."

"Are you sure?"

She looked at him skeptically. "Yes, man. I just go on duty when she come down with her bags to check out. Took a airport taxi. She didn't tell you?"

His stupefied silence answered that one. The receptionist clucked at him sympathetically.

Clinging to a last spar of dignity, he said, "Any messages in my box today?"

She made a ceremony of searching for a polite few seconds. "No, Mr. Simmons, not today." She shrugged.

He felt she would be laughing the instant he stepped outside.

He found himself walking along Parliament Street like a man in a dream imagining himself awake and walking on Parliament Street. What a place to have the day shoved down your throat. Nassau looked blank. The town had erased her, replaced her with more lurching tourists. Not a glimpse of her in any of their eager faces, their ungainly bodies. A person disappeared and it was as if the place had never held her.

Where had this stranger gone? Back to Geneva?

She'd gone to the airport, anyway. Disbelieving, confused, he went to the airport.

In the taxi he couldn't think. He felt pummeled by all his doubts being realized at once. They exaggerated the arrogant light along the coast and gave the day a harsh technicolor graininess. Why bother going to the airport? She wouldn't still be there. It was over. She'd simply chosen to end it first. But hadn't she said something the other day about her transatlantic flight leaving in the evening? His mind fastened desperately on this shred of a remark like a mountaineer clinging to a cliff. No one checked in that many hours early for a flight, did they?

Unless she were really trying to avoid him. She hadn't left him a note, her address, even a simple good-bye, after all. The message was loud and clear, she didn't have to type it out and sign it. It was exactly what he'd done to that tank of a young woman on the way to Inagua. No different.

The airport was already budding with lines of passengers waiting to check in for the big flights overseas that night—London, Paris, Rome, Zurich. The last line especially he surveyed from a distance, not wishing to be seen by her. Of course there was a good chance she'd passed through Passport Control already and was on the other side of the barrier in a waiting lounge.

He elbowed his way past some polite Swiss and said to the ticketing agent, in tones of great haste, "I got delayed back in town. Has a Miss Gautier already checked in?"

"You'll have to wait your turn in line, sir."

"Please, we're traveling together."

The attendant punched at his computer with annoyance. "Her name doesn't come up. Are you sure she's holding a reservation on this flight?"

Twenty-four hours ago she'd been stretched out beside

him, half naked, on their beach; fourteen hours ago she'd been telling him her life story, or a version of it, in his hotel room; eight hours ago she'd kissed him good morning outside her door while suggesting they both get some sleep—

He surveyed the other queues. No sign. The Departures board showed only one transatlantic flight had gone out that morning. He pushed through clusters of package tourists in embroidered straw hats, about to feel foolish entering the air-conditioned United States dressed like a calypso and stinking of coconut oil.

At British Airways there was a very short queue. Behind the ticket counter, a brisk young man with fair hair.

"Excuse me. I'm trying to find out if a Miss Gautier was on your earlier flight."

"I'm sorry, sir, we're not allowed to give out passenger lists."

"We were supposed to fly back together. My plane from Inagua got delayed."

Was it the right day? Saturday, Sunday—

"Delayed by two days, in fact."

"Inagua?" chuckled the attendant. "What were you doing down there?"

"Waiting for a plane out, mostly."

"I see." The attendant was pushing buttons. "I've only just come on, I'm afraid." He paused. "That flight left at eleven. Right on time. What did you say the lady's name was?"

"Gautier," said Thomas absently, knowing what he'd hear. That was it, then.

"You're in luck," said the attendant.

The phrase sounded ludicrous. Where was she now? In the middle of the Atlantic, airborne. Probably sitting in first class getting chatted up by the copilot, somewhere over the Azores.

"Gautier, first initial E., Miss. That the one?"

"That's her."

"That's she," said the young attendant with blithe grammatical satisfaction. "Holding reservation for flight 182, nonstop Nassau—London with connection on Swissair for Geneva. Did not check in for the flight, however. I expect she'll turn up any minute for the seven o'clock. You're in luck."

Thomas went over to a row of plastic bucket chairs and sat down. He was pouring sweat. Above him a ceiling fan turned with monumental lethargy. She hadn't taken the flight, then. Why not? She'd found a more direct flight at the last minute. That would be via Swissair.

He forced himself to walk over and inquire. No, this was their only departure of the day.

He returned to his seat beneath the sluggish fan. Of course she could've gone anywhere. Maybe she'd flown down to Rio for lunch and she'd be back at the hotel for dinner.

He knew where she'd gone. He'd known in the taxi. Her canceled reservation only confirmed it. She'd gone out to her father's island. It was preferable, after all, to believe she was a little unhinged than to think she had simply grown tired of him.

He sat there in the overworked air of the overheated airport and wondered what to do. He'd been trying to reach this airport from Inagua. He'd finally made it. Time to get on with his holiday.

He took a taxi into town. Back at the hotel, a different receptionist was on duty; he could inquire about messages without feeling humiliated. None, and there'd be none waiting for him in New York.

On impulse he went across the little park to the octagonal old library, thankfully open for the afternoon—the holiday had ended that morning. It was like being inside a dilapidated lighthouse. Tortoise shells hung on the walls; a fan turned above the shelves of humid books.

There wasn't much on Cristóbal de la Torre. The edition of

the Britannica was from the early fifties, so there was no entry under his name, and no back file of international magazines or newspapers for Thomas to look up the extensive obituaries and tributes. He guessed the drowning had been five years ago, maybe longer. No, six years ago, he could date it exactly. He'd been near Delhi, photographing snake charmers in a tiny village; he remembered reading the obituary in *The Times of India*. Was it worth getting the library assistant to hunt for the microfilm of the *Nassau Tribune* from that year? Probably not.

An entry in a British junior encyclopedia, for "young adults," published in 1975, told him little he didn't already know:

DE LA TORRE, Cristóbal (Lucía), sculptor. (1925–) Born Havana, Cuba. An important modern sculptor, from a very early age de la Torre showed a keen fascination with the plastic arts (see SCULPTURE, Modern; CUBA, The Arts & Literature). The only child of recent Spanish emigrés, his parents were relatively well-to-do. His father was director of a musical conservatory and for a time the assistant conductor of the Havana Symphony; his mother was a fine amateur painter. De la Torre achieved an early success with one-man shows in Havana (1946), Madrid (1948), Paris (1949), and New York (1952). Since that time his work has been represented in leading museums of Great Britain, Europe, and the U.S. (see TATE GALLERY and COURTAULD INST.). De la Torre's work is particularly noteworthy for its concentrated, boundless energy. Stylistically he remains difficult to classify. He has gained renown both for his pieces on a small scale (*The Chinese Puzzle Boxes*, 1955) and on the heroic, like his *Giants of the Desert* in 1958 (see MEXICO, illus. & Landscape).

More recently his work has ranged from the highly var-
ied life-size nudes of the mid-60s (see THE NUDE),
alternately hailed as a return to semi-naturalism or
denounced as "Latin Rodin" (see RODIN, AUGUSTE),
to the surrealistic and massive diorama *My Havana*,
inspired by a brief visit to Cuba shortly after the
Revolution. His charcoal sketches of the Vietnam con-
flict have been compared to fellow-sculptor Henry
Moore's of London during the Blitz (see MOORE,
HENRY and WWII, The Arts & Literature). De la
Torre's wife died tragically in 1971 during a trip to the
United States. Always an artist full of surprises, it is difficult to speculate what direction de la Torre's work may
take. Memorable Quote: "Great sculpture is when you
can take a statue, lop off its head, cart away both arms,
scrape off all the paint, lose one foot at the ankle and the
other leg at the knee, leave it outside for three thousand
years and it still looks good." See also CARIBBEAN,
The Arts and Literature; CASTRO, FIDEL; HAVANA;
MARBLE; MUSEUM OF MODERN ART.

Thomas didn't bother to cross-reference.
Seeing the life laid out on paper, all Esther's talk of seeing
her father reverberated until she was entirely one monstrous
lie, which she'd confirmed by blowing away like smoke this
morning. The Esther he'd met here and fallen for barely
existed. There was only the highly disturbed daughter of
Cristóbal de la Torre, an idea almost too alien to contem-
plate.
Last night—before he'd learned who she was, before she'd
left him high and dry—this young woman struggling with
herself had really touched him. He couldn't pretend otherwise. The shadows that he and she had cast together were
surely still alive somewhere, walking slowly through flooding

afternoon sunlight from the gardens of the ruined hotel.

I must be unhinged, he told himself, to think this way.

He went back to staring at the encyclopedia. They'd reproduced a photograph of the Mexican pieces—printed so small it was difficult to tell how massively they rose from the desert, huge primeval pillars of stone that already seemed worn away by time.

And there was the famous Cartier-Bresson of de la Torre. Gazing at it, he thought again that no photograph had ever made more of a dent on him as to what a portrait should be. It'd been taken in Havana prior to the revolution, before de la Torre left for good: a man staring from darkness, his hands carved by scant light spilling from an open doorway. The eyes penetrating and clear. The high, noble forehead. The mouth a thin, almost feminine line. It was de la Torre's palpable physical presence that so energized the picture. Here was no patient explainer or polite conversationalist. This was someone who shook you by the shoulders or told you to get out of the way. Behind him, a white bird was fluttering in the soft darkness of the café.

The bird's whiteness, the impossibly caught image, had caused endless discussion in photographic circles—whether it'd been released by one of Cartier-Bresson's assistants. Looking at the picture again, seeing the deliberation in de la Torre's eyes, Thomas wondered if it had been his idea, not the photographer's.

It couldn't have been pleasant growing up this man's only child. His wife's apparent suicide had confirmed his reputation as a difficult man. Still, Thomas reflected, this was how it got done. This was the difference between a Cristóbal de la Torre and a Thomas Simmons. Your wife paid for it, the next generation paid for it, but the work got done. If you weren't prepared to commit you shouldn't even walk through the door.

It was significant that he'd never heard of de la Torre having a daughter. She'd never made herself into a public personality, at least not in the States, never traded on her father. She went by her mother's name, after all. So much for family pride.

He looked in a *Book of the Year* from six years earlier, and found a brief entry.

PRESUMED DROWNED. Cuban sculptor Cristóbal de la Torre, age 62; off Key West, Florida, on Dec. 29, after a small sailboat he'd taken out alone for the afternoon was found capsized in calm weather conditions. De la Torre's wife had drowned herself sixteen years earlier to the day. His death therefore was ruled a suicide.

Then the body was never found. No wonder Esther was obsessed with the idea of coming here, with seeing her father. Poor thing.

This was what she'd been heading toward these few days with him, why she'd stayed. It wasn't for the sex, for the talk, for the Junkanoo, or for the scenery. It certainly wasn't for him. It was for her father, or for his memory.

What is strange, he thought, is that when you told me about him last night, and not wanting to face him, it was the first time I felt you were really telling me the truth.

In the little park by the library he sat down in the shade of a magisterial royal palm. He thought: Should I go on? Should I try to look for this woman? Suppose it's as simple as it seems? She caught an early flight that I don't know about. She came here to sell off old family property. I get out there and it's some empty tiny island her father owned. Lots of rich people own islands. Now someone's bought it off her. And she's back in snowy Switzerland.

That's one side of it. On the other hand, what do I have

better to do with my time at the moment? There's an encouraging notion that'll move mountains.

And what if I find her? Suppose she says: Didn't you get the message?

Then I'll say: Sorry. I saw you and went deaf. And at the very least I'll find out whether I'm crazy or you are.

Back at the hotel, the maid was cleaning out Esther's room as he went up the stairs.

In his room the bed had finally been changed. The rumpled sheets on which they'd made love the night before had been replaced by new clean ones, drummed tightly into place. He could've bounced a Bahamian dime on them.

You see how easily it can be erased? he thought. It might never have happened. The gulf between people is larger than you want to believe. You met someone? She has a life too. Stop pretending this meeting has any consequences, stop dreaming, stop edging away from what this woman is trying to tell you. It's a miracle you can make a living doing more or less what you want. Get back to work. Go home.

He went downstairs to the terrace instead. He got slightly drunk and asked the bartender if he'd ever heard of a famous Cuban sculptor living in the islands a few years back. The bartender told him about a painter, a Haitian *immigré* with a gallery on East Bay Street that sold local scenes, very popular with the tourists, reasonably priced. Did he want the name? No? All right, man. All right.

Another rum punch?

That evening, stunned by the day, he ate dinner in a garden restaurant on one of the modest old-world lanes off Bay Street. The town had a relieved breeziness tonight, an airy repose after the tense work of the Junkanoo. Its ease made him feel as jumpy as an assassin. He found himself imagining Esther still sitting across from him. If he could've settled on an explanation for her leaving, even one uncomplimentary toward him, and had it stick in his mind without wavering to another opposite explanation a moment later, he'd have been calmer.

To distract himself he'd brought one of the many tourist guides to the Bahamas that he'd found in the little lobby of the hotel. He was trying obliquely to decide if he should spend the last week of his vacation on one of the Out Islands. Now that Esther had dropped away, he had absolutely no desire to stay in Nassau. What was he going to do? Visit their beach? He could fly out tomorrow, surely, if he could decide where. He wasn't even sure it much mattered where at this point.

It was curious to ponder the descriptions of each island, to wander idly down the map of the Bahamas and think that Cristóbal de la Torre had lived somewhere around here, for a time. Curious that the guidebook didn't brag about it. It wouldn't have been near any of the islands featured on the map, the well-known names like Grand Bahama, Eleuthera, the Abacos, Bimini. De la Torre would've presumably wanted somewhere really secret, to be left completely alone. Half the yachtsmen in the United States sailed down through the Exumas, so he wouldn't have settled among them. Cat Island similarly looked too central. Andros was wild and sprawling and nearly empty, but much too close to Nassau.

And the lesser, remoter islands? Rum Cay was barely a speck, population seventy-three; Mayaguana, where they'd stopped for one passenger en route to Inagua, had perhaps twice that, most of whom turned up by the grassy airstrip to see the plane taxi. Even San Salvador and enormous Inagua, way to the south, each had only a few hundred inhabitants. Weren't these areas of the island chain more likely?

Still, none of them were islands you chose to hide out on. Not with seven hundred to choose from, most of them nameless, and only twenty or so inhabited. And thousands of lesser cays if you wanted to start counting. This was why drug smugglers flourished in the Bahamas; there were innumerable islands waiting to be bought as private property, and who cared what you did there, or who you really were?

It occurred to him that when he'd mentioned Inagua, she hadn't recognized the name. There'd been no reason at that moment for her to pretend anything. So the island wasn't that far south, anyway. Esther had conjured up a small island with only her father on it, dependent on an occasional supply plane. Gossip being the strongest force in these islands, no one had ever known he was there. It was a cay everyone took to be uninhabited.

How do you locate a woman who doesn't want to be found, among seven hundred islands?

9

NATURALLY THIS HAVE TO HAPPEN ONE day, she actually keep a promise and come back. You imagine old Einstein be jumping up and down but surprising how calm he take it. Philosopher at heart. Two months he all over the place like a puppy believing she about to appear out of the sky, you imagine he more grateful. At least by this time he clean himself up, thinking she never show anyway. And he got no idea of it when the plane land for good.

Naturally that damn fool Pinder late as usual even in this new plane of his. Sorry I even mention his name to Einstein in the first place. It a odd thing, family relations. You think someone you cousin he be smart too, but truth is they distribute smart like they distribute cash, and that why one side of good family be poor no matter what other side do for help, and why Pinder be useless as pile of old tires. And he still some kind of cousin of mine. All full of air like tire, too. Bring a plane in here year after year he still bring it down whomp like he trying to smash open a egg. No wonder not even Bahamasair willing to touch the man, he wreck all they planes, set tourism back twenty year.

Meanwhile we standing waiting on the edge of the strip in the weeds and Einstein talking to himself and me in that whatnot English he speak. He pretending he ready to help me unload but really he want to find out what the hell happen up Nassau way few days ago, before Christmas.

I tell him already that some daughter of mine try this with Scully Moses I whomp she back to kingdom come. But she got to be here before you can whomp she, Einstein point out. Can't argue with the man there. I ready to find out myself what happen since Pinder got nothing to say about it over the radio except she turn tail and skip back to Switzerland.

Anyway Pinder bring the plane round on the strip, still good ways away, but my family all got strong eyesight and I beginning to think I see someone else shifting inside. Then Pinder stick his football head out the cockpit window and yell, Excess cargo! while the props still turning. And I think, Oh-ho, Scully Moses, what we have here, eh?

Meanwhile Einstein keep chatter chatter chatter to himself. Must be thinking if only this plane come the other day but she never show. Waiting maybe three year and no plane, no daughter when he want, no doubt he got a lot to say about it. But he keep silent these last days. And I think to him at that moment: Wings of a dove, man. Pray for the wings of a dove.

He not even listening, he worry so hard, then he say some of the old this-and-that to me in Spanish. I not even bother to mention the fact we speaking the King's English in the Bahama Islands. The man has no gift for talking to other people—them Haitian monkeys working here five year and by the end of it I speaking better patois than Einstein.

By this time Pinder pull his damn football head in and the plane finally does stop, in the wrong place as usual, and he go clank-clank to get the door open. Now I feeling sure I see someone else move. And Pinder get it open and stand there adjusting that step down, then he give a wave to Einstein and me like he some idiot Prime Minister here to meet the people. Crooked as hell besides, just like P.M. Then he jump down, Tarzan-style, and put out his hand, and there she is, in the door of that plane.

And you got to admit, she look good. Even you not on a island with the sea rolling in you head six year, she still a fine piece of gal. Look like she just wash, man.

So I gander over at Einstein, and the most unbelievable thing is he not even looking at the plane. He busy examining the way one axle bolt on the pickup joined. The man has got no sense of occasion. Mutter mutter to self, mutter mutter man. And she see he paying no attention. So she start to come over. And I get out of the way. Then he realize nobody saying nothing, and he straighten up and turn and see she there.

He cool enough to let she make the first move, anyway. He say, Esther, my God! I can't believe it! then I lose him in Spanish. But he hold out both hands for she to come. He see she playing it cool, so he play it cool right back.

She take she time all right. Look the old man over like she examining a mango she want to buy or not. Wonder how long it take she to notice he not exactly one foot in the grave. She just stand there in the sun, remind me how my second wife look me down the day she leave for good. Like they rather see you skinned and boiled and on the table than standing there front of they eyes. When woman want to let you have it, she know better to say nothing than say something.

In the end she come over, let Einstein squeeze the hand. But when he try for a kiss she give the old man just a side of the face, like he got something and she don't want catch it. Now Einstein no beauty but still.

By this time Pinder and me busy unloading the plane but not so busy we deaf. They talking away. His Spanish so fast you realize how smart the bastard really is, and she go clackety-clack back at him. Eyes flashing a little and I wonder if the two not arguing already. Something in that Cuban blood must like quarrel. After six year I nearly had enough.

Meanwhile Pinder and me there loading the pickup with food he bring and new parts for the auxiliary generator, trying to look busy. Some excess cargo, eh? say Pinder, and he give a wink and laugh heh-heh-heh like some genius sense of humor he got. This Nassau trash, you teach they to fly a plane, they think it mean the world by the tail.

All the time she look at the scenery like she try recognize it from the last time. I don't think Einstein know exactly what to say to she, now that she here. And not much scenery by the strip, you know, just scrub brush and mangrove and all of it flat and dusty as politician's ass and no shade besides.

Then a funny thing happen. I see Einstein bite his lip like he not sure where he is. And he say in English, Esther, you must remember Scully Moses.

Then she come over to me and put out a hand—nicer than she shake with she father, by the way—and I take it, and she say I glad to see you looking so well Scully after so many year.

What she mean is glad to see YOU looking so well. And I see them eyes as foxy careful as they can be. I think: Oh-ho, watch it, man. This Cuban difference of opinion the last thing you want to get mixed up in, at you age.

Little late for that.

So I say, How CAN I be looking well, missy? You father enough to break the nerve of ten men and Samson too.

She laugh. This not exactly news to she. And old Einstein looking at me like he want to serve me in a pot. And I thinking maybe I gone extract a promise or two, little vacation besides from Einstein in return I keep my mouth shut, before the day through. About whole mess of things he confide in me over the year after year. Not like he about to confide in them Haitian monkeys and they long gone now anyway.

She must have say then she getting suitcases from the plane because Einstein say in English again No, no, I get they for you, and he start in that direction. But Pinder put up his hand, Allow me he say like ain't he some damn film star. Einstein look determined and insist on carrying one little bag. She just stand there watching all the fuss and no doubt thinking Scully Moses the only man not a lunatic on this whole island.

By now I about ready to fly that plane back to Nassau, self.

And then I realize what Einstein doing, speaking English. He try to keep everything public, on the table in front of me where I can understand it. The man want to keep things obvious, you might say. Since he know in Spanish she can say any damn thing she want, make him squirm. But speaking English she embarrass she say too much. And this suitcase business just a act, make she think he banging on death's door. Offer to carry she bags like proud father, but Pinder and me don't let him, see? Reverse psychology.

Tell you one thing, man. That daughter of Einstein got a fine beautiful backside on she. Backside like that make a young man think there ain't no tomorrow. Take a older man to know you can't chew on same gristle forever.

Anyway, Pinder about finish dump everything on me as usual, get most thing wrong as usual and bring enough rice like we got colony of Chinamen planted here.

All right. Pinder finally got no excuse hang around. So good-bye Pinder. Tell you Mama it ain't conceivable you a accident of mine cause if I responsible she produce something more smart and less ugly. Good-bye you damn plane too. Don't you forget we here, neither. I say to Pinder like I say every time, Try to fetch Nassau first try, man. It big enough.

Props turn, he wave, he grin and he gone.

Now just one big happy family. The Cuban quarrel plus me.

I try to act relax, take everyone back in pickup like this normal procedure. Einstein not ready for she so he not sure what to say. Yap yap in Spanish. Look to me like they talking about weather. And you know weather never weather, always mean something else. In the end we put suitcases and she father in back. The man making all kind of sacrifice, give a cough or two when he climb in. He almost ready to cut his own throat make sure she think he ill and damn noble at the same time.

I sit up front with she.

Soon as we get started down track and trees on both sides brushing at pickup she lean in a little like she don't want to get hit. Pickup making plenty noise and she say soft so the old man outside in back don't hear, How he doing? How he doing, really?

Now this about the last discussion in world I want to get hooked in. Especially when that gal preferable for other kind of discussion, you know. So I say, Gal, you see how he doing, don't you? You got two good eyes, eh?

Maybe I don't say exactly that way but she get the message.

She say, Seem like he not bad.

She speak like she surprise at this. What kind of damn fool nonsense that old man been writing she? I think.

Not bad, no, not bad, I say back.

By now I sweating like a dying dog and trying to pay attention to where pickup head, since Einstein lazy when it come to cut back a tree here and there and with that steering it a matter of luck anyway. Never imagine that Cat Islander like me end up after sixty-three year running all kind of boat in and out these islands, man, the local gals too, working away, how many year in Nassau on the docks, you never imagine I end up doing the gardening and the cooking for some famous Cuban bastard pretending he dead and wise as Solomon. Never imagine I end up like this. Some steep fall from justice and when I get back to Nassau one day I tell that goddamn two-face minister Hawkins the works and let him stick his fool hand out and preach about fall of Adam and Eve after that. They swift on the rise compared to falling Scully Moses.

Still, me and Einstein and them Haitian monkeys build the biggest damn thing ever happen to a Bahama isle, probably the whole Caribbean, and not one body know about it but us at the moment.

Then she catch me. I too busy paying attention to where we heading. Forget she smart as Einstein and woman besides.

And what about the doctor? she say.

Doctor? I say. Which doctor you mean?

She look sharp at me, and I think, Too late, man. Einstein gone to catch hell for that one. But how I suppose to know what nonsense in these letters he send? You start with lie, man, you finish with lie. We say that on Cat and it true everywhere else.

Though you ask me, in Nassau you start with lie, you finish in Parliament after a slow walk through the bank. But that a whole other story.

So to cover for Einstein I say, Oh, you thinking about that doctor for you father. Yes, yes, missy.

She look at me strange and I see she suspect. But maybe I too suspicious by nature and I cover O.K. She not convince either way, I see that. She say, That doctor tell you anything he don't tell my father?

Well, well. Let me see.

I say this, concentrate on driving. Figure we almost there, if we arrive I can get out the way.

Anything at all? she say. He look quite healthy to me.

You know this Bahamas climate good for the body, I say. Man look strong down here right up till the day of his death.

That true, too. Even my last wife acting strong right before she go.

I know that, she say, meaning the climate. I just wonder if he might have gave you any sense of how long my father has got.

No, missy, he don't give me no sense of that at all.

And just at that minute we finally there. Enough to make you believe in God. I jump out quicker than you ever see snake move. Help Einstein and take she bags and let they sort out doctors for self. I figure she gather something not right but from now on she his problem, not mine.

Einstein send me a look when I help him down and I send him same look back. Don't want he think we in this together but want he know to watch his step.

So he say in English he sorry but we not sure she was coming. So she room not exactly ready anymore. Maybe she like to have a swim while we get it ready. Or maybe she hungry.

By this time it around two and she say no, she not hungry. Maybe a swim relaxing after the plane. Say she gone to help me prepare dinner later. I say I know what she mean, one hour in a plane with Pinder enough to drive anyone daft.

Last thing in the world I want is she in there with me cooking and asking questions. Figure I get dinner ready while she in the water. Get out of that one in a hurry.

All this in English, you know, for my benefit, and I get the idea they drop this polite yammer and start in Spanish, they at each other throats in no time. I put the bags down and she take out a swimsuit and say she remember the way. Einstein call after she and I figure he saying not to drown.

This man gone to exhaust me. He grab my arm the second she leave and haul me round behind palm tree like spies everywhere, listening and watching, not like this some deserted island, just me and some unhinged lunatic. And he say, What she say to you? What she say? What? Like kettle about to boil over.

I say, Keep calm, man, keep calm, let go my arm or I smack

you. Then I tell what she say, maybe I embroider a little just to watch him sweat. It a hot day but I still never see a man sweat like that. He mop a hand all over his face etcetera then I say, You know that expression, Einstein? Silence is golden, man. That mean silence got a price. How much it be worth to you? A month vacation?

Then he start calling me names. I not paid to listen to insult so I just leave him standing there and go get the food unloaded into the deep freeze before it go bad. Then I get to work on that generator before it go bad and bust too. Figure old Einstein sweat some more, he soon come round.

10

WHEN THE MOMENT WAS UPON HER TO
enter her father's last house, the roofs among the palms that
she'd seen from the plane, she could not do it. She stood in a
clearing of rapid sunlight before a doorway of shadows, their
shared house for as long as she chose to stay, and it stared her
down like a barrier of electrified force. Even the veranda
seemed hostile.

Against clusters of royal palms stood two restored old
Bahamian clapboard houses with thatch roofs. Both had
been small hospitals early in the century; for twenty years the
island had been a leper colony, and failed even at that. It had
been wild brush before and completely abandoned afterward. The smaller house, originally for the doctor and his
staff, belonged to her father; the other, for the lepers, had
been used by the Haitian workers and Scully, who had it to
himself now. She gazed around the clearing, thinking about
the rough airstrip and the tortuous track from it, saw how
many months of labor had gone into making it all habitable
again. One day, she thought, this place will go back to the
jungle. Who'll bother to resurrect it the next time?

She watched Scully and her father dealing possessively
with her bags on the veranda of her father's house. A flamboyant red poinciana tree flourished at one end. The houses

were a burst of color amid the fervent green of the palms. Her father's was cream yellow with white trim; its slant thatch roof shaded the veranda a story below like a broad-brimmed straw hat. The larger house, one long story, was painted a vibrating blue and red. How like her father, so adept with rewards and bribes, to keep Scully working by giving him an enormous place all to himself.

She gazed at the two wooden constructions in the clearing and tried to imagine her mother here. Impossible—this island was alive only because her mother was gone.

Her father was speaking to her in English, out of a kind of deference to Scully Moses. Or perhaps he was scared to begin talking to her in either language of her childhood. He looked tanned and fit, surprisingly well, standing there burnished by the healthy light. It was hard to see any marks of death on him. She found herself searching for those subtle signs that the doctors could read clearly, but she didn't want to go close enough to touch him.

"Your room isn't ready. We weren't sure you were coming."

His polite way of putting it.

"Are you hungry?" he asked.

"The plane was too hot. Thank you, no."

"You'd feel better after a swim. I always say it begins the day again."

He sensed her reluctance to go inside. She tried to control her anxious breathing.

Scully Moses was watching them with either deep fatigue or deep annoyance. She wondered how clear her father had made his plans—to stay on until he died. And that would be how long? Before another Christmas? Before the summer?

Nearly all her life, since her mother's suicide, she had considered herself experienced with death. Around her she'd watched her friends begin to go through the same pattern—a parent's illness and then the inevitable—and they had always spoken to her as if she were wise, having practiced in the experience for so long. First her mother's suicide and then the famous tragedy of her father's supposed death had steeped her in it. Now she realized, looking at him, that she knew little about it at all, could not even recognize the brush of its fingertips on him any more than she had, as a child, with her mother. His apparent good health made her feel foolish and blind.

I wonder, she thought, if Thomas Simmons would guess this is a dying man.

He said, "Perhaps you'd like to see what I've built you. It's on the way, I can come with you."

"I'll just swim for now. The plane was hot."

"Was the path still overgrown when you were here before? I can show you—"

Fidgeting for an excuse.

"It's all right. I still remember the way."

She pulled a swimsuit from her bag and set off down the path through the palms. From up ahead came the unearthly screech of a peacock. Here the path branched toward her father's latest effort. She could feel its finished weight dragging at her through the camouflage of trees. She kept her head down and walked on with determination. She told herself she'd promised to come see him, not to see it; she'd refused the last time, on her sole visit. To see it would mean she approved of his coming here, his enormous deception; would make her even more his collaborator. And she refused to replace a whole world of his attentive admirers.

More and more as she grew up it had dismayed her to see his work. It had come to seem a half-lie, only the more flattering side of the story. He'd managed to put the best parts of himself into his work and leave out all the faults—the selfishness, the ability to destroy those closest to him—as if he'd contrived since his earliest successes to convince the world that Cristóbal de la Torre was really a very fine fellow. She waited in vain for the scholars and biographers who occasionally tracked her down in Geneva to realize this for themselves; instead they got lathered up over his sketchbooks. Of course he was somewhat untouchable by virtue of becoming a political exile, but it struck her as being significantly different to be unable to go back, rather than being unable to leave. After all, he'd quit Cuba long before Castro; he'd have stayed away in any case.

She saw clearly enough in his work his pure enthusiasm, his unassailable sense of beauty, his ability to transform others' ideas to his own ends—like the Italian pool surrounded by realistic statues of imaginary creatures, monsters and angels, from many ancient mythologies. Or the delicate wall of that naïve church a half-kilometer underground in southern France, begun by an obsessive madman and finished by her father. But where was the rest of him, the larger truth of the man?

Once, on the advice of a therapist, she'd tried writing a small essay about her father's work. It had come to more than a hundred pages; she'd destroyed it a year ago, in a fit of anxiety that one of his biographers might someday get hold of it. It'd codified what she already suspected, that at the core she could find no genuine warmth in his work, found it persuasive in only the large gestures and never the small. Like the giant Mexican desert sculptures: they were convincing only because they were so immense. Or what the world believed his final work, the statues of fighters in the Spanish Civil War, laid out a half-century later across several thistly hills in northern Spain, so you could wander gaping among those dying in battle. Shrink them down to fit on a tabletop and they'd lose all their sense of artistic command.

To see him as an artist was the only way she could begin to approach him—as a father he was only a destroyer.

She felt this way about the work of most artists who'd done well in their lifetimes. It was why all of poor Van Gogh's work was intimate and why Picasso's was intimate only until he became famous. She didn't count it as failure, any less of an achievement, only less touching. Fame had restricted her father's creative imagination, success had made it shy away. No matter how hard she tried, no matter how impersonally she managed to look, she felt touched only by her father's work as a young man, like the carved marble busts of his parents, now irrevocably in Havana. She could even imagine her mother being seduced by him through the early work. But how had her mother fallen more deeply in love with him through the work that he had in fact done for her, as a kind of courtship just after their marriage?

These were the nudes. Her mother in many materials: several woods, marble, granite, silk on wire, whorled steel, transparent lucite so you saw the world through her; even one in origami on a large scale, in white cardboard. She saw the folded curves in paper and thought: Those were my mother. Those were their life of passion.

They had all been done before she was born, but the last in bronze was her mother carrying her. This was the one she couldn't bear to look at. Here everything she had lost was preserved, metal burned to liquid then shaped, cooled, and hardened to outlast her mother and herself. It had become so famous that she couldn't avoid seeing its image reproduced in photographs everywhere, hovering on the edge of turning into a cliché, like Brancusi's bird. That it'd been her mother's favorite in the series made her feel a traitor.

Over the years those public sculptures had come to seem divided from their inspiration, irreconcilable with everything Esther remembered. People came to Barcelona from all over the world just to see them, but what had these sculptures, "these elemental shapes of a startling eroticism" as one art critic put it, to do with her mother? Where was the person she knew behind the erotic?

He had entitled the series *Mi Inspiración*.

Hadn't her mother already been dying slowly during all that time, carrying the impulse of self-destruction inside her since the beginning of the marriage? Hadn't that been the real seed planted by her father in all this passion?

Surely her father must have known, surely her father who could envision a woman in a block of faceless stone could have seen his wife was waiting to die.

And what did the critics know about any of this? They saw a set of masterful nudes and they measured the cost in so many tons of stone, so many months of work, so many sketchbooks. As critics they were investing in futures: Chagall futures, Cézanne futures, de la Torre futures. Cost to them was something paid until the work was done and shipped out of the studio.

But cost, real cost, was always measured long afterward, paid off ceaselessly throughout an entire life. When she saw the nudes of her mother, she'd think: Would the world be so much poorer without them? As poor as I have been without her?

Around her the light was fractured and brittle through the palms. The stunned heat of afternoon. A dormant sea, blue-green light innocent across it. The cries of idiotic birds. The palms began to scatter from the path and as she came through the ruined arch of blanched stone, the trees ordered themselves into a splendid line that swept up the beach to the end of the island. Up close the water was so brilliant, a sheet of corrugated tin, that it made her wince. Her bare feet wobbled woozily in the sand.

He owns everything I can see, she thought. He owns the waves curdling in, he owns the path I followed, he owns each palm.

By now Thomas must know she was gone. What would he conclude? That she'd come here at her father's beck and call? That she had no control of her life, utterly subject to someone else's whim? Or probably he'd imagine she'd gone back to Switzerland. Either way, he'd feel well rid of her, the more he considered.

Those distant days had no presence here, under this light; that time seemed less substantial than this water.

Watching the water, she remembered the landscape of her mother's death, that wintry coast as the night came on. In the fresh tropical wind, she shivered.

She could not bring herself to change into her swimsuit and go in the ocean. She knew nothing would feel better after the tension of the night before in Nassau, the nervousness of that morning and the sweaty constraint of the plane and her arrival. As a very small child she had been absolutely fearless about the water. But since her mother's death she could not bring herself to go swimming alone, with no one else in sight. It was such a rare situation—she swam nearly every day at the pool of her health club in Geneva—that she'd forgotten how deep the fear ran in her. She stared at the ocean's transparent invitation and refused it. Under the shade of a palm she flopped down and leaned back against its rough hard body and closed her eyes.

The act of abandoning Thomas in Nassau was only beginning to catch up with her. She'd telephoned Pinder from her hotel room as soon as Thomas left to sleep in his own room. It seemed inevitable to her now that she should have left him as she did: what choice did she have, with her father dying so near? It wasn't her choice. If she'd tried to explain to Thomas she'd inevitably have given her father's identity away. Thomas already knew more than anyone else ever had, even if he didn't realize how much he knew.

At least she hadn't named the bank where she worked.

She'd been careful not to give the hotel her new address; the one in her passport was obsolete. She wouldn't be that easy to track down. Her telephone in Geneva was unlisted. Anyway, it was senseless to imagine a chance encounter, a brief affair with this man could lead to anything.

She was so exhausted now, not having slept the night before, that her time with him had taken on the suspect air of a barely remembered dream. Now that she was here, their affair seemed already final, a long-completed interruption within a shaky but direct journey to her father's island.

The rainy July night her father had first announced his plans to disappear, to die, to come here, she'd been twenty-two, done with university for a year. After a week in Paris with an older lawyer she was breaking off seeing—who, in retrospect, was probably the kindest man she'd ever been involved with—she'd taken a *rápido* to Barcelona and caught a taxi home from the train station. Her father, whom she thought of as journeying through South America, surprised her by being there in her apartment.

At first she thought someone had broken in and was waiting to attack her. The apartment was all darkness except for a small lamp in one corner that discerned the shape of a man sitting on the sofa. She was so startled she wasn't able to back away or speak. She thought, absurdly: I shouldn't have splurged on the *rápido*.

Behind her the light from the hall silhouetted her in the doorway. She heard the man suck in his breath, as startled as she, sensed him staring at her outlined form. Then he said one word, quietly.

"Thérèse."

She froze at the name and lost her breath. She thought she was going to fall. She had the sense to hit the overhead light.

Her father was sitting on the sofa, staring at her.

She collected herself and said, "I beg your pardon."

"In the darkness you looked just like her. Her shape."

He didn't say: Sorry to frighten the sacred shit out of you, daughter. Sorry not to warn you I was coming.

"What are you doing here? When did you get here?"

"I've been here for four days," he said. "Waiting for you."

It was, after all, his apartment. He insisted on calling it the "family flat," though he'd purchased it a year after her mother's death, to have somewhere to stay when he came to visit while she was living with her great-auntie around the corner. At least he'd had the manners not to bring his mistresses here.

For nearly five years she'd had the flat to herself, several high-ceilinged rooms in a wistful old section of Barcelona, hung with mementos of the past: portraits of him by Picasso and Matisse and Cartier-Bresson, paintings that were gifts of admiring colleagues, several of his own mother's watercolors of Cuban country scenes. All Thérèse's books were here, and two oil portraits he'd done of her, and even an upright piano that had belonged to his father, bearing the inscription HAMBURG 1884—brought out of Havana by sheer lucky timing just before the revolution.

He was so rarely in Spain that during her years in university she'd had full use of the apartment. When he did come to visit she would stay with a friend. In those years she had several boyfriends, usually long-haired university socialists who dressed affectedly in the conservative suits of another era. Their talk of ideology and revolution annoyed her father, and it was some time before she realized that those affairs tended to coincide with his impending visits and end shortly afterward.

That summer she was gradually moving back here from Paris after nearly a year away, carrying a remorse that would only deepen at the loss of an older lover far readier than she. Searching for a career, not yet having had the idea of being a translator, she'd studied acting and supported herself by occasional modeling. She'd made some quick money at it, partly, she knew all too well, from her name. A few months of it was plenty: it made her feel like a sculpture. And Paris did not let you live anonymously unless you were established.

Seeing all those actors and mannequins experimenting wildly with different names gave her the idea to take her mother's surname and drop her father's. Twice she'd invited him to come see her act in small productions, but either he hadn't received her letters—on the move constantly—or he hadn't been free, because he'd never shown up.

She'd come back to Barcelona that night with money in her pocket, no lover, a new passport with a new name, ready to travel for a time, only to find her father slouched on a divan beneath a Picasso portrait of himself as a young man.

She took in the comparison hurriedly: her father looked more drawn with charcoal in real life than in the Picasso.

He said, "Can you keep a secret?"

She thought: You're getting married again. Who's the lucky lady?

"I'm going to disappear, Esther."

She was tempted, then, to say, "How will I be able to tell?" but as always she left these remarks unspoken, so that over the years they'd become a rambling monologue that went unheard except in the theater of her mind.

"I've been meeting with the lawyers. In fact, that's all I've been doing. I couldn't get an answer at that Paris number you sent me."

"I was finishing up with someone," she said. "A lover."

At that age it seemed a daring thing to say.

"Serious?" With the word he became serious too.

"Not at all serious."

"Aha." He had cognac before him, she saw, but she couldn't read any purpose in his face as he sipped. In any case she preferred gazing at his younger portrait.

"This apartment is now yours," he said idly. "So is the house at Nerja. There are provisos. You cannot sell either of them until you're forty—they'll be made over to you from a trust in bits and pieces. A bathroom here, a window there." The prospect amused him. "A doorknob. A corner of the garden. A plate or two."

She felt a stab of suspicion. "Why?"

"I'm not finished." He was positively jovial. "I am also leaving you what remains of my entire estate. I did extract a good deal of cash from it. You're wealthier now than I am. You could open a museum. Have some cognac."

"No, thank you. I don't understand."

"Who understands lawyers? It's in their hands. They'll protect you."

"I don't know what you mean."

Beware El Greco bearing gifts, she thought.

He smiled. "If you make a bad marriage and change your mind, your ex-husband will not make off with any of my work as settlement."

"What a relief."

"I knew you'd think so. Imagine how relieved I am."

"Why do this now?"

"Good question." He took another sip of cognac.

Fresh from acting classes, it was clearer than ever to her what a ham he was. I'll outwait him, she thought.

It didn't work. He had the whole speech worked out in advance. He leaned back on the sofa and beamed at her.

"Why? you ask yourself. Because I'm going to die. This year."

At last she sat down in an armchair, slowly.

He lowered his head into the snifter of cognac. "Not unusual, really, for a man in his sixties. A little touch of cancer here and there. Like birdsong in the night."

"What?"

She hadn't caught on, at that moment, and he played arpeggios around the maudlin theme for as long as he could.

"Nothing drastic. Yet." He gave a modest cough. "When I look in a mirror I must admit I look a little green. I thought a spell in the tropics would do me some good."

"If it's not drastic yet, can't they do anything about it?"

"The cancer? Only a ghost, a faint shadow. A phantom in the stomach. A specter in the throat. I'm not worried," he said magnanimously, giving cancer the benefit of his doubt. "There's some work I want to get to and I've found the place I want to do it. And the easiest way for me to be left alone there is to die. You see? And the only way to do this legally, without any complications for you later on, is to leave you my estate now. Don't worry, it will look like an accident. Not, I hope, a suicide."

She wondered what her face showed at that word. His face showed nothing.

"So when I finish making all the arrangements," he went on, "I'm going to disappear."

At last she understood. She said nervously, "There's no need for you to do this."

"That's what our lawyers said. Perhaps you should become a lawyer. I convinced them."

"You haven't convinced me. What are you going to live on?"

He smiled. "It's very thoughtful of you to worry about your father. I've transferred a good deal of money under a different name to a numbered account in a bank in the Bahamas. None of this is illegal, by the way. That account, when the inevitable finally transpires, will go to you."

"And what if you need more money?"

As if money were the issue.

"Why should I? There's nothing to buy where I'm going. Perhaps you'll visit from time to time."

This last was said with such sly cunning, a little nothing dropped into the conversation like a touch of garlic, it wasn't until she replayed the scene back in memory that she saw how subtly he was setting her up.

"Where's there?"

"I've rented an island. Under this other name. I hadn't decided on the Caribbean until I got the latest doctor's report. Much healthier climate than the Mediterranean, you see. My work will be too big to move. A small Bahamian island is the ideal permanent setting. You'll have the greatest say in what happens to it afterward, naturally."

She wasn't about to give him the satisfaction of asking what the work was, though he seemed eager as a schoolboy to tell her. She said, "I can't believe you're contemplating this."

"It's the best idea I've had for a long time. Want to see where my island is?"

She noticed that her atlas was lying in a corner of the sofa.

"I know where the Bahamas are."

"Actually, it's too small even for the maps. Uninhabited since 1921. You'll have to come visit me. Once I die, you see, I can't leave." He grinned. "Or I should say: I can't return."

"Millions of people go to the Caribbean every year. Why do you have to put on this absurd performance just to do the same thing?"

He put on his pained, was-ever-a-man-more-misunderstood look.

"No one will know but you. No one will visit me there but you. Do you understand? No reporters looking over my shoulder. No parasites dropping in."

"Lots of people own private islands," she said. "And they don't play dead. Marlon Brando owns an island. In the South Pacific. Do you think people drop in on him?"

"This was not done lightly, you know. It took me three

months alone to find the right men in Haiti to help me. I've spent nearly a year planning. Organizing complicated legal affairs so my daughter will have the most benefit. Outside my lawyers and my workers, no one but my daughter knows or must know. Now I am simply asking her if she will visit her father—who will have no other visitors—from time to time. Is that so very difficult to understand?"

He was nearly shouting.

She said, with deliberate carelessness, "Well, when you put it so nicely, how can I refuse?"

He made his usual grimace and sipped more cognac and stared straight ahead. She watched his jaw line tighten, the pulse beating angrily in his neck.

He said, "I wanted to make something special and dedicate it to your mother."

She got up on the pretext of opening a window. She did not want him to see her trembling. Because she had grown up away from him she could never stand up to him, even through sarcasm, without feeling fear—the fear of his anger, always a threat ever since she could remember.

She said, "I thought you'd already done that."

As a child she'd felt certain that if she weren't well behaved, weren't subservient, he would stay away longer. Even though she came to see that his comings and goings had nothing to do with her, she could not get around her anxiety. To stand up to him tightened her chest and made her breathless, on the verge of the asthma which always came to threaten her at moments of extreme tension, a delirium of the chest that expanded until it gripped her whole body.

He said, "I'm not asking you to join me in my enterprise. I could hardly ask that of someone who has just inherited all you have. I was simply asking you for a little of your time every now and then. I'm not doing this in order to encourage visitors."

You won't have to worry about that, she thought.

"There won't be a telephone. There'll be a supply plane every couple of weeks. I'll give you the pilot's address. You'll be able to write me there. Under this other name, of course."

"What is this other name?"

"Christophe Gautier."

Her mother's maiden name, naturally.

She was still at the window. She glanced down to the street: a crowd from the Palau de la Música at the corner was just streaming out, liberated by a concert. She turned back to him and said, "Why the disappearing act?"

He looked elegantly puzzled. "I told you. I want to be left alone."

"You are left alone. Who bothers you down in Nerja?"

He said, "I bother me. I don't know how long I have. These cancers will grow, at least one of them. One is enough. Perhaps I have two, three years of good health if I'm lucky. This is work I want very much to do. This seems the easiest way to accomplish it. And it organizes the situation for you, too."

What on earth is he talking about? she thought.

"I guess I should thank you."

"No need. What are your plans?"

She saw he was as dissatisfied as she with the shape of their conversation.

"I saved some money in Paris," she said. "I was planning to do some traveling. North Africa, maybe. I have a friend from school who lives in Geneva. I thought I might visit her when I got back."

He said, "It would do for you to be somewhere available toward the end of December. You might have to fly to the States. To keep up appearances."

To keep up appearances!

"I'm not sure where I'll be."

"Trust me," he said. "They'll find you."

Sitting now in the shade of a palm, she thought: Look at how the years increased for him here. I wonder if he came to believe this moment would never come, of time running out for him on his island. What a strange, lonely end to this man's life.

The more foreign it seemed to her the more she felt she saw it all clearly.

"What about your friends?" she'd said. "What are they going to say? Aren't you going to tell them? Or are you going to hope they show up at your funeral?"

"How many friends do I have left?" he said easily. "The ones that matter are all gone. The others—" He shrugged. "For a year I haven't seen them. I haven't missed them. They haven't missed me either, I suspect. Not as I will miss you."

She'd said nothing to that. Remembering her silence now, she watched the procession of light across the waves and thought: Will I come to miss you, when I know you're actually gone? Do you imagine it as going to join my mother? Can you see her? Where is she?

Frozen in the distance somewhere, trying in darkness to stumble home across the ice.

———

When she wandered back down the mile or so of path her father was waiting for her, shirtless in his baggy khaki shorts. Tanned, he looked as steady as a goalkeeper with his hands planted on his hips. He ran a hand through his white hair and said, "Did you have a good swim?"

"Not bad."

"Your hair's not wet."

"I kept my head out of the water," she said.

Her bags were still on the veranda.

"Your room's ready. I didn't want to move your things up if you weren't happy with it."

That one time she'd visited, three years earlier, he hadn't been so concerned. The Haitians had been there then and all of them, including Scully, had been out at work soon after dawn every morning. They worked right through the end of the day and sometimes into evening, using torches, then turned in early. She'd sat and read and resisted his attempts to coax her into keeping them company hour after laborious hour. She tried to use the excuse of waiting until "it" was finished to see "it" all. He was beyond understanding that whatever it turned out to be (wanting to surprise her, he would say only that seashells were involved), it represented everything she found repellent in his life here.

His requests, then his demands, that she see it and admire it, then his cold shoulder, brought back all her childhood anxiety—when he was hard at work, he was absolutely untouchable. After four days of the best intentions and a scorching argument over why she wouldn't promise to return in three months' time, she left.

She said now, wanting to avoid any discussion, "I'm sure the room is fine."

How exhausting it was to actually stand near him. To think that this person had fathered her, that she was connected to him by a line of force that couldn't be severed, that would be there through to her children and back to him, if she ever had children.

She said, "I brought something for you."

"For me?"

His easy delight, his readiness to receive a surprise, a gift from her, was oppressive. It was like the facile pleasure of a too-eager suitor at every remark she made.

"A Christmas present." She pulled out the cigar box. She'd abandoned the idea of gluing on the shells—so little effort it would've taken, such pleasure it would've certainly given him. A way of protecting myself, she thought, to keep something in reserve, to know it's there and not being offered. There is more of me in the shells not glued, not given.

Just as it was deliberate to give a man battling cancer cigars in the first place, when he'd written her that his doctor had made him give up smoking.

She said, "I might take a nap."

He appeared not to have heard. He was slowly, painstakingly unwrapping the box of cigars from the ordinary trademark paper of the tobacco shop on Bay Street. Savoring the long-awaited moment.

She said, disowning the offering, "Not much of a gift."

"Wait a minute," he murmured.

He pulled out the box and threw the wrapping paper aside like a child. He gazed at the flamboyant trademark longingly, arched his eyebrows, ran the edge of the fragrant box beneath his nose.

She thought: He'll make some joke about Castro, I know it.

"I suppose you know you're propping up a dictator's economy." He ran his thumbnail through the seal and said, "I suppose someone has to, eh?" He laughed in lavish enjoyment of his own joke. "Someone has to!"

He was admiring the cigars lined up like individually wrapped torpedos. She knew he would've leaned over to kiss her had she not been standing several paces away.

"Monte Cristos for an exile! What could be more appropriate? I am the Count of all I survey!"

She said, "I'm going to lie down. I didn't get much sleep last night."

"I'll take your bags."

"I can take them."

"Don't be silly." He put down the cigars and lifted the

bags with a cough. "You've got a room all yours now. I hope it's more comfortable than the last time."

The last time she'd slept in his study downstairs, an open room that sweltered in the mornings. She didn't see how he concentrated there, except that possibly it reminded him of the heat in Havana. It'd been disturbing to sleep in his work territory, among the meandering overgrown paths of his mind. The drawings taped everywhere, exact anatomical sketches of different seashells with mysterious notations; watercolors of island views, tossed off when he had nothing better to do; the pile of paperbacks in one corner: several anthologies of poetry, a copy of Columbus's journals, an encyclopedia of American baseball statistics and a handbook of Caribbean cooking. She didn't want to sleep there again.

This time she was to sleep upstairs, apparently. He said, "It'll give you more privacy. In case you want to stay longer."

Already, she thought, already it's started.

He held the screen door open for her. Within she had trouble adjusting her eyes to the shade. Off to one side she could see through a cracked doorway her father's bedroom, the rumpled corner of an unmade bed. Personally fastidious as always. The larger room, his study where she'd slept the last time, had been whitewashed recently. The sketches were gone, now that "it" was evidently finished. Instead, lined up along the floor stood odd sculptures of dried coral he'd stuck together, apparently at random, that had a haunting haphazard geometry. An old day bed with a few Nassau cushions functioned as a couch; screened glassless windows let in the breezes and palm-fingered light. A small table was precariously piled with art books. A bookcase in one corner was full of more.

Along the back wall, looking out on Scully's small vegetable garden, was a long table with sketch pads and pencils. Two small Goya lithographs hung on the wall over the long table between the windows—the giant, and a woman hand-ing an old beggar a mug. They seemed out of place only because she knew they were genuine. In one corner stood a tall Chinese folding screen, cheap in style, with red dragons among golden clouds. Sometime since her last visit he had painted elaborate mustaches on the dragons. She remem-bered that the screen hid the remains of an old-fashioned privy; thankfully her father had put in new bathrooms in his first months here.

He led her upstairs.

Three years earlier the upstairs of the house had been a ruin. She felt a pang of dismay at seeing such evidence of what he wished from her.

He and Scully had refashioned it into something like a small apartment, with an old Bahamian fourposter bed at one end. A wood-bladed fan hung from a central beam in the matted thatch. A plywood wall protected what was undoubt-edly a little toilet and shower; a metal bar had a few clothes hangers, some towels were arranged in a corner. There was a crude bookcase by the windows and a couple of chairs. Up here the breeze was more alive and persistent. Between each window hung framed pictures.

She moved closer: they were sketches her father had done of her as a little girl. She'd long thought them lost.

He said tentatively, "I want you to feel at home here."

Beside the bed was a small chest of drawers. On it was a framed print of the same photograph she already had with her, the three of them in Paris with the fountain pluming up into the sky. His was more faded than hers.

He said, "These old photos lose their color, don't they. Do you have the negative somewhere?"

It might've been Thomas speaking.

"I'm not sure," she said, though she knew exactly where the negative was.

"That was a different light. No one talks about how the light alters in great cities over the decades."

She said, "Will you wake me in time to help Scully with dinner?"

"He doesn't need help, that's why I pay him."

"I'd still like to help him."

"When would you like to see what I've worked on here? It's finished now."

"You wrote me that it was."

"For nearly a year," he added.

He was looking elsewhere around the room, anywhere but at her. "Perhaps you'd like to see it before dinner. The light in the late afternoon is lovely."

"I don't think so," she said. "I'm very tired."

"You've got your own shower up here now." He gestured. "Plenty of rainwater at this time of year. Very refreshing."

"It must be." She sat down wearily on the edge of the bed. Only late last night she'd been on another bed with Thomas Simmons. How remote that seemed.

He said, "You'll be glad to know I gave up on my autobiography. I saved what I wrote. Mostly about Cuba. It has some historical importance, you know. I lost interest after my parents died."

She said, "Why on earth do you want to stay here?"

He smiled. "Where else on earth would I go?"

"Maybe somewhere you could get better medical attention."

"The medical attention I've had here is excellent."

"Not to someone who lives in Switzerland."

"We both know what the outlook is and has been. I refuse to have chemotherapy or radiation. I will not waste my life trying to prolong it. When the time comes—and I can feel it coming—I will go, without protest and without surrender."

"You can't want to be ill here."

130

"I cannot think of a healthier place to die. Or a place I love as much as this one. I have done the best work of my life here and I will not leave, just for the sake of a few doctors. Believe me, if you lived here for any time you'd understand."

"Perhaps you can be cured," she said quietly.

He said, "There's no cure for old age. I don't want to become some creature kept asleep and breathing and carried twitching in and out of hospitals. I'm not in any real pain, yet. I can take it when it comes. I suppose it'll be like a slow summer evening settling in."

She felt a bile of pure hatred come up in her throat. As if he were mocking her mother with all his noble talk of twilights. She said belligerently, "So you expect Scully Moses to look after you as you get weaker and weaker."

It was clear what he expected.

He shrugged. "He has a daughter who's a nurse. He's talked of bringing her out here if we have to."

She said, "Where do you want to be buried?"

"In the sea near here." He paused. "Like your mother."

"Like my mother!"

"Yes."

All she could say was, "It's a very different ocean."

"I disagree. I've been staring at it for a little while now, I should know."

"I suppose you should."

"Anyway," he went on, "Scully understands what I want done. I've asked him to take my body beyond the reef and drop it overboard. I don't mind nourishing a few fish. They've fed me well."

"And the whatever it is?"

He flinched at that.

He said, "I've got the island on a long lease. Another twenty-five years outstanding. With the government. They don't know what we've done here, they don't have any idea who I am. As long as no one complains that we're smuggling drugs, they don't care. When I die, the lease stays in the family. All paid up, don't worry. There's nothing they can do about it."

"Then?"

"Then it's up to you."

She said, "I don't want the responsibility. I can't be the curator for your open-air museum."

"Let the jungle grow over it if you want. It belongs to you and your mother."

"I wish you wouldn't say that."

"You can let people know how it was conceived, how it was made. I think while Scully is still alive as eyewitness this might be a good idea. The Haitians will be a little difficult to track down."

"Not for a good hagiographer."

He said mildly, "I'm lucky to have had this long. To think I imagined finishing in two years! I was dreaming. It takes longer when you work with primitive methods. I see now—"

She couldn't listen any more to his outpouring of egotism. His work. What he'd thought earlier. What he thought now. As if she cared. Did he want to know what her apartment was like in Geneva? Did he want to hear about what she saw every morning on her walk, or the café where she ate lunch most afternoons? Did he want to know who her friends were? Did he wonder if there were any men in her life? Had he read any of her translations? Had he ever made the time to come see her act, at a time when that had mattered most to her?

Interrupting him, she said calmly, "By the way, I forgot to tell you. I met a man in Nassau. A photographer. An American. That's why I didn't make it here for Christmas. I spent it with him instead. I told him about you the second night I was with him."

Savoring the whiff of blunt confession, she added, "Father."

That's put a dent in the conversation, she thought.

He said tightly, "What did you tell this man?"

She said with exaggerated ease, "I told him I'd come to the Bahamas to spend Christmas with my father. And that I'd decided not to. He convinced me to stay for other reasons. I wanted to make love with him, so I stayed." She enjoyed seeing him flinch. "I was ready to go back to Geneva. But I found I'd talked myself into coming to see you after all. You know how women tend to open their hearts to someone they're sleeping with."

He watched her with darting, untrusting, betrayed eyes.

She said lightly, "Don't worry. I never told him who you are. And he doesn't know my real name. You'll never see him."

He let out his breath. "I'd better let you sleep. I'm glad you did come, Esther. For whatever reason."

Then he turned his back and shuffled away. She heard him clomping heavily down the stairs—a slow, rueful descent.

Already his presence had transformed her time with Thomas, and made three days of truthfulness sound like treason.

In the mirror in the tiny bathroom she looked filthy and flushed from the sun. She rinsed her face but didn't bother with a shower. She lay down and tried to will herself to sleep. The fan whipped above her head like helicopter blades ready to descend.

When she awakened the thick night of the tropics was falling rapidly. The room was nearly all darkness and at first she thought she was in some weird dream of the Amazon. She went to the window and could just make out the palm limits of the clearing. Below she heard the clanging of pans, water running in the separate shed of the kitchen. Fireflies were beginning to dart like individual meteors through the viscous shadows. An orchestra tuned up as night came down: a toad ratcheting somewhere, the purposeful chat of a single bird, wild ululations of several others, a creature that sounded like some clacketing percussion instrument being painstakingly wound up then let loose.

She saw her father come padding along. At first she thought his hand was on fire. He was carrying a torch. He walked steadily around the clearing in the gathering night and lit flickering lanterns on several wooden posts that sent the shadows scurrying. He made his rounds of the lanterns slowly, like a litany he was accustomed to reciting every night. A wooden table with a blue cloth had been put in the center of the clearing. The torchlight caught the knives and forks and the glasses and gave them an eerie glow. Her father lit a candle on the blue-robed table where two places were set.

He glanced as if on instinct up toward the window and she pulled herself back involuntarily. The faint recollection of what she'd said to him sickened her. She'd come here for purely selfish reasons—to rid herself of guilt. That small guilt had evaporated after an hour here, replaced by the urge to do damage and a lacerating anger at being forced to lie constantly on his behalf.

An ocean away, she'd constructed a life for herself that had as little to do with him as possible. As soon as she made a move in his direction—look what had happened in Nassau with Thomas—her own truthfulness got eaten away. Beside him at last, she was reminded unwillingly of how much power he had invested her with. It made her giddy, tempted her to take advantage of it, to attempt to pay him back. As if no matter how hard she tried her father brought out the worst in her, not the best.

She took a shower, and with reluctant inevitability put on

her mother's dress, knowing why she'd brought it, knowing she should not have—the strange remnants of a childhood desire to please him, to keep him from leaving. She went down through the suggestive shadows of the empty house. Now there was no one to be seen outside. In the clearing great moths like black bats swooped around the lanterns and battered themselves senseless against the glass. The cracked door in the kitchen shed spilled streams of bright light. She heard Scully swear. She went to the clearing's edge and peered down the path, all darkness and palm silhouettes. Down there somewhere off a branching path was her father's precious work, waiting patiently for someone to see it. Suppose it got overgrown, swallowed by Bahamian bush. Who would ever find it? After he died here, without fanfare?

Her father came from the kitchen, squinting in the lantern-light. He carried a bottle of wine. He said, "We can sit down now."

"Should you be drinking?"

He looked at her curiously, then glanced proudly at the bottle. "Romanée-Conti? My doctor recommends it to all his patients."

"Did he encourage you to take up smoking again?"

"Only patriotic cigars." He winked expansively and moved to pull out her chair. She was barely quick enough to seat herself.

He said, "If a man can't have an occasional drink with his daughter, he might as well live alone on an island."

"A man could always go live beside a Swiss lake. With the finest health care money can buy."

"Not a man from Havana. Who wants to swim in such cold water? That's enough to kill anyone."

He was tapping the blue tablecloth impatiently, avoiding her glance and sucking on his lower lip: the ghost of a sound, an inward hiss, that she remembered. This man really is my father, she thought. The candlelight shivered on his solid skull, the flaring white hair around his ears that slid down the back of his neck, his perturbed imperious eyes, his steady wide swimmer's shoulders, his delicate mouth used to laughing at its own jokes, his broad forehead. There was so much animate life within, like one of those lanterns atop a post, blazing durably through its window from a rusted cavern, that it was hard to imagine he would ever die. She could not believe that the wooden post of him was rotten and one day soon would collapse, eaten away from inside by scavenging termites.

He said, "I wondered what happened to that dress. Did I ever tell you about when I gave it to her?"

"Several times."

"She made that man's seamstress do it over twice!" he crowed. "Because it wasn't right. No matter what his reputation. She knew exactly how it should be. She was more exact than I was."

Scully brought out plates of grilled fish and spiced rice with Bahamian peas and set them down in silence. In an apron he looked long-suffering and absurd, a yellow T-shirt wrapped around his head to keep the sweat from his eyes. As he came and went his silence had the weight of spurious disapproval.

Her father said hesitantly, "How long do you think you'll be able to stay?"

"Only a few days. I have to return to the bank."

"You haven't told me how your literary work is going."

"I've finally gotten some good commissions. Translating for a French publisher." She mentioned a few works by a well-known Spanish writer in his fifties; the assignment had been a real coup for her.

"His work never impressed me," said her father.

"What was the last novel of his you read?"

"I can't remember. It must've been twenty years ago."

"You should give him another chance."

He shrugged. "Never take artists more seriously than they take their work."

"You've got it backwards. You all take yourselves much too seriously."

He said amiably, "You sound just like your mother. Right as usual. It's because of this we didn't have a very good visit the last time. I take myself too seriously. As everyone knows, I'm one big joke. If I had two wheels I'd be a bicycle."

"That's not why at all," she said. "I just thought it a little unreasonable for you to ask me to come live here."

"I agree," he said triumphantly, as if this were the very point he was trying to make. "It was totally unreasonable. Just an ordinary request from your unreasonable father."

"I'm glad you see it that way now."

"Now I see it as reasonable. What can I do here? All alone?"

"There's Scully."

"I don't need to be so well informed on Bahamas politics."

She said, "Why don't you write one of your former mistresses? The last one's still quite a beauty. She turns up in the Alpine resorts all the time. It must be skiing that keeps her fit."

"No, thank you," he said quietly. He looked down at the plate. "That wasn't necessary. I've written you how close I've felt to your mother here these last few years."

"It's your vivid imagination," she said harshly.

They were quarreling over the possession of a ghost.

Scully came out of the kitchen bearing coffee. "Well, well now," he murmured. "It obvious for miles around everyone like my cooking."

"Go to hell," said her father.

"And a good night to you too, Einstein," the Bahamian said. "Sleep well, missy."

"Good night, Scully."

Her father stared into the blurred darkness. He said, "Esther, I don't have much time. I would like to spend as much of it with you as I can. The great regret of my life is that we haven't had enough time together."

"I work for a living. I can't upend my life to stay here."

"Your bank has a very important branch in Nassau. Couldn't you be transferred?"

"It's not so easy as that. Suppose someone got suspicious?"

She was grasping at straws, and he knew it.

"No one's suspicious," he said. "You don't need the money they pay you. Why do you think I left you everything?"

"I haven't touched the money you left me."

He said, "I always knew people lived in Switzerland to avoid living somewhere else. The country is synonymous with indecision."

"You wouldn't say that if you'd spent any time there. And it was you who encouraged me to try it."

"I had more time left then."

"Do you think there's any bravery in pointlessly hanging on here?"

"You call it hanging on? Waiting three years for your only daughter to come see you, while your health deteriorates day by day? Bravery, I think so, yes. I could've taken the coward's way out. Like your mother. I loved her more than you can imagine, but she took the coward's way out."

"She took the less painful way out."

"What pain do you suppose she was avoiding? Not the pain I inflicted on her—"

"No, no, you were a picnic in the country."

"Let me finish—and not the pain of being your mother—because you were a joy as a child, only a joy, to her and to me."

"What does it matter now?" she said with exasperation. His unexpected praise had caught her off guard. "It was a long time ago. We were different people then."

"What kind of psychological crap is that?" said her father. "People don't change, life just falls on them differently. Like light. Neither one of us has changed a bit."

Is that all you can see? she thought. Is that all?

He said, "You have this notion that I stood by and let your mother kill herself. If I'd had the slightest warning, do you think I'd have let her?"

"How could you not know?" She realized sharply that she was breathless and on the verge of an asthma attack. Instinctively she reached for the dress pocket to see if her inhaler was there and remembered it was upstairs, on a table in that shadowy room. She said, "Even I knew something was about to break in her. I wasn't even seven. How could I know and you not know?"

He said, "You're closer to her than I could ever be. You came out of her body, after all."

Mistaking her sweat for tears, he stood up and moved his chair to the head of the table, to be able to reach over and comfort her. She said, "Please don't touch me."

Around the table in the snakeskin shadows, grotesque dwarves carried her breathing away on cushions of brocaded silk.

Her father handed her his napkin. She didn't need it, she had her own. She was gasping. She took a deep wheezing breath. "I'm still revolted by how you acted after she died."

Jesus, couldn't he see how this conversation was hurting her? She willed her breathing to return, her chest to slow, willed her lungs to pretend that nothing was wrong and she could say anything she wanted.

"You take things too literally. You did so even as a little girl. What I meant—"

"I don't care what you meant, I'm telling you what I mean. What happened to me after she died? Did I suddenly acquire a contagious disease by having a mother who committed suicide? You treated me as if I had leprosy."

He laughed nervously. "That's a strange comparison. This

island was a leprosarium a century ago."

"A century from now it'll be Bahamian bush again."

He stiffened. "That's as my grandchildren wish."

Grandchildren? The man was delirious with posterity.

"They won't see it." Attacking him, her breath had returned. "I'm not going to abandon them to your reputation the way you abandoned me. Do you suppose it did me any good as a child to hear from my classmates that you were having affairs all over the world? Strange, wasn't it, how people stopped talking about your work."

He said, "I didn't trust myself to bring you up. It would've been impossible to follow the same life we'd had together when Thérèse was alive. You were starting school anyway, so it would've had to change."

She said, "It would've changed because Maman wanted a divorce, and you didn't want to give it to her."

"I wanted to keep trying."

"How magnanimous."

He said, "Thérèse thought she wasn't a good enough mother for you. She wanted to divorce me, yes. But she wanted to leave you with me."

She couldn't speak.

He went on. "I tried to convince her that she should give herself a holiday. She told me she didn't think a holiday would be enough to make her a good mother again."

She said falteringly, "I don't believe you. She was a wonderful mother."

"That's what I said to her. But she was far past the point of believing anything anyone could say to her."

"She wanted to leave me with you? No—"

"That's exactly what she did."

"What a shame," said Esther, "that you were so very busy at that time. That after a decorous period of mourning you felt free to change mistresses with such frequency. Maybe you don't see these books that come out about you. About us, I should say. There's a bookstore with a fine selection two doors down from my building in Geneva."

He said, "Find another apartment. You were just bragging about your little affair in Nassau. The hungers of the body don't go away. Even with the death of someone you love. They haven't for me yet, even here. Even with my illness."

She said, "I'm glad to know my father can still get it up. Even though he's far above all this now. At least you knew her. You knew her as a grown-up. All I have are a child's memories. And a lot of biographers' dirt about you. That's not enough." She pushed back her chair. "I'll see you in the morning."

She thought: I should've stayed in Nassau.

"Esther."

She ignored him. She heard him start his death's-door coughing before she was even inside his house.

Once upstairs she looked down into the clearing. The lanterns made it into an arena waiting for someone to fight for it. Her father was gone. She listened, but he did not come into the house. Fled away into his island.

Maman, she thought, you are so far away from this place. How can he feel you have anything to do with it?

Remember scent of her, crook of her neck and cheek and pillow of soft dark hair. My place to put my head on her. Her face nuzzling the back of my head, her arms everywhere around me. Today was the twenty-sixth of December; in three days, then, it would have been twenty-two years ago. Remember oh remember.

Nothing takes away her arms, ever. Or the scent of her. All that is taken away is the feel of her letting me hug her back. For all these years she has been giving to me constantly, giving all her love. But never once has she been there to take mine away with her. And how much more she must need it now.

Remember building the sea wall of sand together on the beach in Brittany. When he was gone somewhere to work. Remember the story she always read about the cat who walked by himself, all on his wild lone. And that night in Havana when the yellow-and-red horse buggy stopped for us with the bells jangling. Or the burst of flowers she bought me in Charleston, I think. Remember telling stories of the wild tribes of the Amazon and how we would go there by canoe one day and capture a headhunter and carry him back on our shoulders. Learning English together that last winter and telling me not to be afraid no matter what happened and to look after Father. Remember how I must love him with all my heart.

Remember him asking me afterward what was she wearing, where was she going, why did she say she was walking alone? And I said, All on her wild lone. I told him I asked her, Let me come with you, and she said, No, not this time. Remember to love him with all your heart.

How hard it was not to let that winter, that December, obscure all else of her mother. They were living on the Massachusetts coast, a wild rocky place, while her father supervised the quarrying of some granite nearby for a project in Boston. It was so cold that she and her mother spent much of their time watching television together, trying to learn English. That afternoon her mother said she was going out for a walk, they always did at that time. But never before by herself, and without a coat.

Remember her kissing me, giving me a quick hug. Not enough. Remember the door shutting behind her. Too quick. Remember the sea frozen along the beach, then black. Too cold. Late afternoon, nearly night, gray everywhere. Last light, last look.

Her father was somewhere in the house they'd rented, sketching, working, planning, and it was getting dark earlier and earlier; she saw all the lights from the far opposite shore start to come on across the water like sad candles. And she felt her mother falling somewhere out there. She called out to her father that something was wrong, and when he didn't answer she knew he'd gone out without telling her. He never ever did that. Then she looked, she looked out the window and she saw him.

Before her again was the jumbled expanse of ice and the empty black ocean, bearded white.

She saw him trying to get across the ice, as fast as he could; he must've seen her mother hurrying coatlessly away. Through the window she heard him faintly calling her name. *Thérèse, Thérèse.* Faint sound carried on a faint wind. And she pressed her face against the hard cold of the window and saw that the ocean was the only thing out there where he stood, on the last sharp rim of the ice; and she knew, like a bolt of iron in her chest, what had happened.

Later that night a terrible storm came up and lasted for days. It swept her mother's body far out to sea, rolled her under, picked at her and fingered her clothing and dragged her down: they never found a trace. She remembered waiting dully for days at the window, bald daylight glinting on the froth of ice where the blank waves were frozen a half mile out from the beach. She remembered shifting in and out of a place that was like madness, thinking: Maman must come in from her walk soon.

All she'd wanted, those breathless days, was for her father to take her in his arms and say to her what she knew but couldn't say, that her mother wouldn't come back. Instead there was the desperate meager story about her having gone away for a little while. And in the end it'd been her great-aunt who'd flown over—hobbled into the room, blinking behind thick glasses—and told her and held her while she sobbed and sobbed.

Remember the long grace of her fingers. Never to see that hand again, knotted ring she wore.

Downstairs now her father came into the house. She heard him moving about familiarly, shutting the door to his bedroom. In the clearing the lanterns had been put out but the moths still fluttered with contentment against the faintly luminous wicks of the candles within the lanterns.

Last light, last look. Last look.

11

His dreams had been confused and they were in tatters by the time he tried to hold on to them. He was making love with Esther and she kept looking at her wristwatch. Her father was seated in a chair by the bed, saying, "Of course you can take my picture, but I won't show up on the negative, because I'm a dead man, ha-ha." He'd tried to explain tungsten film to de la Torre, how it would work with tungsten film.

Yesterday evening, he'd been (he thought) philosophical about her leaving. This morning he was infuriated. What had she told him that was true? He felt like the last person in Nassau to guess the truth about Esther. Passers-by at breakfast regarded him with scorn. The waiter sneered at him. Orange juice? The hemlock of fools.

At the tourism bureau in the pink colonial buildings in Rawson Square, a porcelain-pretty girl told him, "I never heard of any famous sculptures in the Out Islands."

"Sculptors."

"You better try our other office."

The other tourism bureau was farther down Bay Street in a seedy new concrete complex sandwiched between delicate older buildings. The emotional woman behind a cluttered desk looked unhappy to see him. Her unhappiness filled the dismal office.

"This not the office for the public. We got a public office at the corner of Parliament Street."

"You mean Rawson Square?"

"Okay."

"They sent me here."

The woman considered this to see if it deserved an answer.

How many conversations in my life like this one? thought Thomas. How many in the Caribbean alone? In Arabia, with official interpreters who speak no English? Or on the sub-continent? Can you tell me, please, surely you know, which way is the snake charmers' village?

"I'm doing a story on a famous sculptor. Named Cristóbal de la Torre. He died a few years ago. He owned one of the smaller islands."

She shook her head.

"I was hoping you might be able to tell me which island."

Anyone here know the road to Molar Bund? Chagroonimalatinapore? Anyone want to sell a border pass? Anyone here found a lens cap?

She kept shaking her head.

"Does that mean you can't tell me or you don't know?"

She stopped. "That mean I don't know."

"Can you think of someone else I might speak to?"

Talk them, woo them, bore them into submission.

"Your boss, perhaps."

She said, "I'm the general director of this office."

"There must be a Ministry of Tourism."

"You're in it."

He'd learned in the Middle East to recognize that moment when an information ministry was about to lash out. He stood up and said, without a trace of anything but genuine gratitude, "I can't tell you how helpful you've been."

"Okay, darling."

Into the morning heat feeling dry-cleaned.

Back at Rawson Square, he found a land registry office in one of the little wings of the government houses. Echoes of Empire right down to the sober lettering of the signs. Behind an ornately carved old desk that looked much too big for him, a studious young man in a white shirt and thin scarlet tie was seated beneath a merciful fan. He seemed to be copying something with a nib pen from one sheet of paper to another. The breeze from the fan regularly flapped the sheaf of uncopied forms held down by his elbow. He inspected his handiwork while Thomas sat down in a chair to one side.

"Good morning, man."

"I wondered if you could help me. I'm trying to find a gentleman who owns an island in the Bahamas."

"You supposed to meet him here?"

"On his island. I don't know which one."

"Are you a Bahamian citizen?"

"American."

"Do you own land in the Bahamas?"

"Not yet."

"But you considering buying this gentleman's land."

"I need to have a look at it first."

The young man smiled. "Look, man. If he want to tell you, that his business, you know. But I can't do that."

"There must be a public registry, no?"

"You're in it."

"The problem is," said Thomas, "this gentleman isn't even alive anymore. His family still owns the property. They were going to sell it off. They might even have done so. The name was de la Torre."

"So you thinking about buying the property, eh?"

Not a bluff he could sustain.

"To be honest, I'm here for an American magazine. Called *The Geographer*."

"Yes, man? I get it every month."

"I have to do a story on this gentleman's island."

"So you're a journalist."

"I'm a photographer."

"Travel a lot, eh? Not like being stuck in Nassau all day."

"A lot of people wouldn't mind being stuck here."

"So you say. You know what? I bet you go talk to those people in the tourism bureau and tell them which magazine you from, they offer to put you up any fancy hotel you want, room service, credit at the casino, long as you like."

Thomas said firmly, "I'm happy where I am. But I really need to find where this guy used to live, because I don't have that much longer here."

"I understand this," said the young man. "But what you're asking me for is to break the law. Why you don't ask his family? Any of them in Nassau?"

"They live in Brazil now. I've been trying to call for months."

"Brazil, eh?"

The land registrar thought about Brazil.

"Look," said Thomas, "I'm not trying to buy anyone's property or invade anyone's privacy. I need to take a couple of pictures of this guy's island and then go home. I don't even think anyone lives there anymore. I'm really backed into a corner here."

"I got you, man," said the young man. "I'd like to help, you know."

"There can't be that many families with their own islands."

"You're right," said the young man. "There can't. You want to know why?"

"Why?"

"One, cause an island is expensive. Two, cause we got something called the Immovable Properties Act."

"I see."

He didn't see anything, except no, no, no.

"Now what the Immovable Properties Act mean—" The young man savored the phrase like fresh mango. "—is that since everyone start buying up these little islands, cays we call them, smuggle drugs in and out, now if people want their own little island they got to lease them, cause the government decide not to sell them off so easy anymore."

"So rich people rent an island? Like a hotel room?"

"Look, man, I'll do you a favor. I can't tell you if this gentleman's family own an island, but I can sure tell you if they don't."

"His last name was de la Torre. But the island might be under the name Gautier. Unless they've just sold it."

The young man smiled. "I can tell you positively that no family of those names owns an island in the Bahamas or has for the last twenty years. That help you?"

"Could you could tell me if they rent an island?"

"That outside my jurisdiction. But you wasting your time you try to track the place down that way. Could be he rent year after year from someone whose name I got here and I don't know it. Could be he rent direct through whatever local district he got near him."

"I don't understand."

"Let's say you off Grand Bahama. You renting from some local registrar office on Grand Bahama. You see?"

"I see." He stood up to go.

"Say! I got an idea, man. Got just the right idea for you."

He was shaking Thomas's hand.

"I need the right idea."

"So you say. Listen. You go out the end of the island. Nice beaches there. Empty as can be. Take some pictures." He shrugged. "Nobody know the difference."

"That's a great idea."

"You just keep going. Past Love Beach."

"Thanks. Thanks a lot, man."

He stood outside in the untiring sunlight and felt embattled.

Where next? It was barely nine o'clock. Where did you go for missing persons?

There was a police bureau in a corner of the park. He walked through pleasant patches of shade and said to the desk sergeant, who was standing outside, "I'm trying to find someone."

Perhaps you even saw her here, walking along, yesterday—

"Has they disappeared?"

In a way.

"Yes."

"Okay, then. C.I.D., man. Criminal Investigations Department. Ask for Sergeant Hugh Symonette. You know where they are?"

He took a taxi.

In the turbulently air-conditioned C.I.D. building, toward the center of the island, Sergeant Symonette received him with the efficient air of a man who was used to dealing with even the most complicated matters that very day.

"Yes, man. You got someone missing."

"I'm trying to locate them."

"That a different thing."

He concocted an elaborate story about Esther, the magazine, a photograph of her father's island, a missed rendezvous.

"So she not actually gone missing, eh?"

"I'm trying to find out which island they live on."

"You check the phone directory?"

"It's a very small island."

"And this Spanish gentleman never want no one find him."

"He enjoyed his privacy."

Sgt. Symonette grinned. "Well, he pick the right place.

How you going to find him, man? You got three thousand island out there to choose from."

"I thought it was only seven hundred islands."

"We say three thousand. Morning God made the Bahamas, he had peas for dinner the night before. You can't find no one here don't want to be found. Maybe he squatting the other end of Bay Street all you know. Maybe he off jumping up and down some rock in the middle of the sea. Now, you charge him with some crime, like he go after his old lady with a lead pipe or he smuggling cocaine, we got a whole different story. But until that time—"

"I understand."

"Why you want to go find him, anyway?"

"I can't find him, because he's dead. I'd like to take a picture of his island."

"Yes, man?" The sergeant gazed at him skeptically. "Most folks we trying to find in the Bahamas, we got their picture already. We busy trying to match it with the body."

This was getting him nowhere. It was almost ten now; soon the government offices would be closing for lunch. He took a taxi back to the airport, this time to the one-room terminal solely for small-plane flights within the Bahamas.

Lining a wall was a series of counters with removable signs for the island-hopping airlines, some of which had only a plane or two. Several men leaned against the counters, joking with each other; a few had the insignias of the little airlines stitched on their sleeves. Thomas walked over and waited for a lull in the conversation, then nodded and said, "'Morning. I'm trying to find a pilot."

"Where you want to go, man?"

"Haven't decided yet. I need to find out where somebody else went first."

"Then you going to follow them, hey?"

A broad-shouldered man said, "People fly all day long out

of here. No questions asked. That's why people like the Bahamas."

"I'm not looking for trouble, I'm just looking for a woman."

"You not the only one, man."

"I think you'd remember seeing her. Fairly tall, late twenties. Half Cuban, half French."

"Best of both worlds," said another.

"That's right."

"Gal like that cure the common cold, eh?"

Another pilot, who'd kept silent up till now, said, "What you looking for this girl for?"

Heavyset, oblong, he carried a certain air of authority, and Thomas realized the other men had been expecting him to speak.

"I've got something I need to give her."

"You a friend of hers?"

"That's right."

Truth was the first casualty, in love as in war.

"Can't you send it to she?" said another.

He realized unquestionably that these men had seen Esther go off with one of them.

"It's not something I can send through the mails."

"This gal didn't leave you high and dry, did she, man?"

"I had a thing like that to deliver once."

"Don't forget, two Nassau gal a day keeps the memories away."

He said, "What I have to give her concerns her father."

"You better off working on the mother, man. That the strategy I always use."

"Sometimes you find yourself in greener pastures, too."

The oblong man said, "What you got on this lady's father, anyway?"

Well, well, he thought. "Some legal documents."

"You looking for the post office, then."

My life has been spent on conversations like this, he told himself. Days and months of them. Always for that one photograph. The one that's theoretically going to make all the difference. And it never does.

He said irritably, "I don't think this lady would be very happy if I put her documents on a mail boat. Especially when there's a pilot who knows the island."

One of the men said with patience, "So, man, you looking to hire a plane. Which island you want to go to?"

Back to the beginning. It was all right, he had another week.

"I'm not sure."

He couldn't think of any way round this.

"You got to be sure in a plane."

Bahamian laughter, American silence.

"You know whereabouts in the Bahamas? General area?"

This from the oblong man again.

Guessing, he said, "South-central Bahamas."

"Seems to me if this lady knew you trying to contact her, she let you know where she is."

"She doesn't know I'm trying to find her." Thomas could feel the men tiring of the game. "Her name's Gautier."

The name didn't register on their faces.

He said, "I need to get out there, today. I'm sure it won't be cheap."

Listen to you, he thought. Old Moneybags.

"Man, if we thought it was going to be cheap we wouldn't be having this conversation."

"You got any identification on you?"

Reluctantly he handed over his passport.

One pilot opened the accordion of extra pages and stretched it out. "Travel a lot, man."

He took back his passport. "I'm a big supporter of small airlines."

The oblong man said, "Best thing I can think of is you

leave a copy of these legal documents with us. We spread the word, and we hear of anyone going out that way we give it to him to take."

"I'm not authorized to make copies of these documents."

"That up to you, man."

"It's not up to me."

The oblong man spread his hands. "What can we do, man? We offer to help."

He said, "I'm staying on until tomorrow morning. At the Hotel Rawson. My name's Simmons. If the pilot turns up, ask him to contact me. If not, well, what can you do. See you guys later."

He felt their eyes on his back until he hit sunlight.

Outside the terminal he bought a Nassau paper from a strolling boy. He read it in the taxi on the way back to town, the breeze riffling the pages. Anything to settle his mind. The front page was all about the upcoming election, full of accusations of corruption on both sides. Voter turnout was expected to be massive. Every island was fought for, even those with minute populations, because they each had at least one representative, one vote in Parliament. He imagined little settlements on these cut-off islands divided by beery arguments and harangues from each party's visiting representative.

What if there were some census office? Or some general accounting place that kept a tabulation of all the islands' populations, for voting purposes? There must be.

This time the taxi took him right past his hotel, past the post office buildings on the hill, past the white statue of Christopher Columbus gazing stolidly out to sea. On the second floor of a modern glass building, looking down past the back of the Royal Victoria, he found a sleek air-conditioned office filled with chattering computers. A neat young lady in a business suit received him courteously. He introduced himself, mentioned the magazine, and said he wanted to do a story on the islands with the smallest voting constituencies. Human-interest pictures.

She said, "In the past certain people, unscrupulous people, have shown a tendency to try to vote on several islands at once. We had to put a stop to this kind of unsociable behavior, you see. Without a census, there had been some difficulty in ascertaining whether voter tabulations were correct."

"I see."

"Bahamians are very proud of their status as a sovereign nation. They enjoy exercising their rights in a democratic society. Voter turnout is very high. Because of these certain unscrupulous people, who are bound to worm their way into any democracy, we need to be particularly careful about numbers. It has taken us years to complete a full and accurate census."

Once wound up, she kept running.

"This election, for the first time, each name and residence will be checked and counterchecked against our census. Voters on the very tiniest cays will have to go to the voting post on a nearby island. But they are able to do so up to a month before election day if they so desire."

That'll guarantee a clean election, he thought.

"And the smallest voting post?"

"That would be Rum Cay."

"What's their population?"

"Just a moment." She went through a folder of computer printout paper. "For our purposes, eighty-one. The real population is probably somewhat less due to people going to Freeport or Nassau to work. That figure includes children, of course. Several foreigners as well. In all we have thirty-seven eligible voters on Rum Cay."

"Aren't there any smaller islands?"

She smiled at being asked to pour out so much valuable

information. "Of course there are. But the people on those islands will have to go elsewhere to vote. You said that your article wanted to portray the smallest voting islands."

Had he really said that? He'd told so many lies that morning he was getting tangled in their loose wires.

"Do you have the smaller ones listed separately?" he asked. "They're the ones I'd be most interested in." Perhaps a little lubrication was called for. "We want to show how in the most remote geographical situation, Bahamian democracy reaches out to its people."

He caught himself mimicking an editorial from the morning paper.

"Here," she said, pulling a handful of sheets from the back of the dossier, "are the twenty-one smallest constituencies. Some of them, now, are private islands—"

His heart leapt.

"—where indeed a property might be foreign-owned. You'll note that foreigners who are not residents, and this includes foreign corporations, are not eligible to vote. These are indicated by N/A after their names. Often, however, they do have Bahamians working for them in some capacity. Usually—" She gave a school-marmish sniff. "—doing the heavy lifting. The computer always distinguishes between population and voting population. For example, on Solomon's Cay, we have a private residence and marina. Population twenty-four, voting population nineteen. The owner is Swiss, with several year-round friends. The rest are staff. They'll go to Grand Bahama to vote. Here's another. Population one, non-voting."

"Who's that?" He tried not to sound too excited.

"A gentleman from California. I understand he's writing a book about how to live alone on a desert island. He goes over to Andros every Saturday for the boxing matches, though." She added confidentially, "They say he gets so drunk they worry he'll get lost some night on the way back."

She was flipping rapidly through the dossier and he was following through the papers with her, as best he could, upside down. Evidently this was the person to talk to if you wanted to know what anyone in the Bahamas was doing last weekend. As she went past one page, he spotted a name and nearly grabbed it from her.

"Pardon me. May I?"

"Of course."

It was labeled: *Desirada*. In the dot-matrix computer type, he read two names. The second had caught his eye.

MOSES, EZEKIEL A.   (V)
GAUTIER, CHRISTOPHE   (N/A)

Gautier, Gautier, he thought. And Christophe probably French for Cristóbal. Got you!

Then he remembered: this was a dead man.

"When did you hold this census, anyway?"

The woman said primly, "In some areas, this past February. In others, I'm afraid our data goes back many years indeed. As much as seven, eight years."

At least he'd found Esther's island.

"And where would these people vote?"

She glanced at the page. "They vote—rather one of them votes—hmm. I don't know where this cay is. Just a moment." She was scanning some gobbledygook letters at the bottom of the page. "That's the code for San Sal. So they vote on San Salvador. The cay must be in that neighborhood somewhere. It could be a considerable distance away, though. Are you planning to visit some of these smaller constituencies, Mr. Simmons? Most of them are going to be quite difficult to reach."

"I imagined they would be. Yes, I am."

12

ANOTHER MORNING ON HIS BEACH.
First swim of the day. Deep sigh of the palms. Sea perturbed
this morning. Clouds in the southwest. Man-o'-wars unsettled in the trees. Storm approaching.

From far away her foraging mouth took him, twirled him,
uprooted him and carried him away.

Away: we will never come back. Never again to that place.

In the largesse of the hotel suite's bed they'd lain apart,
broken and separate sculptures. Thérèse's breathing was
deep and even: he thought she'd fallen asleep. He was wondering if she'd packed Esther's valise for their departure to
Havana when he felt her stir.

He sensed her watching him in the darkness, fully awake.

"Are you asleep, Cristóbal?"

"What is it?"

"Something."

"You should try to sleep."

"I don't know," she murmured.

He waited.

"I'm not sure I can explain it."

He sensed suddenly that she'd been waiting hours to have
this disjointed conversation with him.

"Try."

As if she could scarcely believe it herself, she said, "I—I've been passing through something. But it's over now, I promise."

What could she mean?

She said gently, plainly, "I've been seeing another man."

His ears started to burn. Only inches away in the darkness, it was as if she were talking to someone else in the room, a stranger rendered invisible. Why was she not speaking to him? Then he realized it only seemed thus because he wished it so, he did not want to hear her say this to him.

"No," he said, almost inaudibly, hearing his voice meekly utter the meek word *no*.

"Tonight I told him I'd never see him again. That's why I was so late." She paused. "I wanted to make love with you one last time before I told you."

She spoke as if she feared he would interrupt or she might lose her nerve and have to begin again. He felt his face tauten into a grimace, his eyes squeezed shut as if from contact with smoke. She had nerve to spare—what could he say to such a tactical assault? Now the third person in the room was sitting on the edge of their bed. He opened his eyes and light from the other room came chattering under the bedroom door.

I shouldn't be surprised, he thought violently, that you chose to take it this far. You've proven your point.

Dissipated, as insubstantial as the air stirring in the obscure bedroom, he said nothing. Trying to slow his brain accelerating back, searching for individual nights it could've happened. Their first visit here a year ago, surely, when he'd received the commission. When else? Did it matter?

He said dully, hearing in his voice how much the world had altered in the last few seconds, "You met him here last April."

The question, the other questions implicit, hung in the air.

She said, "I saw him once in New York and here a few more times. Not many."

How many is not many?

"Is he younger than I am?"

"Cristóbal, that's not the reason, listen to me."

Beneath the grief and the guilt in her voice he heard the exaggerated enthusiasm of someone who has wanted to tell the truth for too long and now wants to tell too much of it.

He closed his eyes. "How did you meet?"

"At one of the parties for you."

"Did I meet him?"

She sighed heavily. "I think you did. You probably wouldn't remember him. He's not the sort of person one remembers."

There was a curious sadness in her tone, as if she were speaking about herself rather than this person between them. Why are you telling me this? he thought. I don't want to know any of it. Telling me about it is more of an action than having done it.

"Did he ask you out at the party?"

And all the ready women I've turned down since I met you.

"The next day. You were meeting the museum people. He saw me on the street and introduced himself again."

A shiver ran through him. "I remember that day, you got back to the hotel late in the afternoon. After I did. Esther said you hadn't called."

She said, "I've told you, it was different than you think."

"Meaning it was exactly as I think." Rage around his head now. "You were supposed to have been with Esther!"

"I can't be with her every moment of every day."

He reached across her roughly and switched on the bedside lamp. It made her face seem vulnerable, partly in shadow: beauty racked with a force it was not sure how to endure. Another hallucination generated by the illusion of light. He saw, too, signs of satisfaction in that torment.

For an instant he stood apart from the turbulence gathering in him and wondered if he still believed it was impossible for them to leave one another, only death had the power to make that happen.

He thought: I could break everything in this room.

He saw himself clearly, at that instant, grotesque: he wanted to know only how this man had taken her. Feeling the jealousy come up like bile in his throat, he knew with a stabbing clarity that it was this taste she wanted in his mouth. He fought it down.

"Does he have a name?" he said at last.

"Raymond," she said.

"Raymond what?"

"Do you have to know?"

"If I ask you," he said, "you have to tell me."

She said, quietly, "Raymond Harris. He owns a paper company."

Ramón. Ludicrous. His wife had been stolen from him by a man who made paper.

Next year, he thought, it will be a man who makes rubber bands. The year after, those things you put in drains to keep the water from running away. The year after that—

Someone who doesn't make you jealous every time he tries to get some work done. Someone who gives you his complete attention, all the time. Someone who makes paper hats and paper airplanes and probably toilet paper for a living. Someone whose work isn't worthy of your destruction.

"Why did you do this?"

As if there could be a surprising answer.

"How can I say it so you'll understand?" she said. "I knew it wouldn't be for long. I saw him only four or five times. I'm not curious about other men. I needed to understand why I'm with you. No, that's not right," she corrected herself. "Why you're with me."

Didn't she understand she was the only person who'd ever freed him from the banal, local prison of himself? Didn't she feel any wonder at together having made Esther to carry out time for them?

He sensed the beginnings of a vast and uncontainable rage, and tried to slow his breathing. What was love, if it could not conquer rage? And yet rage could be as clear in sight. Beyond two closed doors, thirty feet away, Esther lay asleep. What did she know of this? What damage done there? How used-up, how petrified he felt. Between his legs he had shriveled with the cold withering dark that followed sex.

Up until this moment he had been able to enjoy the unalloyed sensation of knowing that, no matter what, Thérèse was in love with him. Now that idea had lost its purity, was in fact sinking in Charleston Bay. Forty-six: he felt two decades older tonight.

He never imagined those two decades, the longest of a long life, would be spent without her.

"Which one is it you don't understand?" he said. "Why you're with me? Or the other way around? Choose one."

She said, "I don't understand. I never have. I don't understand why I hurt you. Why I hurt us." She covered her face with her hands, and shook her head slowly.

This is pathetic, he thought. The only thing to understand is why you're so selfish.

His mother's voice, vague with the intervening years, came back to him: he was Wednesday's child, he could overcome woe. So much for the obsolete beliefs of a believing mother. So much for twilight-blue eyes of utter devotion to him. As Thérèse's eyes had been before.

He thought of Esther asleep in the other room, of the years travelling a limitless world with this woman.

Where oh where are the people we were?

"There's nothing to understand," he said wearily.

Nothing indeed.

I was a fool, he told himself those decades later, to think I could forgive her so indifferently and have it count. A fool not to recognize a cry for help when I heard one. A fool to have asked her to live a life that would play upon her weaknesses. It was I who forced us to travel so much, from commission to commission, that she never had a chance to establish herself anywhere for more than a few months at a time. A fool to think being with me would do anything to bridge the inward distances in her. A fool to think having a child would help. A fool to think someone incapable of belief could risk believing for long.

A fool not to realize taking a lover and telling me was the last way she could think of to reach me. She would find one more.

If only every night we could have made love as we did that last night we loved.

That is all a forgiving lie, he told himself. Why forgive either one of us? She knew I was a man of costly nature when she married me. From the beginning I knew exactly the person she would always be, I saw that all her passion only covered up the deepest lack of self-belief I ever encountered. Those apologies of hers that always terrified me, because I saw they were only an excuse for the next assault. And her unending irritation and insistence that I do something about the hollowness in her. She was one of the unsatisfied ones, and I made the mistake of loving her.

She had said, "What if you were to cancel the project near Boston? We could spend the winter in Paris, and go to Nerja in the spring."

That had been her offer, that might have changed everything, but how had he responded? What small amount of his life had he been willing to give up to spare her death?

The sightless words stared blindly at him from a distance of twenty-two years.

He said, "It's too late to cancel, I'm supposed to be there in two months."

What had he understood of her? Nothing.

"Are you sure it's too late?" Her voice rang strangely.

He said, "Why don't you take a week's holiday after Cuba? In Aix or somewhere. By yourself. Esther and I can stay in Paris. Then we'll all go to Boston. I'll find us a house on the shore. Somewhere calm."

She said, speaking away from him, her voice muffled by the pillow, "You think I need a holiday."

"Perhaps it would do us good."

"You need a holiday from me."

"I don't." Even though he was all but demanding one. Would it have been different? Had he canceled the project, as she asked—a stupid big abstract whatnot for a corporate headquarters that, in any case, never got made. Or would he have come home one afternoon to find she'd swallowed sleeping pills in the Paris flat? Or swum out to sea off the Spanish coast at Nerja, to a warmer end?

Slowly he felt her body adjust to his. He shifted so she could be encompassed within his arms, and she moved backward into them. One body, sealed once more. She looked again over her shoulder at him, blinking back tears, and a thrill went through him at the wildness in her face, the naked soul in those cheekbones; the answering look on his face relieved her and she closed her eyes and settled against him. Through the window, with the breeze rustling, he sensed the midnight clouds scudding, the alliance of stars, and he felt their intertwined lives whirled upwards and away.

Away: we will never come back to this place.

Their intertwined lives were over; those phantoms had nothing to do with the separate people on this bed. She had been right: one last time.

Tears ran down his face. They blurred the ceiling until he

reached across Thérèse, now sleeping easily in his arms, and shut off the light.

Who can ever put this back together? No God in heaven I ever believed in.

What a prayer, he thought those long years later, what a smudge of words to excuse anything he wanted them to excuse, what a dull echo it had made sitting in that cold house, wrapped and shivering in the worn coat the policeman made him put on, Esther so small staring out the window, saying nothing, seeing where he'd run an hour earlier across the ice, seeing the insolent sneering curl of its lip where Thérèse must have stepped off into the hurrying black water, where he would dream over and over of seeing her turn back and catch his eye for one startled instant, seeing the look of pure despair on her face that he'd put there, he'd painted on her as if she were a worthless statue he could shatter and cast again whenever he wanted. That was only a dream, he hadn't seen her; he'd only stood helplessly at the edge of the ice, shouting her name.

So much for prayers, so much for the years washing memory away and making life acceptable. He remembered the scrape of his shoes across that ice, he remembered the satisfied shriek of the wind, he remembered the arrogant speed of that black water. He remembered Esther's open disbelieving eyes. The end of all belief.

And she still innocent of the full truth of those years, he thought, because I chose never to tell her any of it. The days of broken work and the nights of broken sleep. I should tell you that story, Esther. So you have all your mother. Not some dream of her I can never live up to.

"Esther!" he roared.

Around him, hidden by trees, his peacocks shrieked and cowered and shat in terror, birds went scattering in torment at the urgency of his passing; the fronds of palms bent towards the golden pangola grass and stayed out of his way.

"Esther!"

Scully Moses turned in the clearing to see him coming.

"What you need, man?"

Cock crow from behind the house. Bougainvillea bursting scarlet and purple this morning.

"Where is she?"

Beset by masked devils, he thought his head would explode.

"Esther!"

She appeared in the doorway, in shorts and a T-shirt. No echos of her mother there. She said quietly, "What is it?"

"Promise me something. Promise you'll come with me now, this morning, and see the shrine."

"I won't promise anything until I've had my coffee."

She'd spoken in English. He saw what she was trying to do: enlist Scully's support.

"Promise me."

"I won't promise."

"It's five minutes' walk!"

"I'm here, isn't that enough?"

"It's not enough." How could she come this close and refuse? Was she so frightened by the possibility of being moved by what he'd done?

Around him the sunlight was insatiable.

She said, "I've thought about this Nassau doctor of yours. I think you should be somewhere you can get serious medical attention."

"Serious? Most of his patients are millionaires. Don't you think he knows how to pay attention?"

"I've asked you over and over again to give me his name. Every time you refuse. I want you to have him out here while I'm here."

"He's much too busy to come out on such short notice."

"No one's too busy for you, surely."

"You should see the bills I get."

"I'd like to."

"I'm not protected by insurance anymore, you know."

"What's his name? I'll find him myself."

"I tell you what," he said. "Spend the day with me, let me show you something. Then we'll talk about the medical profession."

"I want you to go see some proper Swiss doctors."

"How am I supposed to get to Switzerland? In disguise? Hidden in a sack of coffee?"

"In a shirt and trousers. Like everyone else. They'll probably treat you for free."

"Scully, you want to go to Switzerland and see some doctors for me? You think I need to see a doctor there?"

"You an important bastard, Einstein. Tell the man fly here. We always happy to let a doctor land. No discrimination there."

He said, "What if we promise to fly one of your Swiss doctors out here to see me? Will you come look at what I've built for you then?"

He heard his own voice pleading. Didn't she see he didn't care what happened? At least after she saw what he'd made?

The answer of all forgiveness lies not a half-mile from here, he thought. Feebly, he said, "Can't you give me one day?"

"Why are you determined to avoid what's inevitable?" she said. "You're going to have to leave eventually. You shouldn't be here. You should be seeing doctors with some competence. You should be—"

"The hell with your doctors!" he burst out in Spanish, fed up with this feminine harangue. "Why are you stalling? I don't need a doctor!"

"Go easy, Einstein," muttered Scully.

She stared at him.

"That's right! What I need is to be allowed to live in peace on my own island with my friend and my daughter for another ten years! That's what I need! And if I did need a doctor, I promise you, Esther, I would cut my throat or get someone to cut it for me rather than submit to being pushed, prodded, needled, wheeled about, tested and re-tested and pumped with chemicals and shattered with radiation. When the time comes I'll go to it, and stronger than the moment I was born, and I'll do it myself, on the day of my choice, the place of my choice, the death of my choice."

She said, "What did that doctor tell you?"

"What doctor? No doctor! Never any doctor here! No doctors allowed on this island! No governments! No journalists! No art lovers! Only daughters and wives!"

"You told me in Barcelona, before you came—" She faltered. "And in all those letters, how ill—"

"Remission!" he said triumphantly, eyes ablaze. "That's what this sea can do for you. I've given the Caribbean two honorary degrees. One for each cancer it's washed away. Better than any doctor. Do I look like a man who is going to die? Do I look like a man ready to submit to being coaxed off his island? Do you think after all I've given up to come here, all I've won through to stay, I will leave now?"

She said wearily, "My mother was right."

13

IT TOOK THOMAS TEN MINUTES TO pack. The only difficulty was deciding what to do with his exposed film—he couldn't risk taking it with him. It'd be one thing to explain soberly, to a normal person, what he was about to do; to try explaining to his editors that he'd lost seventy rolls of film en route would be worth paying money to see. Realizing he'd have to pass through Nassau on the way back, he got the burly receptionist to put the film in the hotel safe.

The flight down the islands, stopping briefly at Georgetown in the Exumas, left promptly at noon—he made it at a run. Nearly everyone on the aged Bahamasair plane got off at the bustling Great Exuma airstrip. By one-thirty he was standing on San Salvador.

It was oppressively humid. The air clung to him and the sand fleas were bloodthirsty. The small town straggled around a bay banked up the coast by white sand. There was a modest stone church with an unflattering carved portrait of Columbus, a tumbledown bar, a wharf with a mail boat under repair. He saw no tourists and made inquiries—not a single guest house, though an enormous hotel was under construction on the south coast to commemorate Columbus's first landfall in the New World. It seemed a bit late as a business opportunity, but that was apparently how things went around here.

Seated on a stone bench outside the little church, watching with poisoned nostalgia the bickering mail boat crew on the wharf, his motivations for having come even this far seemed laughable. To make himself feel less rejected, less stranded? To prove something? He'd been only a fling for Esther on the way back to Geneva or Paris or somewhere. Her father was a long-lost sea-picked skeleton. That census information was a decade out of date. Why spend any more time chasing these phantoms?

Or perhaps he was only trying to insure he didn't have anything resembling a calm vacation. No, that might entail being forced to think things over a little too clearly, and not like what he saw.

They'll cancel the next plane out, he thought, and I'll be stuck on another limping mail boat. That'll use up the rest of the week, and I'll go back to New York with diarrhea.

He was contemplating the prospect when a schoolgirl in a blue smock offered him fried conch from a paper plate. She turned out to be a nun, teaching in the island's only school.

"Sister Jessica," she said amiably. "Call me Jess."

He introduced himself and asked if she knew where he might rent a boat.

In the plane he'd pored over a detailed navigational chart found at the last minute on Bay Street; in his camera bag he had the compass he'd bought for Inagua—worried about getting lost on the labyrinthine salt lakes. He also had his small collapsible tent and bedroll. The odds were, of course, he'd end up camping out alone until he got sick of mosquitoes lunching off him.

"Where you trying to get, eh?"

He estimated that Desirada lay about twelve miles east-southeast of San Sal. A tiny unnamed cay lay between, otherwise only the usual Bahamian system of shallow water over sand bars and unexpected ocean trenches. The distance didn't worry him; he'd sailed for years and felt comfortable handling a small boat alone.

"I want to follow the coast," he told her. "Maybe have a look at the other side of the island."

Sister Jessica said, "I can introduce you to a old man who got a couple extra boats. You interested in taking a picture where Columbus landed?"

"Do you know the spot?"

"We got three monuments on three different beaches. They say his footprint was still on a rock on one beach. But then the rock disappeared. You know how these things happen."

"When can I meet this old man?"

"Right now."

The venerable Mr. Wilmott, who'd received a letter off the mail boat, told him to watch out for the weather and accepted a deposit of four hundred dollars in the form of a personal check. People were trusting on San Sal; being introduced by a nun didn't hurt. And, just like that, the boat rental was accomplished.

His journey had gone fluently—he was used to things going swiftly and irrevocably wrong. He had nearly three hours of daylight left. Instead of hunting up a room for the night, he crossed the cracked road to the little grocery and stocked up on enough water and provisions to last a couple of days. He filled two extra tanks of gasoline. He thanked Sister Jessica, and got going.

The boat was a stalwart Out Island skiff, high-sided and layered like a clapboard house, with an old Evinrude 45 depending from the stern. Its red paint was flaking all around but he felt how seaworthy it was just kneading his way through the approach to San Salvador. He began to relax, leaving the island's whiteness behind for an hour until it became a sliver of beach with sandy hills like humps of snow that disappeared in the waves.

The sea was calm and shallow, sand bars milkily wavering through the green water. At one point he saw a hammerhead glide below him. The sky was the palest pink with blue tints, the sun molten. Way off the sky was shaded slightly darker, like a smudged thumbprint. He went over the chart and decided that the Exumas were getting five minutes of rain. They were probably happy to have it.

Still plenty of strong light, even at four in the afternoon. He took a mental photograph of his legs stretched out and the high sharp prow evenly and cleanly dividing the water before him as the skiff plunged rapidly on.

He passed a few massive outcroppings of reef, significant enough to qualify as dots on the map, and then the larger nameless cay, identified as H-231, nearly due south, where it should've been. He estimated Desirada another six miles ahead, maybe less. He wondered a little nervously what visibility would be when the light began to wane.

Now the distant thumbprint of rain was inkier. At the stern the engine roared on with satisfaction as around him the water deepened to violet. There was still daylight when he realized the thumbprint was being blotted all over the sky. All right, he thought, you're going to get a little wet.

He'd been in storms on the water before, and in smaller, more vulnerable boats, but never in the tropics, and never so isolated on the sea. He lifted his head to the wind and tried to reassure himself that the rain would miss him, blow past before he got to its territory. The sky before him resembled a dark scrim draped down from distant clouds. If he found shallow water anytime soon perhaps it'd be sensible to let down the anchor and let the rain pass by. What a nuisance. Why hadn't he had the brains to wait until tomorrow morning to leave? It was happening with incredible quickness, like a hand passing magically over the water from afar, getting nearer.

His natural skepticism made him reluctant to accept that he was ever in situations of real danger. When he admitted what was going on around him, he got the tent out of his canvas bag and, while he could still see what he was doing, covered all his gear securely with it. He checked that his palm-sized flashlight was working, then put on one of the life jackets stowed under the seat. He told himself it must be only three miles to Desirada.

The wind had stiffened, no longer the cool breeze of day's end. The skiff was being slowly pushed about and he had to keep the prow into the wind to stay on course; the incited waves made his headway sluggish. The skiff felt ungainly, a land animal struggling in the water.

Then, far behind him, in seconds, the sun went down at the edge of a gray sky in turmoil.

He watched its descent with real panic. There was still light, diffused across the sea's surface and being sipped up thirstily, but he couldn't see any island ahead. Only he could have done something this stupid. God in Heaven, why was there only deep water here?

Waves were slopping over the starboard gunwale. He had no choice but to quarter—veer off the wind and waves—and try to stay approximately on course. Why didn't his compass have a luminous dial? Because he'd bought a cheap one, why else. He secured it and the tiny flashlight in his shirt pocket.

Somewhere astern the unnamed cay was gone from sight. He could admit to himself now that he was really worried. What an unbelievably foolish effort this had been! To leave so late in the day simply because all had gone so well. Ridiculous to have trusted so much to instinct. If he missed the island he'd end up loose in the Atlantic.

It began to rain as night came down.

The rain was warm, but it flew straight at his face and hampered any chance to see ahead. With the waves chafing higher and higher, the skiff slamming into them, he rapidly lost all sense of direction. In the slippery rain he couldn't manage the flashlight and the compass and steer at the same time. It occurred to him to toss the anchor and hope it caught, but he was in open water; anchoring wouldn't help. The wind whined and shrieked around the sliding boat and as he watched, the gathered darkness became complete. He couldn't even see his own huddled knees. There was only the loud hissing of rain and the annoyed grind of the engine as the skiff scaled rising valleys of water.

He forced himself to pretend he was back in his studio on East 11th Street—yes, one so often encountered bad weather en route from the darkroom to the bathroom via the kitchen. Bobbing alongside him now were mementos of his journeys—a Guatemalan deer mask with bells and mirrors, a silverized Tibetan monk's skull, a grinning black pirate puppet from Java with red bandanna, an ironwork crocodile devil-god from the Sahara who would protect him from all harm—swept through his apartment past massive camera equipment that the sea engulfed.

The only solution was to crawl to higher ground, the bed loft, and hope the waters would not be able to reach. Or that they'd float Esther up to him.

Hadn't he come here, in fact, to avoid everything the last two weeks were trying to tell him? That night with the secretary en route. The sun-blasted stay with the flamingos and the time wasted on the mail boat. The few days with Esther that ended in a profound sense of futility. Now this ludicrous search for an island that even the government couldn't be bothered to locate. He'd lost all belief in his own life, and what had he done? Bet on some impossible hope of a woman and her dead father.

He had no choice but to keep steering off the wind. He remembered vaguely something he'd read about a small land mass directing air currents. Perhaps the wind was blowing directly from Desirada. That wouldn't be very helpful. Now and then he rode across great sea swells like the long backs of enormous whales. Once when he felt the skiff almost nose under he frantically pulled his gear back toward him.

And then he sensed the wind shift right round. It was an extraordinary sensation—for a few seconds he thought the boat had been sucked into a whirlpool and was whelming down—as if the unseen horizon were revolving about him. All his bearings taken from a fickle wind. His clothes sopping with warm rain.

Trying to steer with one hand, he fumbled the flashlight with the other. In the faint blink of light the compass showed him roughly on his proper course. It seemed so impossible that he thought the compass must be broken and he was lost for good.

Perhaps, he told himself, he'd come this far only to feel he was risking something. In Nassau he'd known that everything with Esther was his imagination except her body and her own regret about her life. Her leaving had been the realest thing about her. She was a work of imagination from the start, as much as the idea of her father somewhere out here. Still he'd convinced himself to come; he'd put himself out in the middle of this. He'd left late in the day, he'd wanted to be here.

Not anymore, bucko. There was nothing out here. Nothing and no one.

Now the skiff was almost planing, the wind and the swells carrying him from behind at an insane speed, bucking like angry horses. Off in the distance he thought he saw a faint light then it was quickly gone. There it came again. He peered fantastically through the fast rain until it occurred to him that he was still clutching the flashlight with one hand

and unconsciously thumbing it on and off, on and off, signaling to himself as the bug of light winked on a metal fitting at the prow.

Had he not felt so alone on those salt lakes, had her body not felt so supple in his arms, had he not felt so drawn to everything he sensed but could not see clearly about her life, he wouldn't be here. Had he not been looking for some excuse to abandon all sense, to make the grand gesture.

He realized coldly that the stress of the last hour, two hours, half-hour, whatever it was, had started to unhinge him. He felt joyous in a desperate way, from speed and the rush of air, as if he were hung from a great height and could calculate how much ocean there was. Waves he couldn't see soaked him, he was licking salt from his lips constantly; he sensed walls of water on all sides, veering off at crazy angles, reaching to the nearby sky.

His storm-tormented mind thronged in on itself, battered him cruelly with questions. After a time he realized the outboard was doing little good, he was simply wasting fuel, but if he let it die he'd never be able to start it again, so he kept it working, even though at moments it was tossed free of the water entirely. He put the flashlight and compass back in his shirt pocket and with his unoccupied hand he made crude attempts to bail with a sawn-off Clorox bottle. The rain around him was as warm as a hotel shower.

I am going to die out here, he thought. I really am.

At first it seemed unbelievable. Of course it must always seem that way, if you had time to think about it. A couple of years back he'd photographed soldiers dying in the desert in insufferable heat; they'd accepted it quite naturally. Being wounded must shatter incredulity at death, in both body and mind.

A short time later he felt an encompassing peace descend upon him. It was comforting to have his camera bag wrapped dryly in a tent at his feet; he could feel the hump of the camera body and the lenses. Strange that he could have garnered so much affection over the years for a machine that was easily replaceable, for its familiar weight in his hands.

He felt lulled by his own helplessness against the sea and the multitude of winds hurtling around him, testing the immensity of the black sky. There were no shades to this night—it was an amazing claustrophobia of darkness. Without the flashlight he couldn't see even the prow of the skiff, plunging against the ocean, nor the white plastic of the bailer, nor even his hand when he put it right before his face. It was like going entirely blind. There could not be a more absolute darkness; it seemed to have flesh, to be a palpable, living thing, seducing him into falling asleep.

He tried to keep himself awake by pinching his thighs through his shorts. He realized suddenly that he wasn't drowsy at all, but desperately wide awake: he had been on edge and alert for so long he wasn't even aware of it anymore. How many men were given the chance to experience this, surrounded by the rough ocean, the night sky, the wind at full force, the sense of all space whirling around them? If it was to be tonight then let it be tonight. Better than in his stale studio, in the middle of a strident city.

He tried to sing, so his mind would have something active, not merely reactive, to do, but he couldn't make himself heard over the storm, only a weird honking in his skull. His back ached from fighting to steer for so long. After a while he began to feel he was dissolving into night, he was not anyone anymore. Thomas Simmons was slipping away. He tried to read his watch with the flashlight, but it was too faint. Surely one night could not be this long. He had imagined dawn only a few hours away. Surely the storm could not go on all night.

The wind had shifted again and the rain had lessened

slightly. At least he didn't seem to be getting as wet. Perhaps it was that he could no longer tell any difference.

Then he looked up and saw a few thin stars beginning to show amid the clouds—abruptly he could see clouds. The storm was blowing elsewhere, to trouble other boats and other men. He felt a wave of energy lift him as a wave lifted the boat carrying him, a fragile bubble of his hopes and contrivances and luck. Angry with himself for thinking he was already dead, he searched the cloudy sky for other stars.

The rain slackened and then ceased altogether.

For what he guessed was around two hours—the flashlight was broken now—he waited for the moon to come out. There was only the faint light of a few stars. They were enough to let him know where the horizon was, where the boundaries of sky and ocean tilted; he could discern the faint trail of the Milky Way. Though the rain had abated the wind still hurled the skiff wildly and relentlessly forward. Immersed in night, he sucked at his shirt collar because the bag with his provisions was too far forward in the skiff.

Then he saw the edge of the moon, and in the distance, a brooding darker silhouette just above the horizon. His ears caught the crashing of white water; moonlight fell on waves breaking across distant reefs, foaming before an island; and the wind held.

It was another hour before the wind and the currents brought him near. The wind was still strong but the ocean calmed and the clouds were clearing. The moon was out like a beacon. By his watch it was barely three. In another hour it would be neither night nor morning but he would reach the island before then. He supposed it to be about three miles long, and low-lying. Beyond the fringe of surf across the reef he could just make out an even line of palm trees, billowing in the wind, their heads enormous in the frayed silvery moonlight.

He was near enough to see a seething mass of white water

where the reefs lay. He could see no break or breathy slackening of the foam, no way in. He stood up clumsily, his back in agony, and saw, too late, just how close he was. For the first time he realized there were no oars in the skiff. Impulsively he reversed the outboard to back the skiff away from the reef, but the engine jammed and died on him. Cursing, he tore at the starter cord, trying to get it going, perhaps the points were soaked. No matter how furiously he yanked it wouldn't start, and he felt all the pent-up desperation of his helpless night unleashed. He was being taunted with this island, he could still die, the skiff could be smashed to pieces on the reef and he could be flayed to ribbons on the coral. Of all things, to lose now because he couldn't yank a starter cord fast enough.

The white water was around him, catching the blue light, and he could do nothing but grasp the gunwales and hope the water wasn't deep beyond the reef. What if it wasn't even the right cay? What if there was no one here? Of course there was no one, there hadn't been for years. And if the skiff got staved in and he was stranded?

Being swept through the maelstrom of white water, reefs darkly present around him, used up all his fear that the storm in total darkness had not. An excited froth streamed all around the boat like the manes of white horses, the waves roared as they detonated and destroyed themselves on the gnarled coral heads. He saw the palm trees waving at him, huge in the moonlight, and he gulped in lungfuls of salt air rich with the land scent. He could smell mangrove, sea grapes, wild limes; then he whirled and the reefs were behind him, begging to be bade farewell, and he realized he was babbling at them. Pale sand of a curved beach was coming rapidly toward him, glimmering. The wind whipped at his head. The skiff surged forward again and again, as if the swells, acting on behalf of the entire ocean, were trying to cough him up. He stood up in exhilaration and wobbled on his feet. He felt his head spin.

The propeller bumped, scraped, then the skiff heaved beneath him, and he was thrown sideways and out. The welcoming water warmly embraced him, soothed him under, and he floundered in it with the life vest before he realized he was only knee-deep and a few feet from shore. He grappled at the prow of the skiff for the anchor line, thinking of his camera and the food; he managed to get the anchor to his chest and stumble out of the shallows and onto the beach. He pitched the anchor as far forward as he could, in front of him, toward those wavering palms. Then the hard sand came up to him fast.

He awakened to the languid light that followed dawn. His head throbbed and his body felt ponderous, lying prone, encrusted with wet sand. Before him as the light came stealing up, the mottled gray trunks of palms revealed themselves, a few coconuts lying plopped in the sand, green fronds scattered everywhere by the storm. The anchor rope ran past his body and the anchor itself lay like a weird pronged sea creature eyeing him face to face. He spat out sand and pulled himself gingerly to his knees. Hunks of the beach were matted in his hair, his clothes, his sneakers.

Yet it was like civilization to be on land again. The apparent peace of this beach, these palms, the quiet water he heard chuckling behind him, a place he had imagined coming to and could not quite believe in yet, reminded him how lucky he'd been, how fragile his hold on life was. He gripped gobs of sand greedily in his fists. He lived because of the whim of wind and a few currents and rain. He could as easily still be out in an open boat, slowly dehydrating and starving. Or else already a sea-drunk corpse, bloated and bobbing.

When he stood up hesitantly and turned around he took in almost without comprehension his skiff idle in the lapping shallows, cool in the easy light, and the graceful palms along a naked beach. The sea was perfectly flat, there was no wind. So much for the storm. He could barely spy a ridge of gentle froth across the reef.

When he turned to look in the other direction he was so startled he let out a yelp of surprise. Halfway down the beach a dismasted, aged Bahamian sloop was pulled up, looking like it owned the place. He stared at it dumfounded.

Someone else is here, he thought. Or was, anyway.

He heard his own breathing. He realized his fists were tightly clenched around wet sand. He let it go.

The right island? The right someone else?

The thought of her now was stranger than ever. He had come through so much to find her and yet it was difficult, this stunned morning, to summon back her face.

He kicked off his sneakers and got out of his shirt and shorts and rinsed the sand from them as he walked into the water. When he felt clean enough he wandered over to the skiff, spread his clothes on the gunwales, and rummaged around in his bag until he found the bread, the processed cheese, and a plastic bottle of mineral water. His mind wanted coffee; he hadn't realized how very hungry he was. He ate a terrible breakfast standing waist-deep in the shallows. Then he tilted the engine forward and pulled the skiff up until it wedged firmly in the sand.

By the time he was done he needed another swim. Naked in the water, he thought: So where is everyone? Still asleep.

He brought his bags out of the skiff and laid them within the shade of a clump of traveler's palms. He dressed, and with his camera bag over his shoulder, he started off down the beach.

Behind the palms lay a forest of lemon sunlight, a great

expanse of yellow-green pangola grass from which rose taller palms and some stunted trees he couldn't identify. Fronds broke the light into fragmented gold that lay on the deep pangola grass and made it into the floor of an illumined lost world. He saw it extended inland until the trees thickened into shadows.

He walked on, expecting to come upon a house set back in the palms. The beach continued to curve in a slow embrace. The water was only now taking on its first aquamarine tints of the day. A fragrant breeze was awakening bird cries. He got out the longest lens and used it like a telescope, patiently sweeping the beach and the stately procession of palms to the end of the island. No house, no other boats, no signs of human presence at all.

He was considering whether to give up and try the other direction when he saw that just ahead the palms broke briefly. Here was a path, and framing it, half-ruined, an arch of stone, bleary and salt-stained, sun-whitened. It showed signs of recent repair, some cement to keep it standing. The texture of the aged stone was wonderful in the slant light. He photographed it from both sides, unable to decide whether its ambivalent invitation was to enter the island or to leave it.

The path—white sand punctuated by fallen coconuts and fronds, shaded by a long colonnade of palms—led away through the dense foliage for a quarter-mile, then curved abruptly out of sight. Obviously it was being used every day, otherwise it would've grown over.

He set off confidently down the path. The slight breeze died as he went inland. He took off his shirt and carried it loosely in one hand, feeling shadows from the heaven of crisscrossing fronds stroke his naked back in benediction. He looked back and, knowing it would look like nothing special in a photograph but wanting to remember, he took a long shot of the beach and sea through the arch.

Birds in the palms marked his passage. A parrot flew from a tree near him to another down the path, from which it watched safely. As he approached, the parrot gazed gravely at him and uttered a burst of speech, like fragments of an ancient garbled tongue. When he couldn't reply it nodded, richly green and pink against the shadows. The light was precisely what he wanted. In the stillness each ratchet of the camera shutter seemed harsh.

He walked on, feeling his weariness from the night before, wondering what lay at the end of the path. Another beach, with a quietly booming ocean. Perhaps a house. Or perhaps no one, no one at all. That would be less strange, this morning, than a dead man's daughter.

He had come to a curve in the path when he detected movement in the pangola forest, among the many palms. He caught his breath as the grass parted. A male peacock, its tail folded into a gray broom, stepped onto the path a short distance before him. The imperious black eyes sheathed in gold mascara glared at him, the little royal blue head jerked nervously, the enormous wagon of tail swept behind.

The peacock screamed once. Then its mate, a peahen with a stumpy brown tail, followed it out of the pangola grass. The peacock screamed again. A shiver ran through its tail, which lifted slowly from the ground and fanned open like a card-hand unfolding. The tail spread into a great ordered universe, green and gold and blue eyes in each of the feathers like the eyes of angels, lit by hurrying sunlight, all those eyes turned to impress the female and past her, instinctively, Thomas. He raised his camera and shot away.

Clearly they didn't care how close he got; they were used to humans.

After a moment of arrogant display the peacock wandered off the path, his tail neatly descending and tucking itself in again. The female followed. A few broken cries issued from the foliage. Thomas peered through, saw another forest of deep pangola grass, and the two peacock heads bobbing over the canal made by their passage. Soon they were gone in shadows.

Inland the storm had done little damage and the path was bare of fallen debris. As he wandered on, the palms lining the path stirred their fronds like the idly fluttering fans of high-born Spanish ladies. But he could feel no breeze here, how could that be? A brief desolation, silent as a cloud, passed over him, and he sat down wearily on a flat rock. The sea was just visible back the way he'd come, shimmering beyond a thumbnail of beach. He mopped his forehead with his shirt then rolled it like a towel and laid it on the back of his neck, to soak up sweat. The camera bag hung heavy at his side, the camera dangled against his waist.

When he stood up a wave of vertigo assaulted him and he had to put out a hand to the rock to keep from falling. He closed his eyes: shards of sunlight wheeled against the black backdrop of his brain. Suppose no one lived here now? Maybe peacocks in the wild simply didn't frighten easily— they could've been left alone here for ages. And that sloop might've been abandoned years ago; he hadn't bothered to go take a closer look. What if he'd found the wrong island entirely?

He shook his head to clear it, and opened his eyes. Where the path seemed to branch, a shaft of dusty sunlight beck-oned.

He was walking slowly. Above him the sky was bare of clouds, as if a huge lens were focusing light on this island. The path branched quite severely. To the right it continued through the colonnade of palms, to the left it ran along a rock wall. He decided to pursue the left branch, thinking it would end soon enough and then he would retrace his way and follow the other. It wasn't yet eight o'clock and the morning was already hot in these close trees. A big mistake not to bring a water bottle.

He came quickly to the end of this branch of the path. It was muffled by the shadows of heavy vegetation hanging ponderously over the rock wall. Odd outcropping for a Bahamian island.

He began to follow the rock wall as it curved farther left, to see if it led to anything. Then he staggered; the breath whistled out of his chest; he couldn't move.

A man was watching him.

He was more than six feet tall, slightly over life-size, and in mosaic on a panel of rock. His hands were spread in welcome and he was smiling slightly. His eyes were green. He wore a white shift of the kind in Greek or Roman mosaics but the face wasn't Hellenic or Latin. It was the temperate face of a middle-aged man with brown hair and a broad nose, the forehead high, the chin square and resolute. A face full of life.

Here he is, Thomas thought. Straight out of the photograph.

It struck Thomas forcefully that this man in mosaic was even taller than he. There was no mistaking him for anyone else: Cristóbal de la Torre stood before him, in ambush from the rock.

So he wasn't lost. And Esther wasn't entirely nuts; this really had been her father's island.

Thomas walked closer. The mosaic was made from hundreds of shells and bits of coral, pressed close together. Why hadn't their colors faded? He put out his hand to the shells but his fingers retreated from their hard surfaces—they'd been treated with something, undoubtedly, but it wasn't a glossy varnish. Their colors seemed as vibrant and pure as if they were still undersea. Behind them the rock wall had in places been filled in with some artificial compound to make it flat enough for a mosaic but still resemble pockmarked limestone.

This close, the man looked down with something close to complicity. A magician's knowing smile and intent gaze. His skin was pink with crushed shells, his coral hands large with tendril fingers, his gaze direct, as if asking Thomas—

To keep walking.

He lifted his camera. Through the sight the man looked bemused. Thomas swallowed. Why not simply take the photograph? His skin felt under siege by ants.

I'll come back for you later, he thought.

He walked on, following the bare rock wall as it bore sharply left from the watching man. The stone was gray and jagged, not rendered flat as it'd been beneath the mosaic. Above him hung dense vegetation, and the air was clammy near the rock face. In shadows the rock suddenly made a hard right-angle turn right that he didn't perceive until he was in it.

A roaring filled his ears. He stood in glaring sunlight, looking down a corridor of rock about a hundred feet long and fifteen feet wide. The walls on either side rose several feet above his head. They offered no sense of what lay behind them. Every inch of both walls was covered in a mosaic of seashells, and at the end of the corridor, on a wall facing him, was another image of the man he had just seen, again beckoning, but older. At a distance his face held echos of another, living face.

For as far as he could see the left wall, divided into panels by vertical borders of tiny shells, showed an ocean, growing steadily wilder, of blue-and-purple butterfly shells. They were arranged in overlapping pairs so the waves seemed to be made of wings. Among them fish leapt flashing, made from sea-smoothed bottle glass. The detail was extraordinary: the fish had fins, and eyes, and mouths, made from—coquina?

Angel's wing shells? Above the waves, reaching to the top of the rock wall, was a coral sky of flat fans stained a pale blue, and clouds made from white lumps of coral.

Farther down the left wall the ocean rose up, the clouds fled and the sky darkened, with black coral fans making the night. The opposite wall showed a coral shore, crowded with human figures, gaping in desperation at the unleashed ocean across the corridor. Some were mere faces peering over each other's shoulders. All were robed as the watching man, but the sashes of their white shifts were one long sash extending the length of the wall, binding them to each other. Men comforted their alarmed wives; children cowered at their parents' feet; a golden-haired girl held a yipping dog in her arms. Behind them loomed craggy mountains tufted with mists.

So this, he thought numbly, is what de la Torre did those years he lived here. God Almighty, how long did it take him? Surely he can't have done it alone. How long has it been here, waiting?

He walked on in dreamlike disbelief, faces staring past him at an angry ocean rising to destroy them—always with the same startled expression, as if there was so much they wished to say that they could barely catch sight of now that their end was upon them. Among the frightened people stood a deformed tree whose branches were bare of leaves but weeping bright tears.

Past it was another twisted tree, bearing crimson fruit like pears of blood. Seven girls, their breasts bare, knelt around it, hands covering their faces. Their hair was clumps of dried seaweed. Their eyes, between parted fingers, froze his heart. In the center of the tree trunk was the terrible face of an old man, consumed with wrath.

The old man's eyes made Thomas shudder; he knew those haunting eyes.

His heat-dazed mind tried to grapple with the labor that

had built this place. He tried soberly to convince himself that the best thing he could do would be to go back to the first image of the watching man and take his time photographing. He couldn't escape the sensation, perhaps because of all those faces, that there were other presences here, watching him.

He'd come to the end of the corridor. His shirt, draped round his shoulders, felt foul. He wiped sweat from his eyes with the edge of it. His neck was damp.

How can it be no one knows this is here? Or am I the first? Like stumbling on the Grand Canyon. Or the caves at Lascaux. No wonder she didn't want me to follow her.

And again facing him at the end of the corridor stood the watching man, arms outstretched. The face was no longer as open-hearted: the man stared him down.

He stepped closer and saw the detail—the implacable gaze, the exact fall of the shift, the dusty bare feet. The hands of the watching man upturned. He reached out to touch the fingers; this close they were only seashells. Two steps back and the man who had built this place regarded him from the wall of rock, urging him to keep walking. Assuring him his face would be there at every turn.

Behind the watching man were shells charred black like deep space; around him were seven birds, most of which Thomas recognized. A peacock with tail closed. White dove, small nightingale, hawk. A parrot much like the one he'd photographed. An eagle. And a peculiar striped bird with a crest.

There is more life, more grip, more meaning, he thought, in any of these birds than in any image I made on Inagua. More of the human in their faces. I should throw away my camera.

Instead he raised it, took a couple of half-hearted exposure readings, lowered it again.

In the sunlight at the end of the corridor he saw at last the confirmation of what he sensed: he was in a maze. On both sides he was being led into stuttering corners and mosaic corridors, with glimpses of corners beyond them that surely led to more corridors; some corners were half-domed. Already it all had the labyrinthine persistence of a dream. Had any wall not been covered with mosaics he'd have tried to pull himself up to see out, to see how much maze there was.

Exahusted, trying to maintain a repeating pattern so he would be able to find his way back, he turned the corner again left and entered another open corridor, not so long. At the end stood an image of the watching man. Even from a distance he looked older.

The right-hand wall once again was a shore filled with people, but the country was different. The mosaic showed a harbor crowded with ships from antiquity. The sea was calm, and a king and queen stood onshore, wearing golden crowns. People gathered around them, and the queen had one hand raised high, clutching a golden ring. A dove flew toward it from a pale blue sky of shells. People were waving; down the wall three ships set out, and the coral fans forming each ship's sides made them many-winged.

The left wall showed ocean again, the dove aloft with the ring in its beak, leading the ships. Farther down the wall green islands rose from the blooming sea, beneath a twilight sky jeweled with periwinkle stars. He recognized the images as Isabella's dream, in which she'd given a dove her ring. It had flown across the sea and finally let the ring drop to the waves. Where it fell, islands blossomed; a dove had shown Columbus's ships the way.

He had given up all thought of photographing the maze now. He tried to hold back the apprehension that he was completely powerless here. It occurred to him to sit down in the narrow shade of one of the walls and rest for a few minutes, but he wasn't sure he'd be able to remember which way he'd come when he stood up.

Why keep this place secret? Why not tell the world?

Before him the man was not watching, not beckoning. His hands covered his eyes, and his shoulders sagged, bent as if he was crying. His hair was streaked gray.

Once again the walls went both directions. What had he missed the last time? He went left and encountered, on a junction wall, a watching man like the one in the first corridor, though this time with eyes avoiding his, looking away. Several other complicated corridors in shifting colors stretched off at devious angles.

Was it only yesterday, thought Thomas, that I kissed those eyes? That faint smile? Two mornings ago.

He retreated, turned, tried to retrace his few steps and found himself beneath a half-dome coming out of a corner, showing those seven birds again in space. He followed a wall of two white peacocks right and was brought up short by a brief wall facing him as the principal way went left again.

Keep moving, he thought, the way out of a maze is to choose a scheme and stick to it.

This brief passage showed on one side the weeping tree, on the other a yellow dawn over the sea. Here the three winged ships were reaching an island. Native canoes, small boats of stained razor shells carrying bronze-skinned men, rode across the waves to greet them.

He fought the impulse to hurry, to run, to lose what he was trying to follow on the walls that hemmed him in and led him on.

He obediently turned left, into another corridor.

From both walls the colors blazed at him, a conflagration of fire coral. In an otherwise calm blue sea the three ships went up in flames, the white fans of their bellying sails cracked into pieces, the hulls of the ships were charred black.

Out of the sky—out of rolling blue clouds echoing the waves below—winged creatures were falling, creatures with the heads of men, mouths snarling, eyes afire, stubby arms protruding from beneath their wings, claws flexing. They swooped down on the white men from the ships and the brown men from the small boats, and on the two groups who cowered together on the shore of the island, arms raised to ward off the raging attack.

He walked aghast down this corridor, glancing from wall to wall at scenes of bloodshed as these winged creatures, which seemed part man, part bird, part dragon, wreaked destruction. Men of both races lay disemboweled and headless on the beach. A row of heads stared wild-eyed from the water's edge, some right at him, some fearfully skyward. De la Torre hadn't been sparing of detail: a few scattered eyes floated bleeding on the water, and the beach in places was soaked with blood. Near a clump of palm trees a winged creature breathed fire at a running man. Far down the wall a palm with a burning man still clinging went up in flames. Several winged creatures had cut their way through a group of escapees. One man was split down the middle, entrails spilling onto pale sand. Other men fell from heavy wounds and lay bleeding on the beach.

The scenes were grotesque, but slightly at a remove. On both walls Thomas looked down as if from above, through the eyes of one of the winged creatures. On the left wall, above the ocean, they hurried upward through strands of white mist, their faces rapt with the joy of bloodlust and destruction. Above them ran another ocean of foaming blue clouds laced with white, waves cresting. Faces gazed from those cloud-waves, and from the shelter of every wave's curl eyes peeped out.

Far along the corridor both walls changed. The blue sky deepened to twilight and then night, with watching moon and stars. Above the ocean, near the clouds, a group of winged creatures hovered. He saw they were crying tiny shell-tears.

Across from them, on the shore, beside the clusters of dying white and bronze-skinned men, a man in somber robes knelt on the sand with face upturned and hands clasped in prayer. Just above him hovered one winged creature, looking down at this feeble praying man. But the winged creature's claws were folded away, entirely hidden beneath its out-stretched wings—he could almost feel their buffeting wind—and its face was benign. And Thomas realized that all these triumphant attacking creatures, their wings spattered with blood, were angels.

What would it be like to walk through here and think that your father had made this? That these were his dreams?

He'd come to another junction. Night on all the walls around him. On the sand several men who had survived hud-dled prone beside a small fire. On every other wall the night sky was full of those watching eyes.

He tried going right this time, found himself face to face with another image of the weeping tree. Its vining branches grew up across a half-dome. He went left, found he was back at the end of the corridor of ships. Did it all end here? Ahead of him a little farther the corridor of angels ended with another watching man. This time his eyes were uncovered, looking downward to the earth at his feet. He bled from a cut on his broad forehead; presumably an angel had attacked him. Unconsciously Thomas reached up and touched his own temple. He was dripping with sweat. In the driven sunlight the watching man's face was lined, his hair now entirely gray.

No, the maze didn't end here. Along the walls of night pierced by many eyes, just past the watching man, was another cleft in the rock. Thomas had to go through side-ways. Here the maze cornered right, directly into another corridor. This corridor of shell mosaic seemed narrower. At least its walls were higher; the impression was that the maze was closing in.

He guessed it must be the last corridor. It finished in a solid wall of honeycombed rock whose heights were covered with thick vegetation. On a flat central panel was a last image of the watching man.

The right-hand wall showed the shore again: the surviving men had built a lean-to, a small shrine, from palm trees. A few men were dragging felled palms across the beach to add to it. The back of the lean-to shrine showed a peacock with tail-feathers spread, crudely imagined.

On the left wall, in morning light, the sea's eyes were awake and watching. The level of the waves seemed to have risen from the previous corridors.

On his right, in another panel, the peacock on the lean-to shrine caught fire.

Facing it across the narrow corridor the ocean surged up, eyes alive and furious.

On his right, in the last panel, the men grappled with each other and died on the sand, hands at each other's throats. Nearby their peacock shrine went up in flames. From a palm tree several angels watched with satisfaction, serene with their dragon-wings folded. Across from them the ocean engulfed the entire left wall.

So that was the end of it. So much for any chance of escape: the men had killed each other as the ocean came to sweep them away and the angels watched. And the fragile shrine burned.

He saw there were no more corridors. He would have to find his way back somehow.

Facing him for the last time from a wall of otherwise barren rock, the watching man stood surrounded by his seven birds with their different guises, their nearly human faces.

Behind him flowed the blackness of deep night. Suspended above him were the dove, the nightingale, the eagle, the parrot, and the striped crested bird, freely aloft. The hawk perched on his arm. At his feet a peacock with tail folded glanced incuriously out at Thomas.

The watching man was old now, his hair as sparse and white as fine thread. He leaned upon a gnarled stick and gripped it with a gnarled obsessive hand. His white shift was torn in places, and his pink skin, of fine crushed shells, showed through. His green eyes, heavily lidded, were full of sadness, and the cut on his forehead had scarred. Ravaged and tired, he had seen enough.

Why did you do this? thought Thomas. For whom? No one knows about it. For yourself alone?

He heard a scratching behind him in the sand. He wheeled.

A white peacock, its lacy tail-feathers folded, surveyed him from about ten feet away. It took several nervous chicken-steps sideways, cocked its head, let out a loud shattering scream. Then it came purposefully at him.

He found himself retreating against the solid back wall, against the watching man. The white peacock took no notice of his attempts to wave it off. It came to within a few feet, idiotic eyes glittering, white head bobbing aggressively.

He tried walking directly at it. The peacock pecked at his legs and blocked his way, the oversize caboose of a tail dragging in the sand despite the regal bearing.

He wondered if there might be a bit of candy in the camera bag that he could toss to lure the creature to one side.

Shells scraped his bare back. He glanced behind, shivered; they were de la Torre's hands. He really was in a corner. On his right the mosaic of furious ocean joined the wall he was backed against, of the watching man; the left corridor ended in a final panel of mosaic, bordered by lianas and mosses trailing down. Maybe if he could get to it he could pull down some vegetation to throw at the white peacock, waiting for him to make the next move.

The final mosaic showed a naked man lying on the same sandy shore. The man's body was motionless; he might have been drowned, flung up by the sea, or only sleeping. Near him an arch of stone framed a peacock with tail spread, eyes in the feathers. Waiting for the discovering man to awaken.

Thomas gulped. There I am, he thought. That naked man.

He edged along and the white peacock followed, effectively closing in. He scrabbled at some of the mosses and lianas beside the mosaic to get a clump he could pull away, and his arm dipped into the rock. Anxiously he bent down; a small cavern. A glint of light showed through the cavern darkness.

He felt something scrape his other arm, then jab. He whirled in panic as the peacock, glaring at him, stabbed again at his arm. "Get away!" he yelled, and as the peacock screamed and came after him he ducked into the cavern at a crouch and nearly banged his head.

Great, he thought.

The peacock blinked at him from outside, but didn't follow him into the dense shadows of the cavern. Bent over, his camera bag slung over his back and the camera dangling at his chest, he turned on his hands and knees and saw that past a jutting rock was a muted flood of light. It wasn't a real cavern, only a brief low passageway through the rock. For several yards he scrambled along on his knees. The peacock had given up, at least.

Squinting at the brightness just ahead, he crawled out and straightened up.

Sunlight blinded him. He felt his legs go weak and his chest tighten. He was conscious of sand beneath his feet and sweat in rivers on his back, but that was all. A hurricane carried off everything from the surface of his brain.

He was at a back corner of a vast garden whose only

plants were a few brief clumps of straggly grass in the sand. It was a garden nonetheless, full of trees and birds and people, alive in seashell mosaic on the long high walls of rock on either side of him—a hundred fifty feet long, he guessed—that bounded the garden until they ended in a vast wall of rock perhaps a hundred feet wide and fifty feet high.

The walls on either side made the garden alive. They were covered with a background seascape, blue ocean married to paler blue sky. In the foreground a white coral-shore of sand flowed, at the walls' bases, from the real sand on which he stood. On that mosaic shore stood tall palms and men and women looking out at him, not in fear or desperation but clear-eyed welcome—the men with the bearing of heroes, looking across the expanse of sand separating the two side walls so that as he came forward he was caught in the crossfire of their gaze.

Not all of them looked out. Some gazed up, into a sky in which many birds flocked, as if trying to perch on their shoulders. Above them, too, were angels, just below the rolling waves of heaven. Among the men, hands linked, stood their women and children. One man balanced a bowl of fruit on his head; birds flew down to feed from it. Another brown-skinned man at the water's edge dangled a fish temptingly over waves where dolphins sported. Wild animals wandered civilly among the people: jaguars, bulls, gazelles. A lion with a look of sleepy boredom was allowing a child to play with its mane. Silver fish threshed the surface of the sea.

All the faces—several dozen of them—were different, but all had the same quality of happiness, of play, as if the previous violence had been taken in, won through to gain this peace.

But what was most miraculous was the scene he faced on the front wall. Real stunted palms grew from the grassy summit, billowing in a breeze. Below, at the top of the mosaic the rolling waves of heaven began again, and among them faces looked down, the faces of the winged creatures, now forgiving angels. Beneath the clouds lay blue sky, and at the bottom a coral shore that merged with the real sand of the garden.

Only now filling most of the rock wall, a vast flock of peacocks stood on the shore with mosaic tails spread, glowing in greens and golds and blues, an entire veil of eyes stretching from earth to heaven, so bright they were almost blinding. Their pure stare paralyzed and then relieved him; he felt his breathing subside.

The eyes in the peacock tails slowly drew him forward into the center of the garden. On both sides he felt presences—people, animals, trees—and beyond them the immense blossoming of a long sea petalled with shells. He stood astonished in an inhabited Eden, won from life after all the death behind him in the maze.

What were all these shining eyes, the vast tapestry of feathered eyes, watching? Not him, surely. Not just him.

Eyes looking at him, everywhere. Eyes of the mortal around him, on both sides; immortal eyes, the burning gaze of those peacock feathers, in front of him.

What eyes lay behind him?

When he sensed he had reached the middle of the garden, he deliberately looked down at his sneakers in the sand and turned uncertainly around, then raised his head.

He let out a grunt. Suspended before him was an enormous white canvas tarpaulin, made from many old sailcloths stitched haphazardly together. It draped down from high above, lying flat against what must be another wall.

He felt a pang of arrogance at having made it this far, having discovered this place. The blind courage of being the first man here. He went forward and tugged at the cloth to test how it was attached. It resisted half-heartedly; a few small rocks rolled off the summit. He grasped the edge of the cloth and took several steps backward and heaved as hard as he could. He felt it slide, heaved again, heard a couple of larger rocks giving way above. He heaved once more, then the whole cloth came sliding down the wall and he stumbled backward to get out of the way as it fell slow-motion and crumpled with a thud into the sand. He picked himself up, turned—

— and looked up to a gigantic mirror covering the entire wall of rock. The hurled sunlight flashed in the mirror and threw his own image back at him, blinking like a fool with his back turned to the many blazing peacock eyes watching him with blue and gold and green fire, threw their own inviolate gaze back at them, back at him, as if to say: This is all. There is nothing else.

He felt suddenly and completely alone. He couldn't hold himself up anymore. He flopped down wearily in the sand. Before him his legs extended like the legs of someone else. In the mirror the peacock eyes now seemed mildly sympathetic toward him, and this made his heart lift. He glanced around him and all the people who had won through somehow— how?—seemed also to be sympathetic, watching him. They were waiting to see if he would get up. That was it. As he stared into the mirror all those eyes became a blessing, telling him he was wrong, he wasn't alone, and he felt their gaze also on his naked back.

But where was the watching man? Thomas forced himself to look around again. He wasn't here, anywhere. So the watching man had given up, having lost all his hope back in the other corridors; now he was the one with no place in the Eden he'd built. But surely whoever entered this garden took his place, earned it by passing through the rock. And turned to the mirror waiting behind in ambush, to surprise you with your own image within it. Whoever came this far became the watching man, and created the garden of the peacocks anew.

All the eyes in the mirror seemed genuinely curious as to what he would do next. He was conscious, as if it were a long-dormant memory, of his weariness from the night before. He wiped his face with the sweat-soaked shirt and got to his feet, stumbling in the sand, and caught himself. He'd made a foolish mistake, not bringing a water bottle. He sucked at his shirt and the salt taste cut through his dry mouth. Clumsily he pulled the shirt back on, to protect himself from the sun. He wondered if there were a path through what resembled a slight opening in the corner of the front wall of mosaic, at least as reflected in the mirror. Somewhere beyond this place, he reminded himself, was that beach, and that sea with its promise of peace.

The morning was getting on. Time to get to work. Serious work. He faltered on his feet and took several steps backward in the sand, back to the center of the garden. He lifted his camera. It wouldn't be long before there'd be much too much light.

Then as he gazed wearily through the camera into the motionless depths of the mirror, seeing himself there, he felt his believing mind shatter. The watching man had come to life. He ran from the corner in the front wall, an old man glaring at Thomas from beneath a thatch of wild white hair. His skin was deeply tanned and he wore a ragged white T-shirt that resembled his robe in the mosaics. He clutched a large coconut with both hands, and as Thomas let his camera drop from his face and watched incredulously in the mirror, the old man ran at him from behind, across the sand. The watching man's hands came up, then hurtled down, holding the coconut. It smashed the back of Thomas's head, and he fell forward as his skull came apart.

14

IN HIS NIGHTMARES THE STRANGERS usually arrived in hordes, not singly or in stealth but in swarms of airplanes and noise, like his own winged creatures falling from the sun. Now a shape inhabiting his dream had come to life: the man lay sprawled, arms askew, camera coughing in the sand. Not even the satisfaction of a little blood.

Cristóbal fumbled at the back of the camera, still looped about the man's neck, and extracted the film. He went over to a corner of the garden, dug a small hole with scrabbling fingers, and buried it.

Chest heaving, he went back to the body. A hooked fish battered into submission. He peered at the unconscious face, trying to read it as other men might read a newspaper. Some strength in the brow, a pressure of thought around the eyes and mouth. A certain bleakness: good to have in a man's face.

He picked up the coconut from the sand. There might be more men scattered through the shrine.

He ducked through the corner passage into the great semicircle of the Havana corridor, then escaped his maze and headed beachward.

The path no longer seemed innocent; the forests of deep pangola grass and coconut palms were haunted by shafts of dusty sunlight, the smaller palms whose tender sway always reminded him of young women watched him anxiously. All as threatened as he by any stranger. He ran. Not far away he heard the sea clattering across the reef. Fronds brushed his face and scraped his arms, sweat stung his eyes. As if alerting him that at any moment his wounded glance might fall on another trespasser.

Across pangola grass spangled with organized golden light, he caught a clear glimpse of spacious blue sea and sky. A quietly revealed glory: only man painted moments of revelation as gaudy and grand. When he burst onto the beach, the coconut still under one arm, he saw Scully Moses traipsing toward him. Beyond Scully a red skiff was pulled up, nearer than their dismasted old sloop.

"Einstein! Hey!"

"Keep quiet." His own voice sounded hoarse.

"Look what I find floating on the tide. Been here all night. Must have come over from San Sal."

"Shhh."

"Don't worry, Einstein. I take the spark plugs from these bastards' Evinrude. Can't get away now. We got they all trapped."

"Listen to me. I found one. With a camera." He paused. "I took care of him."

Unexpected delight in the phrase. Before the war, in Havana it was one of the lines from American gangster films that he and his friends loved to try on each other at the slightest excuse.

"You what?"

"I took care of him."

Better delivery that time, more gruff and bitten off. Then he thought of the inert man with his camera lying in the garden and felt diminished. Made feeble by the man's presence. As if there were innumerable similar men cunningly in wait behind him, with their fast boats and their Japanese cameras, and behind them the rest of the world, everyone waiting his turn in gigantic cruise ships.

The stranger's skiff insolently intruding on his domain, violating the perfection of his glittering light, cobalt sea, gentle sand, was like the condemnation of a court of justice. His eyes and his unerring instinct told him this hunter had come here to find him, capture him, and bring him back alive. Like some rare species of African wildlife. The last white rhino. He'd soon see how the man felt with two feet of rhino horn goring through his chest. That was the only way to treat the press.

He said to Scully, "You think he came alone?"

"Don't know, man. Tide come up. But I see only one footprints. Probably he here all night."

"We'll go get him, then."

He headed directly through the palms and the pangola grass, tramping it down into a shortcut. Behind him Scully muttered to himself.

"Exactly like this government rubbish, send they secret agent everywhere. With they camera and they walkie-talkie. Probably got a ship waiting offshore. All kind of electronic whatnot. Turn you back on they and man, they in you house, they in you flower garden, they in you bed, they in you goddamn wife."

To think he'd shared more of his limited time on the planet with this ranting Bahamian than with anyone else except Thérèse.

Cutting through the palm forest, skirting the walls of the shrine, he felt a gasping fear that he would find no one there—no Theseus in the labyrinth. What if the man had eluded his thought, escaped his grasp? But stepping into the open sunlight of the garden of the peacocks, he had the calm satisfaction of hearing Scully's exclamation at the body flopped where he'd left it.

THE GARDEN OF THE PEACOCKS

"You kill the man, Einstein?"

"I should have."

Scully handled the man's head gingerly. He grinned. "You shoot him through the back?"

"I hit him with this." He let the coconut drop.

Scully whistled mournfully.

"What is it?"

"Give you some advice, man. Free advice. Next time you decide to whomp someone on the head, they be better off you pull they out the sun. That way they don't start to go bad so quick. This bastard going to stink soon, he stink up the whole damn island."

"What?"

Scully shrugged with faint regret. "Maybe not, we get him in the ground quick enough. Where you want him? Tell you what," he nodded emphatically. "Better we choose somewhere the ground soft. I not ready to dig ten feet down through rock and it got to be at least ten feet in this Bahamas climate, you know. Grave not a easy thing in hot weather. Why you think these pirates always make a crew dig they own ditch, then be bury alive with the treasure, eh? You never think why, Einstein? Insurance. Keep they mouth shut. Only sensible way. And shut mouth ten feet down the best kind of insurance you can buy. No doubt about it, man, you do the right thing. We just got to get rid of him and that skiff too, so no one got evidence he ever come looking."

"What are you talking about? He's still breathing, isn't he?"

Scully laughed harshly. "You never hear of the last breath left in a dead man's lungs? Too bad we got to bury the camera. Worst evidence of all. That kind of equipment fetch a pretty price over in Nassau. Maybe it new, too, he get it duty-free. And I going to need a little more cash now I mix up even deeper in this old Einstein foolishness."

Scully had busily unlooped the camera bag and the camera

as he spoke. Now he handed them over and lifted the man's shoulders roughly.

"Come on, man. Don't like it neither, but we got to move fast."

"But I only hit him once. With a coconut."

"Traditional way to do it. No second thoughts, man. One day someone give you the same message, you pay attention too. Grab the feet, eh?"

God in Heaven, what had he done? "It was only a coconut."

Scully chuckled. "You a ugly stupid gullible bastard, Einstein. He not even half as dead as you or me. He just asleep. Now we got to move before he wake up and whomp you back. He already catch sunstroke lying there."

"You son of a bitch."

"Heh-heh. Gullible as hell. No wonder you Cuban let that damn fool Castro talk his way in. Believe any old nonsense somebody say and half you own besides."

"Shut up."

"Heave-ho, man. This fellow solid."

Together they half-dragged, half-lifted him and made their way through the corner passage and out of the garden. Scully turned and slung the man's limp arms around his waist. They moved on heavily, in silence.

When they came to the clearing, both out of breath, Scully said, "Rest a minute, man. We decide what to do."

They let him flop.

"Any ideas?"

Scully shrugged. "Why we not bury him after all?"

"What?"

"We got the chance, eh? One down. He make good fertilizer for my garden."

"You mean bury him alive?"

"Why not, man. Some kind of tasty vegetables this time next year."

"Esther!"

He thought the man might wake, yelled to life.

"Einstein, in the Bahamas, it not a question of legal code of law, you know. It a question of upbringing. And my mother bring me up practicable."

She came out of the house in khaki shorts and a white blouse, her long hair wet and combed back. He thought: This will stop her bleating about when Pinder can come fetch her, when she sees we're under attack.

"Look what I've caught. They've started already."

It took her only an instant, in blinding sunlight, to catch on. She did an extraordinary, betraying thing. She said with disbelief, "Thomas?" and hurried to the man on the ground.

He and Scully stared at each other. Two old men.

"What happened?" she said urgently.

"You know this man?"

"Not really." But she spoke without conviction.

Remembering her tirade about Nassau, why she'd been late, he understood everything.

She said, "What'd you do to him?"

"He gave himself a bump on the head, that's all," he said carelessly, as if every other day he found strangers lying senseless at the foot of his garden. "The heat must have knocked him down."

"Where was he?"

Examining the wounded like Florence Nightingale.

"At the end of the shrine. Taking pictures. Every inch of it. Thank you for inviting him here."

"I didn't tell him anything."

"Obviously you told him enough."

"I never told him who you were. I never told him where I was going."

"He got a boat pulled up on the beach," said Scully. "You think he come alone?"

"I don't know," she said. "He must have. I don't know how he knew—" She broke off.

He said harshly, in Spanish, "Isn't it obvious? As you explained it to me, you open your heart to any stranger you happen to be fucking."

She said, ignoring him, "Scully, can you please bring me a wet towel?"

The Bahamian, like an obedient accomplice, muttered, "Maybe better we get him into bed first."

Bastard.

He said, "Leave him here. The fresh air will do him good."

How naïve could she be? Didn't she know by now not to let herself be tricked by the press?

He said, "Weren't you suspicious? What bedtime story did he tell you?"

At least he saw doubts in her face.

"His name's Thomas Simmons," she said flatly. "He's an American photographer. I met him at my hotel."

"We know that part. I want to know who he really is."

"That's who he is. He gave me a book of his work."

"I'm sure he signed it for you. He happened to have it with him, yes? Give them an autograph and turn back the sheets."

"Look," she said, defending an invading disease, "long before I left Geneva he was down on another island, taking photographs of flamingos. He was on his way back."

"And he happened to check into the same hotel. A virile American with a camera."

"He was already there."

"Are you sure? You're sure it couldn't have been arranged to look that way?"

He saw clouds of confusion pass across her face.

He said, "Perhaps if you'd come here discreetly, directly, as we'd planned—"

"If I hadn't met him," she said tightly, "I promise you I'd never have come out here at all."

"Ah, then I should thank him. *Gracias, compañero*." He shook the man's hand, let it go; it collapsed lifelessly. But the man's cheeks weren't so pale beneath his tan. From behind closed eyelids Simmons was laughing at him.

She said, "You can thank him when he wakes up."

He saw she was profoundly glad this man had come. She wanted secretly to bring the whole world down on him, yet she couldn't even take responsibility for wanting. This man's presence here, as journalist and lover, was her deepest desire.

What a long way we have come, he thought, from the evening I first met your mother. What a long way to this spot.

Esther said to Scully, "How long has he been unconscious?"

Before the Bahamian could answer he took back command. "An hour, only. Less. Who's he working for, Esther? He must've given you some hint, no? A newspaper? A magazine?"

If only it'd been Scully who found the man, he thought. Now he's seen me. He must've deliberately gone after Esther to get to me. How many other men like him must already know? How many arriving this afternoon? How many tomorrow? How many more next week?

Better if he'd strangled the man on the cord of his own camera. Better still if Scully had been right, dead right back there.

"Look here, Einstein," said Scully. "This no place to let the man lie. We take him into my house, put him in one of they Haitian monkey beds."

"We'll tie him down. Otherwise he'll try to take more photographs." He adjusted the man's camera equipment around his own neck, wondered whether he should smash it on a rock as soon as her back was turned.

She said, "Give me his camera. I promise you he won't take any more pictures of your precious island."

"Suppose he offers you another autograph."

207

She flared. "And you'll stop him, will you? Club him to death the next time?"

"He fell from the heat. Another blundering American."

"He sure blunder this far," said Scully.

Esther said, "You struck him on the head, I can see the lump."

"He was photographing my property."

"You lie for any reason at all."

"Not true," he said softly. He thought: I've lied for your happiness for more than twenty years.

"Didn't you ask what he was doing here? Before you tried to kill him?"

"I could see what he was doing. I'd been watching him for half an hour."

She stood up. "And you'll defend your island like this from now on? In times of war? You and Scully? Look at you. You're two old jokes. Which of you is the general and which is the army? Or do you take turns, like little boys?" She let out a hiss of disdain. "One of you help me get him inside. If that's not too much to ask."

"Inside?" he said incredulously. "My house?"

"That's right."

Scully said uneasily, "You never see a man wake up after he out cold. Sometimes they get sick over everything."

"Sometimes they're seriously hurt," she said.

Scully shrugged. "All right."

Apparently all that mattered was the invader's welfare.

She said, "Aren't you going to help?"

"I helped him enough by not holding his head under water. Legally, I could do that here."

She said, "Legally, you don't even exist. Come on, Scully, I know where we can put him."

She took Simmons's feet, Scully his head. Feet first they carried him into the shaded house. Instead of going up the narrow plank stairs, they turned into his own bedroom.

This was too much. He went after them.

"You're not going to put him in my bed."

"Then help us carry him upstairs."

But the man had already usurped his place.

On the unpainted wood walls of his room were his early sketches of her mother. He said lamely, "You've seen all these before, haven't you?"

Surely she saw how much she resembled Thérèse. Very little of him, actually, in her face.

His daughter disappeared wordlessly into the small adjoining bathroom. Scully scrupulously avoided his glance and pulled off the man's sneakers. A shame, after all, to have the man's shoes on the sheets when they could have his smelly feet.

There was the impatient gurgle of running water. Esther came back with a damp washcloth in her hand.

"Smother him with it," he said.

He stepped through the house and back onto the veranda, felt the unblinking eye of noon there, waiting for him. He a mere speck on his own island. The man's camera and camera bag bumped against his chest, chastising him. He laid them down on the veranda and pain shot through his lower back. Noises from the past buzzed around him, the insectile din of ratcheting camera shutters from the world outside. Once he had done away with all of it—a maze of dull surfaces that did not flash back the light. Now the encircling world was coming to do away with him. Coming and coming with a vengeance.

Esther, aware of all this, was going along with it. Even desiring and abetting it. The innocent conspirator. He'd always thought there was more resistant strength in her than that. But it would've had to come from him, not her mother. It was difficult to remember that in the end one was responsible, no matter what happened, for only half a child.

You must be content now, he thought.

He opened the man's camera bag and looked inside. Loops of gauze held ten black plastic canisters of film. He put the camera back into its protected padded place. He carefully uncapped each plastic canister without removing it from its little belt, pulled out each metal roll of film, and slipped them one by one into his pocket. Then he zipped up the camera bag and put it neatly in a shaded corner of the veranda.

Help yourself to my daughter, he thought. You're impotent now.

He stepped into the hot daylight and headed down his path to the beach, the pockets of his shorts bulging. A wind was rising. How could he hope to win out? He felt his age this week, betrayed and outnumbered, as full of self-pity as a wound is full of pus. Along his beach the tide would be coming in, already reaching toward the old sloop and the stranger's skiff pulled up on the sand.

When he came to the beach he set off away from the boats, to a place he rarely went swimming because of inshore coral. He waded out in his battered sneakers. Underfoot the jagged coral scraped and rasped at the rubber soles and bit at his ankles. He felt the water penetrate his shorts. When he was chest-deep he emptied his pockets. His water, his ally, took the metal spools of film from his hands straight to the bottom.

15

AN HOUR LATER, WATCHING THOMAS
fitfully wake, she couldn't weed her mind of the distrust her
father had planted. This was not the same man she'd known
in Nassau. He lay like a captured assassin on her father's bed,
admonishing her for having trusted him.

All along he'd known she was coming to see her father. Their
Christmas Eve in Nassau, those nights and days together, had
been a ruse. She was only a way to lead him here. A map to
Cristóbal de la Torre: X marks the island of exhumed treasure.

Thomas's head stirred against the pillow. His eyes searched
the air and found her.

She handed him the glass of water she'd readied. He sipped
from it and glanced around the disorder of her father's room.

She said, "Are you all right? You've been asleep a long time."

He reached up gingerly to touch the back of his head,
winced. He looked like he might be fighting back the urge to
be sick.

"I thought I was drowning in the sea," he murmured.
"Right under the surface." The memory seemed to over-
whelm him; he let out a deep sigh. "It's good to see you
again, Esther."

She said heavily, "You shouldn't have come."

He swallowed another gulp of water. His glance drifted

211

around the room and then came back to her. "I'm really sorry to hear you say that," he said finally.

She took the empty glass from him, refilled it from a pitcher. She handed it back. "You should drink as much as you can. I'm sure your body needs it."

"What day is this?"

"Tuesday."

"What time is it?" he asked.

"About two."

He nodded. "That's all right."

"Are you hungry?"

He considered this as though it were a difficult question. "I don't think so."

The only chair was draped with her father's filthy rumpled clothes. She swept them onto the floor and sat down. "How did you find this place? How did you know I was here?"

He frowned. "It's a long story."

"I'd like to hear it."

He thought for a moment. "I went to the airport. I spoke to everyone in Nassau I could. I asked a lot of questions."

"Did you come by yourself?"

He took a slow sip. "How else? No one would bring me."

When we were having all our innocent conversations in Nassau, she thought, I imagined I could trust you.

He was watching her intently. He said, "I was wondering about my camera."

"It's just outside. It's safe."

He drained the glass. With effort he propped himself on his elbows. He closed his eyes for an instant, then swung his legs off the bed. He set the empty glass on the wood floor.

He said, "I think I'll take a look. I remember I fell on it."

"You should rest. I'll go get it."

Fumbling, he got his shoes on. "No, you're right. I shouldn't have come. Should've gotten the message in Nassau."

He stood up and walked groggily past her onto the veranda. She felt his exasperation and stayed where she was. She heard him unzip his camera bag.

Her father's bed was creased and sweat-stained where Thomas had lain on the sheets. She got up and turned over the pillow.

She heard the camera click open, then shut.

"Someone's taken my film," he said from the veranda.

Her father, unbelievably, had been right. She said coolly, "Are you surprised?"

She went to survey him from the doorway. He was bent over his camera bag, his hair matted. He resembled not the Thomas Simmons who had been her lover, but the weathered and untouchable man she'd first seen in the little hotel lobby. Concerned about the clandestine pictures he'd taken—hadn't he surreptitiously shot her in the gardens of that hotel? And the next morning, with that damned fruit held to her chest?

She said, "My father doesn't want you taking any more photographs. I'm sure you can see why."

He didn't look up. With a small cloth he was carefully flicking sand off a mechanism on the camera. "Don't worry, he convinced me." Businesslike, he replaced the camera and zipped the bag shut. "All he had to do was ask."

"How long," she said, "before you'll be back with more film? I want to be off the island before then. Do me that favor."

He straightened up with difficulty. "What do you think I am? Some slimy paparazzi?"

"Then why did you follow me here?"

He said, "Believe it or not, I really wanted to see you again."

"Because you wanted to meet my father?"

He looked as much amazed as annoyed. "Esther, I woke up and you were gone. I missed you. I was even worried about you. And I didn't think you'd gone back to Switzerland."

"How I wish I had."

He gazed at her wordlessly. For a second she thought he was going to try to pull her to him. Then abruptly he walked down the plank steps and swiftly across the clearing, his camera bag swinging at his side. She saw his back disappearing down the path before she shook herself awake. She had to hurry to catch up.

"Slow down."

His walk veered a little.

"Are you sure you're all right?"

Trees hemmed them in, a parrot flew screeching away.

He wheeled on her. "Look, I went through a lot to get here. Alone. No photo assistants, no reporters along for the ride. Understand? If some magazine wanted a story on your dead father's remarkably good health, believe me, I'm not the photographer they'd send."

More birds went howling out of the palms in a flurry at being disturbed. She put her hand on his arm to stop him striding away again. Behind the exhaustion and strain in his face she saw his gaze assessing her, not liking what he saw.

She let her hand fall. Her two separate lines of thought were so intense and so contradictory, like ranged armies of enemy soldiers, that their opposing forces held her immobile. She said, "But you knew he was here, didn't you?"

She stood there waiting for him to say something and choose a victor in her.

"You really overestimate your father's charm," he said. "I had no idea where the fuck he was. When I found out who he was, though, I decided you must be out of your mind. That's what got to me. Telling me he was still alive."

"So you knew about him all that time—"

"I thought he was dead till this morning. When he attacked me."

"But I never told you who he was. I never told you my father's real name."

He said, "I looked at your passport the night of the Junkanoo. Your birth certificate was inside."

She flared. "You had no right to do that!"

"You weren't telling me the truth. I felt really exposed. I wanted to know more about the woman I was exposed to."

"How was I supposed to explain without explaining? No one knows about him, no one. And I'd told you too much already. More than I ever told anyone. I knew I had to come out here, what was I supposed to say?"

"Look, Esther, no one likes to be lied to. Or left behind. You could've made up any excuse. An emergency call from your office. You could've told me to look you up in Geneva. We could've arranged to meet again in Nassau after you visited him for a few days. Or New York. Or—" He paused. "You could've simply said good-bye."

He was in fact asking her to believe that his presence here had absolutely nothing to do with her father. That he'd have just as readily followed her to Switzerland. This was an absurd idea.

She said, "I wasn't even sure where I was going when I left for the airport."

He heard the lie in her voice before she did. He started walking again, making her keep up.

Damn you, she thought.

"I've never told anyone, Thomas. Any of this. You Americans take it as an insult if you don't tell them all the family secrets in the first five minutes."

"Only when the story keeps changing."

She said, "It's all distrust, isn't it? In the end there's nothing but distrust."

"That's not a very helpful attitude."

"I'm sorry," she said quietly.

They had come to within sight of the sea.

"I'm not sorry you're here," she said at last.

They passed through the stone arch to the beach, into the hard radiation of light-dazed sea. She saw how very tired he was and for the first time she ceased to simply be astonished that he was here and began to wonder how he'd come.

"Around here somewhere." He led her along the sweep of palms. His small red skiff was pulled up on the sand; well beyond it Scully's white sloop lay dismasted. Where the beach began its slow curve Thomas searched for a moment behind several fanning palms.

"You should sit down and rest."

"I left a bag here."

"Perhaps it's nearer your boat."

"No, I remember these traveler's trees."

"They all look the same."

He passed a hand over his forehead. "It was here."

"Scully probably found it." At his look she said, "His man Friday."

He grinned. "Working on that new translation, are you?"

It took her a moment to remember.

"What was in your bag?"

"A change of clothes. Bottle of aspirin."

More film? she wondered. Not a helpful attitude.

She said, "A great deal has changed since I arrived here. In Nassau I told you my father was very sick. For months he was writing to me that he doesn't have much longer to live. This was only a story to get me to come. My father's not sick at all."

"He's a little too healthy, if you ask me." Beyond Thomas the shallows nosed at the stern of his skiff, flamboyantly red against the pale green water.

She said, "This morning I was trying to arrange to leave here as soon as possible. I had Scully radio our pilot over in Nassau. He said the plane engine needs repairs. I don't really believe it, but there's not much I can do."

"I'm surprised planes aren't landing here all the time. That mirror must be visible for miles, when it's uncovered."

What was he talking about?

At her lack of comprehension, he said, "The one in the maze."

"Oh, yes." So it was a maze.

"He didn't build it alone, did he?"

"There were several Haitians. And Scully." She was startled to hear herself add, "I shouldn't talk about it."

"It's a little late for that, isn't it?" He put his camera bag in shade. "I'm going in the water."

"Do you think you ought to?"

"This is supposed to be a vacation," he said.

He wasn't wearing a swimsuit beneath his clothes. Neither was she; suddenly it felt peculiar, even a bit embarrassing, to strip completely. He swam a short span out from shore and did not turn to look as she came naked into the water behind him. She felt it divide cleanly around her—no longer her father's water.

His body glimmered in the shallows.

Everywhere the beach was littered with the wreckage of palm fronds from the storm the night before. The peacocks' din, the lashing rain, had made the night claustrophobic; she avoided dinner, stayed upstairs, and tried to read while her father made solitary noises below. All the time, penned-in as she felt in her father's house, she'd felt a satisfaction at the storm's prolonged violence as it spent itself completely. She'd slept deeply.

This man had come through it, though.

He swam back toward shore. When he was near her she said, "When did you get here?"

"Late last night."

"You were in that storm."

"Storm?" he said. "What storm?"

217

He pulled himself out of the water and ambled dripping across the sand. She watched his pigeon-toed walk from behind, then turned and swam nervously away as he began to dry himself on his clothes.

She could imagine her father surveying them from a camouflage of trees. In a flash of desire she wanted to demonstrate what she'd told him of Thomas—her reasons for staying in Nassau. She took her time walking naked out of the ocean, but Thomas was not watching.

They might have been former lovers meeting after many months rather than after a couple of days. Separation had changed him, changed her; their mutual spell, a short-lived inspiration upon them in Nassau, was gone. Before, there'd been the certainty that one of them would be the first to leave Nassau, their little hotel, the charged circle of their bed. The doubt had been only when: after which last swim, which last conversation? Now even their bodies seemed to have nothing left to say to each other. She realized with a clutch of alarm that it would be only natural for him to take his boat and leave her behind here, as she had left him.

She knew she wouldn't ever have the nerve to go looking for him, to find him as he had found her. At this moment there was no one in the world who knew her as truthfully as this stranger.

He kept searching in the trees while she pulled on her clothes.

The swim had swept his hair back and he had the glistening look of a sea animal with its unexpected sheen on land. He came out of the palms empty-handed and surprised her by gripping her upper arm to help her for an instant as she slid on one shoe.

He let her go and said, "Your father shouldn't worry. That thing would be incredibly difficult to photograph."

It took her a moment to connect. "Yes, I suppose that's true."

"I only got in a couple of pictures before he attacked me. He's got a lot of energy."

"And of course the light was wrong."

"The light was perfect. That's not the problem." He shook his head. "It's unbelievable, what he's built."

Not separation but coming here had changed him. The spell of her father was in Thomas's face like a dose of sunstroke. He might indeed have come here searching only for her, but that search was ended. Her father had gotten to Thomas first.

He said, "You have seen it, haven't you?"

How had he guessed? "I was here three years ago, I told you."

"Was it finished?"

For a man interested solely in her he certainly seemed to have an ongoing biography of her father in his skull.

"Not till last year."

"But you've seen it finished."

"What does it matter? No, I haven't. You must be the first."

"You're really missing something. You ought to have a look at it before you leave."

"I'd like to leave as soon as possible."

He shouldered his camera bag. "I need to get the rest of my gear back first. And I do want to meet your dead father. It's not every day you get assaulted by a great artist."

She said angrily, "You realize he was ready to kill you this morning?"

"With a coconut?" He was rummaging around in the prow of his boat. He said absently, "I'm sure he knows what'll happen to this place once someone sees what he's done."

"No one will."

She heard echoes of her father's arrogance in her own voice.

"They might. I found him in a government census. Under your mother's name." She felt herself flinch. "Along with his friend Moses. I'm surprised no one else has stumbled on him."

"He wrote me once that a couple of yachts put in. Scully scared them off. I think he told them there were drugs coming through that night."

"Lucky they didn't go for a stroll, like I did." He was fiddling with the tipped-up engine.

"After he dies," she said, "I'm to come to terms with the Bahamas government about it. As a sort of nanny. Let them know who he was."

"You'll be explaining for the rest of your life." He pulled open the engine housing and peered in. "Someone's been busy. Look at that."

"I don't see."

"No spark plugs." He shut it firmly.

"What does that mean?"

"It means we leave when your father says we can leave. Maybe you can persuade him to hand them over."

Her father would be around her neck for years: more letters, more pleas, more lies. In the broad heat of afternoon she felt woozy, leaning against the skiff's gunwale. "Couldn't we take the sailboat?"

"I've got to return this skiff."

"We could tow it behind."

"And leave your father stranded here?"

"He's perpetually stranded, that's how he wants it. Anyway, don't believe that lie about plane trouble."

He shook his head. "I don't envy him this life one bit. I couldn't take it. Not for six years. Not even with something like that—" He paused. "That maze to keep me going. I guess it's a maze, I don't know what to call it."

Not having seen it, there was no name her imagination could assign to it.

Thomas said, "Can we sit down a minute? I feel dizzy."

He was moving lethargically. They crossed the beach toward the shade and he collapsed against a palm. He closed his eyes. She watched his face and wondered if he might fall asleep. A moment later she settled herself on the sand near him.

He said gently, "Was there ever a time when you felt differently about him?"

The question startled her. She had been close to her father once: she knew this like a memorized fact but couldn't recall how it had felt. Why were there so few parts of one's life that could not be poisoned by what came after? Look how much damage had been done to a memory of Nassau with Thomas. Their original tentative trust was impossible now. She and her father could never arrive at any real truce, the poison of the last twenty years would always seep in. She could no more resist it than she could describe it.

She knew she had grown accustomed to speaking a contrived language with her lovers, not letting them hear her own words. By sheer accident she'd told this stranger too much; she realized she hadn't reached nearly as far into him as he had reached unknowingly in her. She could not pull back now. She said, "My parents seem happy when I think back as far as I can. It's hard to say. It's like trying to remember the weather twenty-five years ago."

Out there another sea heavily moving, cold—

"One year we were in Italy, near Florence. He was designing some figures to go around a pool, outside one of the museums. He took me to a marble quarry. Deep in the mountains somewhere. To see the men cutting out the blocks of rough stone that he was using."

Her fingers were quarrying the sand.

"The men kept watching us. I remember I loved the different noises of the machines. Huge cranes with mouths that bit out the rock. Then I saw this strange man operating one machine. He was missing both arms. He used his feet to work the gears and levers. He was like a joke to the others. Laughing as he worked. As if he didn't mind at all. Someone told us he'd lost his arms when a boulder fell and crushed them." She paused. "I kept thinking of that man going home to his wife every night with part of him missing. And her having to feed him every day for the rest of his life at the dinner table. And dress him and wash him and help him in the toilet. All so my father could make sculptures from rock and be great."

She felt depleted. Trying to explain away her father created a whole other semblance of him, equally exhausting. She could not cage him in words: to explain was to falsify.

She said, "If you go back far enough logic doesn't help. That man wasn't maimed by my father. But you turn these images over and over long enough and they have a life of their own. You don't even know they're there. But when I came here once before and saw the Haitians working, taking orders from my father for his shrine, I thought about that mutilated man."

She felt the meager truth of all she'd said squatting like another person between them. Sometimes it seemed so simple: as long as her father was there in front of her she could not move past him or around him.

The heat of the day had turned chill. She shivered. She knew, at that instant, that she could never again be the anonymous woman whom Thomas Simmons had happened to meet in Nassau. It was as if she could only exist completely without her father beside her. With arctic clarity she saw that this was neither Thomas's fault, nor her father's. It was only hers.

She said, "I think I can convince Scully Moses to repair your boat's engine. Then we can leave."

"Maybe you can convince him right now."

Scully was coming across the beach toward them.

They were standing by the time the Bahamian loped up to them. He called to Thomas, "How you head, man?"

"Pretty bad."

"You got to try some rum for that. I pour some sense down old Einstein throat too. You smell smoke yet over this way?"

"No."

"You smell it soon enough. Einstein burning."

16

No peace for the devil, man. Einstein on fire all right. Other end the island, he burning down my dock. Time I smell smoke he start a good hour already. Time I get there it too late do anything but watch.

Exactly what he doing, in fact. Sitting there like fat Chinese watching it burn. Took me and them Haitian monkeys three month build the damn thing, only way we ever get all them shells and supplies and mirrors and the truck in past the reef. Einstein know that, too, he the one insist from the beginning and here he pour gasoline on it and ten minutes later you can kiss that dock good-bye.

At first I think it a accident till I see the gas can.

I say, You daft, man? What you trying to do? Attract everyone for miles? Bring in the coast guard?

Like he not in enough trouble already.

He not even turn to look at me. He say, Encourage the others.

Meanwhile it so hot from that fire I wonder how he stand it. All sizzle black like burnt steak at the waterline.

What this mean? Encourage which others?

Keep the rest of they parasites away, he say. Now they got no way to land a big boat.

Like you got no airstrip, boy? I shouting, too.

He say leave me alone, man. I tell him he damn lucky he got no breeze, else he burn down the whole island then he really got some explaining to do. He tell me where Scully Moses can put his explaining. I tell him he keep up this insult warfare I hold his head under water till my dock stop burning, see how lucky he feel then.

That cool the genius off a little. The man is basically a coward, you know. Tell me he want me get busy right away. The man say that and his eyes change. Like he lost in a walking dream. Then like he all tired out he say Scully, get that sloop ready. We got to leave here, man. It not safe at this moment. But this we secret. Don't you go telling the daughter, eh?

And at that moment I don't have clear idea what he really dreaming. It a strange thing. You can know a man deep year after year and think you know him better than you know self, but when it come to a certain day you still don't see what he got behind his eyes. Like we all blind where other fellow concerned. I don't realize till later, else I tell him burn away, man, but you staying right here.

Instead I say when? When we leaving?

As soon as possible, he say.

That soon, I say.

That soon, Scully Moses. Maybe we out on that lifting ocean one night end of the week, even. But don't you tell Esther.

Einstein face like crumple piece of paper. Not the time to ask complicated question. Only time I see him like that once before was after one year here, hurricane come along and wreck everything we done. Pull every damn shell off that first wall so we got to start over with better cement. He ready to quit then and he look about ready to quit now.

Quit what, I don't know.

Not to mention I see he bring a healthy tot of rum with

him. Not sure if rum doing the talking but anyway I head off, look after the sloop, better than listen to Cuban tantrum. By this time I can see tantrum coming from mile away. Like wind on the water.

Smoke follow me across the island along to other beach. And there the daughter sitting all right, just next to that old lady sloop. Like she know everything and she waiting for me. Naturally she American fellow Simpson right next to she. They jump up like lightning they see me coming. Enough to make a suspicious person think he catch they in the act.

I get closer I see maybe they look friendly enough but they not exactly jumping rope. So I explain how the father a little out of control. I got some small instinct maybe better to warn she, at least keep me safe in the middle when Einstein start burning left and right. Too I tell this Simpson fellow I find his bag, I put it where no one about to pour gasoline on it and light a match. He satisfied to hear that, naturally.

You notice I don't tell the man where I put it, though. He smart enough to let that one lie.

Einstein daughter say so what you think we should do about the pyromaniac? Maybe he dangerous.

Missy, I say, you know you father dangerous. But you better off you learn to relax. Let the man burn, eh? You stick you hand in you get nowhere. Einstein get bored and hungry soon enough. Not too long before I gone to get dinner, he relax then.

Because that small instinct telling me it gone to be hard to work on that old lady sloop without answer few more question. And I can smell that Simpson fellow wondering what exactly old Einstein up to. Question of the hour. Simpson busy looking all around, sniffing etcetera, in his position I looking at the scenery too. Probably about this time he begin to ask himself if Einstein daughter taste as good as she look.

Simpson say he notice something gone missing from his

boat engine, does I have any idea who walk off with his spark plug? I say he have to ask old Einstein about that. He look sour but I can't have the man running off to Nassau while we back turned.

I see he still plenty annoy since I tell him I got his gear but I also not offer to give it back. I see all the film he got in there, I see he got his camera now, but he see I got the upper hand.

Then he say is the old man usually so friendly? Whomp everybody on the head?

You the first, I tell him. Man, you lucky you catch Einstein on a good day.

Actually I beginning to enjoy myself, you know. One year, maybe more since we finish here, them Haitian monkeys long gone, nothing happen. Now finally something happen.

And about this time I decide to set that damn Simpson fellow straight. I say look here. Got nothing against fellow man, you know. But some scum of the earth journalist with a camera bother the hell out of me. Only time they try to get me for evasion of taxes over on Cat, was some son of a bitch carrying a camera. And you got a baiting eye and I don't like be baited. You got no fool right come here sneaking round trespassing. You got no right set your foot here without showing the passport. I not exactly average immigration idiot. This sovereign territory, man. You tie up here without permission, got no identification paper, for all I know you smuggling. I not fond of you attitude at all, man. Ever one day you start talking about what you see here, you gone find you ugly face in one hell of a legal situation, Simpson. No hard feelings, I give you some friendly advice, no charge, eh? So you don't get other crazy idea.

I not exactly put it like that but Simpson get the message. He say you the one with crazy idea, man. I come here look for she, not the dead lunatic.

What he mean is maybe Einstein famous but that nothing compare to a fine backside. And I begin to like this American. Man with priorities.

I even a little tempted to let the two of they know exactly what Einstein planning. Any daughter of mine owe me apology or two I let she know in advance what time I walking out the door, give she plenty chance to come crawling on she hands and knees. Christian thing to do. But it cross my mind that nothing stop old Simpson here from playing same trick on me, filch a little something from the sloop. Then we in the same boat, so to speak.

One good thing about this place before Simpson show up, people not borrying everything you turn you back.

So I keep quiet about what Einstein got in mind. Figure they get tired of Scully Moses quick enough.

Sure enough, Simpson say his head hurt, maybe he go back and have a rest if that okay. I say that okay with me but he do better he stick to the path, no sightseeing, cause you never know when Einstein turn up.

Einstein daughter looking worried but hungry. You know what that mean. No rest for old Simpson.

He say he know the way now and he be satisfied no one hit him on the head this time while he not looking. He head off. Einstein daughter following. And I think, That the way, man. Make she run after you and hell, you always running the show.

And I get busy on that old lady sloop. Right next to me sea turning again.

17

THE DAY WAS SLIPPING AWAY, IN THE
heady stench of gasoline fumes and charred wood. He stood
weary, his face seared from an afternoon of fire, watching the
ragged sunset stain a deepening sky. The sun straining down
on the past: here they'd rebuilt the rotted old dock of the
leper colony. Their first undertaking, long before any of the
rest seemed possible. Now gone in flames in one afternoon,
the smoke twisting seaward and away.

A few pilings and odd sticks still smoldered above the
water. Eaten by fire all the way down to the shallows. His
lovely water humiliated by the blackened detritus of the
dock.

His imagination flared with visions of burning the two
houses the lepers had left him, dynamiting the airstrip,
exploding the small truck that had fetched and carried everything. Even walling in the entrances to his shrine. That
would mean weeks of work, how many hours did I have
left? Impatience gripped him like a fever. To burn the dock
had been a futile gesture. But to someone bent all his life on
making, there was sinister joy in destruction.

He felt his island recoil from what he'd done, felt it
entreat him. How much longer do I still have with you, he
thought, before the world arrives? I can't stay. This man is

the first, he won't be the last and the others are not far behind.

The remains of the dock flickered and glowed orange, subdued in the darkening water. Dusk was descending on his scrap of beach. Great arms of the coast withdrawing into the shadows. Thérèse not so far away now, out there waiting. Closer even as his daughter receded.

Surely, he thought, the suicides go to a different heaven. A separate heaven than for the rest. A place for the people who had nowhere else, who tried but couldn't see a way through. A heaven decorated with the illusion of being forgiven by those they left behind.

Such a future rose like a completed mosaic before him, waiting only for his impulse to make it actual. All his life, every work of the imagination had announced itself with such an ultimatum: *Create me or else.* This one was no different.

And if he gave in to his imagination's ultimatum? There must be no doubts this time of what had happened. For years, beyond his horror of what Thérèse had done—mostly the horror of what she'd done to her daughter and to him— he'd held out a secret admiration for the way she'd chosen. Let the ocean perform the deed, dispose of the body, give it back to the planet. Drowning was the most responsible way of all, it left no body on anyone's hands yet took away the hard responsibility of the act itself. Afterward (he'd read many of his own posthumous tributes) the image left was of desperation, rather than self-inflicted murder. There was no blood to clean up, no corpse to clear away. The sea took care of the residue. Original man had come out of the ocean: an original man could go back.

And behind this mosaic lay Thérèse.

He could wait until nightfall on the ocean. Offer to handle the boat while Scully got a little sleep. Then tie the helm and slip overboard while Scully snoozed and the sloop sailed on.

By the time Scully awakened it would be too late.

The few flickering stumps of his dock went out as he watched.

What would it be like to slip into deep water on a calm night? To watch the pale form of the sloop glide away, its sail the last human shape he would ever see, the ocean waiting patiently all around? To swim until his arms began to grow a little tired, then turn basking on his back, and float? To gaze up to a night sky with no palm silhouettes to limit it, all those familiar constellations, to linger amid a last grace and a last enchantment?

And then to give in to that beauty. Simply to become a part of it. How could Esther say this was not her mother's ocean? That he would not find Thérèse, join her somewhere undersea, her hands outstretched to him? Black hair blown back by windy water currents.

With a slow nervousness almost like stage fright he made his way up the stretch of path. Already starting to overgrow, anticipating his absence.

This is how she must've felt, he thought, those few days just before, after she decided.

Then in the failing dusk he came into his clearing, and saw that it already was no longer his. A man with his back turned, torch held high, was making the rounds of the lanterns, setting them afire and closing the little glass doors on each modest flame. The man was nearly finished; the black moths were settled around the lanterns, beating frantically.

Watching the stranger, he saw himself as one of those moths, pointlessly trying to pound his way through a wall of solid glass when the opening was there within reach.

Esther put you up to this, he thought.

As if from already undersea he heard the sounds of a shower running upstairs, the clumsy clanging of pots from the kitchen shed, the yammer of unsettled birds around him in the trees. From up the other path, somewhere near, three peacocks sent up a din of bickering and ragged screams.

This island really has gotten overpopulated, he thought.

He saw that the table was out and three places laid. The cutlery gleamed silver, dangerous in the lantern-light against the blue sea of tablecloth.

Scully was right, he thought. Turn your back and they're in your garden, in your house, in your bed and in your daughter. I could put a knife in this man's back, right now, before he turned around.

He squeezed his eyes shut. He thought: This man has made love to her. She led him here because of it. That's power.

Past the American's shoulder he saw Scully Moses' silhouette in the kitchen shed, back and forth like a carnival shooting-target across the lighted doorway, back and forth.

What is the last thing I still have the power to do? he thought. The very last thing? I did it once before.

—

Thomas had heard someone at the edge of the clearing behind him. He resisted the urge to look, though his back felt exposed. He turned when he heard a match strike.

De la Torre stood watching him intently even as he moved the match from wick to wick. The dinner candles aflame, he shook the match out and threw it aside. His white hair was pushed wildly back, his face and T-shirt were rubbed with smoke. He stank of gasoline and had the dehydrated weariness of someone singed.

This close, Thomas's first thought was that the man still resembled the pictures taken of him over the years. Cartier-Bresson had caught the solid impasse of the artist, the bravado and the urgency. But de la Torre was larger, more solid than that famous portrait suggested, with a swimmer's strong shoulders and a sense of boundless energy and confidence focused from his head right down his spine and into the ground.

There was an unearthly scream from the trees. The night had come down with tropical finality. There was no breeze yet. Above the clearing the night was rich with stars, the constellations looming huge and clear. The air was alive with the island scent, sea grapes and vanilla.

This time last night he'd thought himself dead. He heard his heart beat time rapidly against the methodical pecking of his wristwatch.

De la Torre said, as if to himself, "The uninvited guest always gets served last." His voice was rough; the heavy accent made it rougher, made each barked word a separate accusation. "You shouldn't have done the lanterns so early."

"Your friend said it was time."

"What friend?" said de la Torre. "Scully?"

Who else? Thomas wondered.

From the house they both heard the upstairs shower stop, saw a similar thought cross each other's eyes.

Thomas poked the flaming torch headfirst in the sand. It hissed and sputtered and died, plumed with smoke like a downed airplane. De la Torre cleared his throat. Rage emanated from the old man like an animal stench. He said, almost growling, "Esther told me you come from the States. Which part?"

"Boston. But I've been a New Yorker for twenty years."

"I knew New York four decades ago," said de la Torre. "I wouldn't go back there for a million dollars."

They'd pay you twice that if you showed up Monday morning, thought Thomas. "I'm not there very much."

"Who do you work for?"

"Myself, mostly. A lot of magazines."

De la Torre nodded. "Magazines depress me. Like people who call on you once a month and never have anything to say."

"Imagine working for them."

"I can't," said Cristóbal de la Torre.

No, thought Thomas, de la Torre would surely dominate any photographer attempting a portrait, not the other way round.

The old man said, "These great ruined cities. I remember the last time I was in New York. I said to myself: This city has no future. It has no café life. It has no private gardens. It has no time for useless conversation. It can't flourish or even survive." He paused. "I was wrong. It was the city of the future." He pushed at his straggly hair. "Do you think this is a useless conversation, Mr. Simmons?"

"Not yet."

"Not yet. For years and years I always got dissent from the New York critics." De la Torre shrugged. "The dogs bark, but the caravan moves on. Which magazine sent you to find me?"

"No magazine."

"Esther invited you?"

"I wouldn't say that."

"You think you've achieved something by coming here."

Thomas said, "Nobody's going to find out from me what you've done. You can stay dead forever as far as I'm concerned."

"You had no right to photograph."

"I didn't know you were alive for me to ask permission. And you had no right to take my film. It's mostly blank, by the way."

"You think so? I don't think so."

De la Torre was tapping the tablecloth nervously. Without warning his arm jackknifed sideways and swept one of the candles across the clearing. Thomas had an instant's glimpse of the flame fluttering in midair even as it blew out and the candlestick thudded into the sand.

What next? thought Thomas. Booby-trapped Havana cigars? Exploding Monte Cristos?

De la Torre said, "How long do you think I have left here? To live in peace?"

"As long as you want."

"No."

"You have until the next photographer comes along."

"Then what happens?"

"This is a greedy part of the world. There'll be souvenir stands on the beach. They'll blast a passage in the reef to let the cruise ships through."

"You're a cynical man, Mr. Simmons."

"I've worked all over the world. Everywhere I've ever been looked worse when I went back."

De la Torre wheeled as Esther came out of the house. She was wearing the white blouse and skirt she'd worn in the gardens of the ruined hotel.

Her father retrieved the candlestick a little guiltily from the sand and set it upright on the blue tablecloth.

"Mr. Simmons and I were talking about New York."

She nodded warily to Thomas. "I don't suppose you have any mutual friends."

"Only you," said her father.

Thomas, watching them sit down, thought: These two are more alike than they could ever believe. The same delicate hands. The same small gestures. Fingers pushing hair back behind the ear. The same burrowing concentration and energy. The same pressure of isolation around both, like a fog they can't see through. Except he looks at her like she's haunted; she must remind him endlessly of her mother. But the same natural glory around them both too, like a birthright. No wonder the old man ended up with an island to burn alone on.

What kind of will to stay and build what he made here? What kind of will to refuse to see it? They're like a different species—how long has it been since I felt as much passion for something as they feel against each other?

Well, since a day or two ago.

Maybe she's right. Maybe I would never have come all this way if I hadn't known who her father was. Dead or alive.

Now both de la Torres were staring at him, waiting for him to relieve the conversation. It seemed impossible. He said, "I wonder if your cook needs a hand. I'll go check."

Esther jumped up. "I'll go, Thomas."

For an instant she reminded him of a teenage girl who wants her boyfriend and father to meet and is suddenly afraid to stay for their conversation.

As she hurried away to the kitchen shed, de la Torre said dryly, "The service here is wonderful. But the waitress won't even talk to you."

The lanterns made conniving shapes across his face.

Thomas said, "I guess you have to find something neutral to talk about."

"You mean nuclear war. Or world hunger." De la Torre paused. "Can you think of something? There's not much neutrality left in this family."

"I've only known her a few days."

"You have spent as much time with her as I did in the last six years." De la Torre frowned. "As a little girl, you know, she had a lot of talent as a draftsman. Her mother said, 'Don't push her.'" He made a gesture of dismay. "She works in a bank. I know this doesn't interest her at all. Yet she tolerates it. How can she keep doing something that doesn't interest her, all day long?"

The childishness of the question made Thomas respond as if

to a child. "That's how most people spend most of their lives."

De la Torre made a noise of dismissal. "I don't speak of most people. Most people look in the mirror and realize they cannot ever fulfill all they hope for in what it's possible for them to do. But Esther is capable of almost anything."

"She seems serious about translating."

De la Torre said scornfully, "This is parasite work. For people scared of their own private vision. They hide from it and take shelter under someone else's. Like an umbrella to keep the rain off. The professional biographers are the same. How would most lives look held up to so much scrutiny? How would yours look?"

He didn't answer. Esther and Scully came out of the kitchen shed, their feet scuffling in the sand. Thomas stood up and took a plate from her and laid it at her place. Scully served de la Torre last.

De la Torre said, "The uninvited guest, you see?"

"Aren't you going to join us, Scully?" said Esther.

"No chance of that."

The Bahamian was arranging plates of rice and vegetables and bottles of hot sauce on the table.

"I wish you would," she said.

"Busy man," said Scully cryptically. "Advance cooking."

He glanced at de la Torre and headed off to the kitchen shed. They heard him banging deliberately among the pots and pans.

—

"I wonder what Scully meant by that," Esther murmured.

Her father said, "I don't know why it's so difficult to get a peaceful meal in the islands. It was the same in Cuba. This is why everyone is always so nervous in the tropics. Your digestion is constantly ruined, so you start a revolution."

Stop trying to be charming, she thought, you know you don't believe a word of that.

She said, "We smelled smoke earlier."

Her father only nodded.

"Why burn the dock?"

"Why not burn it?" He indicated the food to Thomas and said, "Help yourself."

She heard the nervous edge in his voice, heard it come into her own. "Suppose something breaks down?"

He shrugged and began uncorking a bottle of wine.

"What about replacing the generators?"

"They come on the plane now. The smaller ones are more reliable, in the end."

She said, "The spark plugs are missing from Thomas's boat."

"Do you really need them tonight?" He was pouring wine, the generous host, sagacious bon vivant of the world, master of his own island, at ease now, having attacked his daughter's lover and burned a dock to get through the day.

"Of course we need them."

"That tarp came down too easy," said her father to Thomas. "Off the big mirror. I thought we had it tied down tight."

"Maybe it got loose in the storm."

Something to do with the shrine.

"Did you hear what I said?" she asked.

"I did. You'll get them back."

Why wasn't Thomas helping? Again the stealing suspicion.

The swim with Thomas had revived her—walking back from the beach she'd felt a truce settle between them. At the house she'd suggested a nap, she didn't need to say more, surely he understood. He'd refused to join her and didn't say why. He wasn't a man who'd resist in order to tease. Was he trying to prove some point? They were still having an argument, she saw that. She could not quite see clearly what they were arguing about.

He'd insisted on napping downstairs. When she awoke from her own restless sleep it was nearly dark and he was outside, lighting the lanterns.

She could not see beyond the next day, beyond the image of their departure. She imagined herself helping shove the boat off the sand into the water, imagined clambering in and their negotiating the reef. After that she had no clear idea of getting back to the island where he'd borrowed the boat. Beyond that island lay Nassau. Then what?

She knew she would not be able to stay anywhere that reminded her of this island. It was easier to imagine Thomas in the clean cold of Switzerland, or beside her on a New York street. She saw herself in the boat staring back and her father watching from the beach.

She said, "We want to leave tomorrow."

"You sound like an admiral," said her father. "Shall we drink to something? What should it be? Departure?"

"If you wish." But Thomas won't want to go, she thought.

Her father said, "I can't give you those spark plugs now. I don't have them with me."

Still in English, for Thomas's benefit.

"Tell me where they are."

"You'll never find them in the dark."

"There's a flashlight in my room."

"Better wait until morning," said her father. "I hid them in the shrine."

In the maze? Ridiculous.

"I bet they're in your pocket."

"Do you remember?" he said. "I used to let you empty all my pockets whenever your mother and I were going out."

Her mother kneeling beside her, laughing, as they went through the incredible contents of her father's trousers pockets. Keys, folded drawings, broken halves of pencils, pebbles he'd liked the shape of. Separating them into left pocket and right pocket and reject piles, while he waited patiently for them to finish. She remembered the objects rippling a white bedspread and the lavish scent of her mother's perfume.

"I did that only once."

"You did it all the time," he said lightly. "Want to try again?"

With one small remark he'd given her back a vivid recollection she'd lost hold of for years. How much more of her mother was stashed away in his idle chat, waiting to be liberated back into her memory?

"I really don't see," said her father hesitantly, "why you both don't stay on here. I'll leave you alone." In the uneven torchlight he leaned back and she could barely make out his face. "I can move in with Scully, if you want."

"There's no need," she said.

"It doesn't make sense for the two of you to stay at a Nassau hotel. It's an awful place, no? And the beaches here are deserted. No one will bother you, I promise. The weather couldn't be kinder. The island's yours."

She said in Spanish, "I don't want it."

Her father said to Thomas, "She doesn't want it. She believes it's contaminated."

It was as if a table fully laid out, candlelit, of food half eaten and wine half drunk stood between her and the rest of her life, and she could not push it out of the way nor push her chair back and walk around it.

She said, "Will you have Scully bring us those spark plugs in the morning?"

"Come with me and I'll give them to you."

"Thomas can go with you."

"Don't you want to see the shrine for yourself? Aren't you curious? You're in it, you know." He waited for this to sink in. "So is your mother."

I could smash every plate on this table. Every one of these glasses. As jagged and gleaming as the frozen sea that night.

She closed her eyes. She could still feel him through her eyelids, his unrelenting stare boring through her and yet not seeing her.

She said, "I have nothing to bring you."

She opened her eyes. Her father and Thomas were looking at her.

You have invested me with powers I don't believe in, she thought, magic powers I don't understand. You confuse me with my mother. There is no healing to be done here.

Her father said, "You don't have to bring me anything. You brought yourself. That's enough."

I am not here, this is someone else, someone who represents me. I am not responsible for anything she does. We'd better go, she and I.

To see Thomas Simmons across a dinner table brought back the faraway shelter of other evenings, before all this had happened. To have him here was a connection with that other life where she could come and go as she pleased and was under no responsibility other than to step around her father's carefully crafted stories and, for her own protection, stay far away from him.

She said to Thomas, "I think I'll go up to bed."

His glance told her he would join her.

As she pushed back her chair to leave the table and go into the house, her father said suddenly, "I feel very tired. It tires me, the way we talk around each other."

"After tomorrow I'll be gone, you can rest."

He said imploringly, "You've got everything you need here. Why don't you both stay on? I promise you, there's no more beautiful island."

"It's not a good idea."

"I want you to have this place. To enjoy it. I've always felt

241

sure that one day you would."

"It's not yours to give," she said. "You only rent it."

"I've rented it for the next quarter-century. It's mine more than anything else in the world."

There's no reasoning with someone like this, she thought. He'll burn down his own dock so he believes he's suffered more than a man he attacked. So he can turn around and be generous with this prison of an island.

She said, "Please stop trying to give it to me. There's nothing here that I want."

He stood up, his voice rising, his arms shaking as his fists pressed against the table. "No? Everything is in front of you and you refuse to look. I hope your friend realizes this. You're the daughter of an artist and you're blind."

His own outburst startled him. He wiped his mouth with the back of his hand and shoved back his chair. In an instant he had stalked out of the clearing—leaving, she saw, before he lost control completely.

She resisted the urge to say something to his back as it merged with the darkness of the path.

"Do you think he's all right?" Thomas asked.

"You mustn't believe what he says. It's a performance."

She added, "He may not even have your spark plugs. Scully's probably got them."

"Why don't you want to see what he's made?"

To you it must seem only selfish, she thought. Now that you've met him. But to behave selfishly you have to have a choice.

"Because he uses it to justify everything he's put me through," she said. "Can you imagine the lies I've had to tell over the years? People are still filming TV documentaries about him. The tragic drowning. He could've just come here to live and work, no one would have bothered him. Instead he made speeches, how it was all being done for me. I begged him not to put me in this position. If I give in, it's as if I accept all of it. This is the last thing I want to do."

"But you kept his secret for him," Thomas said. "You could've easily punctured the balloon and told some reporter where to find him. Why didn't you do that?"

"I don't know," she said quietly. "I thought about it many times. Perhaps those journalists always seemed more odious than he was. Or not smart enough to deserve to know. Or perhaps I was just glad to have him a long way away and know where he was. Pretending he was dead, along with everyone else. And eventually I realized it's what my mother would have wanted me to do for him."

"I still don't understand why he burned his dock. It won't keep anyone from showing up."

"This is his way of getting attention. The grand gesture. He felt like doing it, so he did it. He doesn't really need the dock. He didn't burn his house down, did he? When he starts destroying his wine cellar, then I'll believe he's really upset."

Thomas said, "I can't see what you're trying to get from him."

"I don't want anything from him."

He smiled. "But you came here."

"I didn't think he'd lie to me about dying, just to get me over. I forgot that he has absolutely no limits, he'll say whatever he believes is necessary to get what he wants. Cancer, all these fictitious doctors. And he'll change stories tomorrow, he'll find a new one, don't worry."

"Perhaps he felt he was dying, without you."

You have no idea, she thought. "Do we have to talk about him? Come to bed. You look absolutely finished."

"I feel like the bottom of a river."

They went into the house. This time Thomas followed her up the creaking plank stairs. She felt his eyes on her body as she mounted them ahead of him. A suffusing desire flashed through her and she paused, a stair from the top, and felt his hand come up her skirt, caressing her legs.

He was tall enough to kiss the back of her neck from a stair below. Ocean salt on his lips. She fumbled behind for his hand, snagged it, led it around teasingly.

Then she led him up into her room.

With little moonlight to find her way, she stumbled. Why was she trembling? She knew what she was doing. Darkness hung in the room like a cloud. She turned and came into his arms. Once more the hesitation of a first kiss. Begin again with this man, she thought. Her mouth imploring him not to finish the kiss as his fingers unbuttoned her sliding blouse. I may have gone blind but he has infrared sight, it's his profession, his hands see everywhere. She felt them challenging her skirt. She stepped out of it, then wound herself around him, his arms with no choice but to cradle her, no matter how tired he was.

He saw everything in the darkness: carrying her, he walked directly to the bed and let her down onto it. Her legs reluctantly unclasped. His arms moved lithely, pulling his shirt over his head. Rustle of khaki, the twin echo of his sneakers kicked off. Her own impatient breathing. She couldn't see but felt his eyes hadn't left hers.

A pattering outside, the tune of a light rain. Immediately the air was transformed, acquired a sluggish density. Clouds were drifting in their darkened room. Thomas silhouetted at the window.

"Come to bed." Naked on the humid sheets, she waited.

He turned; a glimpse of his shadowed face, pensive, then he became again a silhouette who spoke.

"Are you sure you want me to sleep with you?"

It was raining in the room.

"Come here and I'll show you."

He sat down on the bed. "That's not what I mean."

Her fingers snaked across his thigh. He caught her hand and held it gently.

"You've got an exhausted man here. I don't want to disappoint you."

Momentarily her hand left his. "Not so exhausted."

He leaned over and kissed her. She held the back of his neck then let him go as the kiss went on.

He drew away. She said, "Again."

He stroked her cheek. "Esther, look," he said. "I came here because I couldn't bear the idea of you disappearing from my life." He hesitated. "I'm sure men are telling you this all the time."

"You'd be surprised."

It was suddenly a full-blooded rain, a loud force thrashing the sand of the clearing. Lightning flash in darkness: she gripped his arm in terror.

His face, illuminated for an instant, remained calm. "There's nothing I want more than to make love with you. But I don't want to be the body on the battlefield between you and your father."

"Just say you're too tired. Leave my father out of it."

"I'm not too tired. I haven't been able to stop thinking about making love with you since I met you."

"Stop thinking," she said.

A crash of thunder cracked the heavy air in the room. She heard herself gasp at its nearness.

Thomas said, "Don't worry, it's still miles away."

"It's nearer than it was last night."

"It was in my boat last night." He kissed her again, softly. "What will we do once your father gives up the spark plugs?"

"We'll go wherever you want."

"Are you sure you won't regret leaving?"

"What I regret is coming here," she said. "He and I have nothing left to say to each other."

"You two don't sound like you've completed anything."

"This is the American way, isn't it? You think you're going to solve everyone's problems for them."

"I can't even solve my own," he said. "I'm only telling you what I see. And I'm telling you I want to be your real lover. Not just relief for your nerves about your father."

"You should've simply said you were too tired." She pulled back the single sheet and crawled in. "At least this once I'd have believed you."

He put his hand on her shoulder. "Esther—"

"If you're exhausted, get some sleep."

She turned aside, facing the window. A moment later he got onto the bed beside her, but he lay atop the sheets. Rain was raging wildly around the clearing now, lightning came from moment to moment, penetrating the earth, and thundercracks shook the house. Petrified, she kept her eyes closed and resisted the urge to fling herself into Thomas's arms.

The rain roared down and the minutes stood still.

Wide awake with the storm, she realized with dismay that he had fallen deeply asleep. At the same instant, electricity surged through the room and thunder slammed her against the bed. She clawed the pillow in terror.

Outside, suspended impossibly high above the ground, his face splitting the blackness like lightning, the old eyes of her father watched her through the window, and watching her, slowly opened and closed and opened again, murderous in their unending sight.

18

He awakened shortly after daybreak. Beside him she shifted a little, distracted from a dream, and without waking made a small sound of acknowledgment. Her shoulders and the gentle rhyme of a breast, its warm aureole, showed at the edge of the sheet. Sweet shape of this woman, he thought.

He pulled himself delicately out of bed. Standing in the pallor of dawn, his feet bare on the wood floor, he wondered what it would be like to sleep beside her every night. He wondered if it were not too late to find out.

He dressed and made his way quietly downstairs. The door to de la Torre's bedroom was ajar, the room as it had been yesterday. He stepped onto the veranda and a faint breeze, still cool from the dawn, swept his face.

Outside, the clearing was similarly deserted, the palms colorless in the dull light, the lanterns vacant. The plates had been cleared away; a rusted thermos stood on the bare table, two mugs beside it. Thomas poured himself some coffee, went to the kitchen shed. It was scrubbed clean. He helped himself to bread and cheese and crossed to the house adjoining, where the Bahamian evidently slept.

He knocked lightly and got no response. He walked in and immediately saw his bag in a corner. The single long room of several beds was immaculate and bare except for a table with a few weary magazines and a crude wooden model of a local boat. Only one bed had sheets, neatly made.

He went to his bag, unzipped it. The spark plugs were in a plastic sack, intact, alongside the bulk of his fresh film, still wrapped in a towel. He put the spark plugs in his pocket, zipped the bag shut and arranged it as it'd been.

He stepped outside and set off down the path. Even this early it was alive with the busy talk of birds, sending their morse code about the man on his way to repair an outboard engine.

The engine was irrelevant, was not the problem. He didn't know how to suggest tactfully that it might be worse for her to leave than to stay—a danger greater than the one she was trying to avoid. He felt sure of it now. As a photographer it was ingrained in him that problems had to be dealt with right away, they could not be corrected later; a missed opportunity was missed forever. Distance had made Esther and her father cowards, vain of their failure, vain of their cowardice.

Heading down the path, he was haunted by how different it had seemed yesterday, returning with her after their swim. He'd felt sharply that he was walking beside someone he had to keep walking beside: it was a need as acute as his thirst hours earlier, when he'd stumbled down the same path alone. With that need came all his doubt of her. She wasn't someone who could naturally pass beyond herself into the entire consideration of another person. If she ever did, it would be to stay. He realized acutely how important the preservation of her walk beside his had become, that he must do anything to protect it.

He knew this all to be nearly absurd but so little had come of the great risks of his life, the years spent on this or that photo project, the damaging expense of energy on a marriage to someone who'd seemed safe and serene at the time, that the greater risk of the moment, all he was contemplating with this unsettled woman, seemed abruptly like the only way out of a trap he could neither adequately describe nor admit. Her trap seemed much clearer at that moment than his own. The entire day before—the storm and his arrival—had left him so exhausted, all that was left was candor.

Esther was not the only way out, surely. Perhaps not even the right way. But a branching of the path out, at least.

It took you so long to get here, he told himself. So many years to admit where and when everything went wrong, why it all just dried up. Pretending a woman you should never have married took your eyes with her. Pretending your failure to fight to get your sight back was because two people failed to get along. Those events had nothing to do with each other, only coincidence. Look at this old man here who lost his wife and daughter. Or destroyed them himself, who knows. Look at how much will he has left in him. Enough to take an island into his imagination and glue his vision onto walls of rock. Your eyesight went away because it was easier than fighting to preserve it, easier to say it was too late. Easier to pretend the man of talent, the man of standing in you was only a young man, and convince yourself he was long gone.

Yesterday morning about now he'd had to stop and sit down from dizziness. In memory it already seemed another island; then it had belonged to him alone. Her father's vast maze seemed part of that other island, not this one.

Not quite—the passage of rock where he'd entered lay just ahead, off to the right, where a rock wall was overgrown.

He found himself considering the half-hidden passage into the maze, with that first image of the watching man, beckoning him in.

On down the path, slowly. Strange to think this old man was what was left after seven decades of Cristóbal de la

Torre. This man's labor had actually made a difference to the world. De la Torre had spoken last night as if the island had become only one more residue of his past, and he was ready to hand it over to Esther, who didn't want it.

How much did I venture, Thomas thought, how many sea-miles did I come to see them wash their hands of the responsibility of the other? Well, not my responsibility. Not my despair.

Esther had come here in the despair of facing her last chance with someone on earth. That part had been a ruse, but now the person was slipping through her fingers, and she was letting him go without a word. He'd seen the equivalent terror in the old man's eyes last night, de la Torre's own quiet despair. They were nothing like the eyes in Cartier-Bresson's portrait, nothing like the wrathful eyes that had come running at him from the mirror. They'd become the eyes of the watching man in the final corridors of the maze. No rage left, only a detached acceptance, but an acceptance without surrender. A turning away, an old man turning his back on all things lovely.

He saw for the first time, deftly concealed by tumultuous foliage, another way into the continuous wall of rock, a passage he hadn't found yesterday.

I might never see this place again, he thought.

He tugged the overgrowth to one side. From beyond the wall came, faintly, a seething blur of argument, of garbled voices.

He passed through a cleft in the rock. Before him, the butt-end of a wall divided passages on either side. From its face a mosaic of the watching man in middle age regarded him dubiously. Thomas went round it on the left and stood in a large semicircle he hadn't come to before. The mosaic ran right round, a complex tableau of Spanish majesty in the tropics: Havana, he recognized the cathedral and its intimate plaza. Figures in cafés and an outdoor nightclub of dancing Amazons, in imitation of the dancing girls on ancient mosaics; the perspective was distorted so the modern scene of colonial streets and decaying interiors looked angular and remote, a life inexorably of the past.

Before them all stood the real watching man, watching him. Around de la Torre, a flock of peacocks stabbed greedily at bits of bread he scattered from a paper bag, shrieking and complaining as they fed.

19

Time had already begun to dissolve around him. He could shape it as he wished: his shrine thronged with ghosts, people already swept away by time, the few he cared about.

I am perhaps going a little mad, he thought.

On the verge of oncoming departure and what he would do that first night at sea, the figures on these walls finally had real life, more life than this apparition before him.

Speak, he commanded it silently.

"I want to talk to you about your daughter," said Simmons.

He knew this tone of voice, the exaggerated interest of someone who had no business speaking to him.

"She asked you to come?"

"She doesn't know I'm here," said Simmons.

He felt himself corkscrewing through the morning, hurtling toward his inevitable last day here out of—what? Two thousand?

"You want the parts for your boat."

"No, I found them."

"Then go. Take her away. What's stopping you?"

Look how quietly the pale light of daybreak is burned off. To a polished glaze across the sea's face.

"I'd like to bring her here first. I want her to see what you've done."

The figures on the walls scoffed. He silenced them with a glance.

"Don't waste your time. In six years she has come no closer than fifty meters. Can you imagine?"

"I'm worried about what will happen to her. After she leaves."

You're worried about what will happen to *her*?

He said, "Esther's a survivor. She survived her mother's suicide, she survived years of having me for a father. You can see she feels no responsibility to other people. I taught her that. It protects her."

He couldn't tell if he'd actually spoken. Simmons was looking around him like someone to whom nothing had been said. Staring illicitly at the walls.

Words are only air: I cannot make them mean anything anymore.

Simmons said, "I didn't see this part the first time."

What did he want, a guidebook? "Now you've seen it."

"Why do you think Esther keeps refusing?"

"She hates the idea of it. She hates that I did it. She hates what it took to do it. She hates what it might tell her. She hates what she might feel if she looked at it."

A belligerent satisfaction in saying these things aloud, to another man who obviously thought Esther cared about him. Around him time kept dissolving, fluid among his creations. His vain peacocks grumbling and departing one by one. Having fed, they conveniently forgot they depended on him for food. And yet centuries before the peacock had been thought vain it had been thought immortal, a bird of incorruptible flesh that time could never consume—the winged assertion of the soul. Who would have guessed that mystical bird, the beautiful with only its beauty to offer, would one day be seen as the ego's gaudy pride, with beauty utterly in discredit? So much for the so-called wisdom of ancient mystics.

So much for the idea of immortality.

He said, "People get it wrong. People who do nothing with their lives. They say I drowned myself in order to atone. They try to imagine what would make them act as I did. What if I didn't want to atone? What if I did it to join Esther's mother? They thought I must feel guilty for what Thérèse did to herself—"

I am saying too much, he thought, and to the wrong person. But why stop? There was faint liberation in the telling.

He said, "You commit suicide only when you can't live with yourself. When you can't live with someone else, you get a divorce. The point of suicide is to divorce yourself. Thérèse always judged herself too severely. The way I judged my sculptures. You can't live like that. She would quote me that absurd poem about choosing between a perfection of the life or of the work. And I would tell her that is never, never the choice. Or even the question."

"Is this what you've said to Esther?"

Simmons spoke as if it were no way to talk to a daughter.

"One time or another. We were still close when she was young. Though I lost all capability to give her anything as a father. So I put her in the hands of my aunt and then the hands of boarding schools. By the time she was old enough to understand, it was impossible between us."

Is that what you really believe? he thought violently. You can't convince even yourself of any of this, anymore.

"She speaks with great bitterness of all that time."

He said, "I didn't want to take away Esther's only saint. I thought one day she might find a new understanding of her mother. But she trusts her memory too much. She blames everything on how horrible I can be. To believe something else would mean she has to open herself to anger at her mother. And an anger at herself for wasting the last twenty years hating me."

"I think she already knows how much those years have cost her."

"She can't imagine. I came here because I didn't want her to waste any more time. I thought I might shock her into understanding. What a mistake that was. If you have an understanding with her, hold on to it as it is and as she is. Don't try to change it."

"I'm not convinced that's best for her," said Simmons.

"She'll choose for herself, don't worry."

Hold on to that treasure, he thought, even if it burns the skin from your hands.

"Maybe she won't choose. She hasn't so far. And a lot of wrong choices get made out of inertia." Simmons paused. "That's certainly what happened to me."

"You don't behave like an inert man. You came here."

"That was to find Esther. I meant in my work. Something happened to it, I'm not sure why." There was bitter nostalgia in his voice. "Before, it always felt natural. Then somehow, when I wasn't looking, I immobilized myself. For years now. And I can't seem to take any photographs I don't despise."

Echoes of difficult years stealing up like shadows in the sand: it could've been his own voice, reminding him.

You want my advice, he thought, my daughter doesn't even want conversation.

He said, "Listen to me. You must put that feeling as far away from yourself as possible. It strangled my work for many years and it has nothing to do with new work. It comes from caring too much about work already done. The vanity of having achieved. But if it was done in the past it was done by someone else. Another person. You must tell yourself that constantly. Then you have to start over, totally. Even though it is more difficult. Always, always start over."

His peacocks were dispersing into the other passages.

"I did my best work a long time ago," Simmons said. "That couldn't be clearer to me."

"You're still alive, aren't you? So you are standing on its shoulders. That means a lot. I would give anything for all the time you have left." And you will remember this conversation many years from now, he thought. "You want to do me a big favor?"

"If I can."

Simmons was staring all around, trying to memorize the place.

"Photograph this island and this shrine for me. As it is now. Before the journalists arrive, and the souvenir kiosks. Just as you saw it first. Like someone alone trying to find his way through. Every inch of it. No matter what happens to me. And whether Esther is with you or not."

"She'll be with me."

Words are only air. And all my peacocks are gone.

20

EINSTEIN NOT SLEEP AT ALL. WAKE ME early that morning like he some kind of revenge in the flesh. Wild as I ever seen him. Want to know why I not busy on the sloop, what he paying me for?

I tell him he keep this up I knock him far as Bimini. He get the message and back off but by this time I awake. So I go down to look after the sloop, better than listen to Cuban tantrum, and couple hours later, right when I tightening the stays, that Simpson turn up. Looking for Scully Moses, he say.

Whole damn island looking for Scully Moses. Like it payday and I got the money.

Simpson conversational as can be. Trying to get me say something obviously, not sure what. Maybe he got a tape recorder hid up the sleeve. I tell him I hope he not trying to trick me, things go very hard if that the case. He say no, no, he interested how I put sloop back together.

So I give the man the life story. Figure I wear him down that way. Tell him about one wife, two wife, three wife. Leave out a few in between. Tell him my father over on Cat, half a century gone, he have a sloop just like the MISS LINDA. Those the sponging days all up and down these islands, man, some year we find our way west on they Bahama banks till sea drop off deep as you can go. Then that sponge disease come, and some year so bad we nearly starve. Got a older brother, heart all shrivel up. Disease like sponge. Nine year old, he give a wave and that the end of him, man. But life go on.

All this time I working on that old lady sloop. I get the mast steep day before.

So Simpson get to talking too. Tell me he feel lucky he make it here other night, he catch a little rain on way over from San Sal.

Rain, eh? I say. You call that rain, boy?

I not gone let the man tell me about bad weather. I tell him he bone dry compare to hurricane I go through few years past.

He got the same look Einstein got when you tell him he daft. So I let him have the whole story. How Scully Moses the only survivor that whole turtling crew, sat on a boat turn over for three days off Eleuthera, while over Governor's Harbour they wailing and weeping in the churches and throwing up they hands and baking bread but too stupid even bother send someone out have a look. I tell him I see everything there is to see those three days, man, looking all around. Seen the ghost of my father, ghost my brother, seen the ghost of my second wife come floating past on she own boat, looking right straight at me. I scared I gone to join she, but I look the other way quick then she gone and I out there alone again. Lucky for me she not able to talk because she got plenty to say, boy, and that not the moment for it.

About this time Simpson start to show his hand. Say he had a talk with Einstein, he seem strange. I say the man strange as hell, that nothing new. Try six year here he want to see strange behavior.

Then he ask if Einstein give me any indication what he planning, once the daughter gone. You notice how they roll out long words when they in a corner.

Now I got to make a decision. Which side the man on? He

got to be on Einstein daughter side by now or else he getting more sleep than I imagine. That mean he not on Einstein side. But maybe old Einstein not on his own side, you never know. Complicated.

Not even worth discussing damn fool question of who on Scully Moses side.

Meanwhile I trying to get few shifty knots unravel. Take my time.

Finally I say, What you think, man? You see me working here on this boat, eh?

So you leaving little later on, he say.

You tell me, I tell him.

Had enough for this island, eh, man?

Maybe that your impression, I say, but that not really necessarily the case. Just to show this American bastard he not the only one with long words up the sleeve.

The old lunatic leaving with you? he say. That very very hard to believe.

Something like that, anyway. I busying away on the sloop. He think another long minute, take his damn time.

Where you think the Cuban decide to go? he ask. Not another Bahama island, sure.

How much you bet me? I say. Thinking all this time Einstein decide be brave, show they journalist trash how fast he think and he know I got good connections all up and down these islands, no one find him if Scully Moses in charge.

Time he leaving anyway, but this no way for man like him. Run off by some shit journalist with a camera. I not exactly sure even he know where he have in mind. And I for one be sorry see the man go. Only man in these Out Islands know how to get something done. You imagine someone else got his kind of patience round here? You imagine someone else make them Haitian monkeys tow the line? Cause Haitian like running water, man, it go where it want. I tell him many times, he got a future in these islands he want it. You offer him a seat in the Parliament, he clean out that Nassau trash before breakfast. Judge in they pokey wig.

But then that other thought come round in me. Left over from day before. Like bad food.

And I tell Simpson I not sure what old Einstein got in mind. Cause after all he not much of a praying man. He a man full of deceit and all kind of whatnot for getting his own way. Maybe he down on his knees more often he not have these problem. But when I think back how his face look yesterday, he got the look of a man who had enough.

Make me cold standing there in the sunlight even think that, but cold like I on the right track. It a real odd thing. I know a gal up Mayaguana way one year. Family say we got no idea she have it in she, how she can do this to we etcetera. Man, I take that gal home one night and I see right away she out of control. One month later, she take she own life. You see someone you got no idea what they say next, what they do next, not to mention they whole life disappearing another someone else pocket, you got to think maybe they capable.

So I say, Maybe Einstein capable after all. You never know. Maybe that why he want we sail up the islands. Leave me behind somewhere. Same trick he pull the last time.

And Simpson say he figure maybe Scully Moses right.

These Americans not so stupid, no wonder they got the whole damn Caribbean in they pocket.

Leave me standing there on the sand. Wings of a dove, man, wings of a dove.

But then I think maybe I got it wrong. Maybe he planning something big like invasion of Cuba, maybe he want I round up the Haitian monkeys again and we put up something else on some other damn island. Why not, man? Biggest damn thing ever happen in these Bahama Isles, only no one know it yet. Maybe we try up Exuma way this time, they never find old Einstein there and I still got a gal or two up that way. That all we lacking here, you know, this the man's big mistake. You know you got a fine piece of pie waiting for dessert every night, you calm down.

And I start thinking about what we gone to need. Already following wrong line of thought. Thinking about being out there on the sea again. Two sails swelling in the deep sight of the moon. Under hungry stars. Pretty, man. Loveliest thing you ever see. So lovely out there you not even thinking woman exist you got none with you. What you need woman for? You got everything else besides.

You say she ugly like ape, but my boat she beautiful, man. Not wavering like woman ashore, but moving so straight she clear self highway front of she. Where sea all tarnish like silver and clouds hanging so low they like a wig. And when she swing and sway like Marilyn Monroe, all the fish lag behind like boys down West Bay Street way. Follow this great big woman mystery, moving cross ocean with stars in she shrouds.

21

HE DREW BACK, INTO THE SHADE OF THE kitchen shed, when he saw his daughter coming down the path through the palms.

She didn't notice him. Resplendent in late morning light, she walked into the clearing as if she, too, were trying to memorize it.

It was shattering to stare at Esther and think this was almost the last time. He found himself seeing her as a blazing, unexpected creature. Not as someone half him, half Thérèse but an entirely new person, someone waiting to unbind herself from all the windings of the past. He saw clearly her beauty and the sense of hindered future. Swimming through a difficult life, having been given as a child such a difficult angel to wrestle with.

He made a shuffling sound and came out of the shadows. He went through the motions of being surprised to come upon her.

"There you are," he said.

They stood looking at each other.

"Did you swim today?" he asked.

She shook her head. "What about you?"

"I've been very busy."

She wasn't even looking at him, she had her head down.

She might have been counting her bare toes.

If you and I had arrived at something different, he thought, I would go back and surprise them all. Let the world know what I've done and turn my back again. There's an active immortality to rub their noses in, eh? De la Torre can produce more dead than the rest of them in good health.

Looking at his daughter, remembering what he had to do, he thought: Both of us will sleep more easily, very soon.

"I understand why you're going," he said. "Still, one day, before the rest of the world arrives, or before the jungle hides it, come have a look at what your father built."

"I've seen it."

What was she saying? What was that in her eyes? Blood pummeled his brain.

"You've seen it?"

"This morning."

"I can't believe it. Really?"

Impossible to restrain the abject pleasure in his voice. No wonder her shy reluctance to speak! No wonder her willingness to stand here with her father like an embarrassed daughter!

"Tell me about how you first went in." He imagined herds of Esthers entering different passages simultaneously. "How did you find it? I was in there an hour ago, we must've been crossing paths with each other—"

"I watched you come out. I waited until you'd gone."

He saw her gazing wide-eyed, dumfounded at the mosaics, reaching out to touch the walls, in wonderment at the shapes her father had made seashells assume, walking along gracefully in the whirling light, all colors at play, letting him draw her in to his understanding—

"So tell me where you started, which passage? There are so many, no?"

"Nothing to tell. I just went in."

"And you found your way through, you saw every corridor?"

No words to match the velocity of his thought.

"You worked hard," she said.

"It's the best work I've ever done."

He had been careful never to use this phrase once in his life since age nineteen.

His daughter only stared at him, as if unsure what to say.

"Come on," he said. "This makes the rest of it look like student work."

Well, not exactly, he thought. But it didn't hurt to be a little modest.

"It's a large mirror," she said.

"I changed my mind about what I wanted there." He added, "You haven't seen all of it, there's more, I promise you."

Come with me, I can show you now, what I made and hid and couldn't bear to gaze on until you were here because it was nothing but hope without you to see it with me—

"I was in there for an hour," she said in a strangely flat voice. "I must've seen most of it."

An hour? Only an hour to see the work of six years and a lifetime? Hadn't it made any deeper impression? Had none of the faces leapt out, meant more to her? Hadn't she recognized her mother in it?

He said, "You don't understand how it began. I did it in your honor, you know."

"You shouldn't say things like that, when you know they're not true." She might have been admonishing a child. "That's the glorious lie of the artist, pretending it's all a sacrifice for someone else. The real genius is convincing people you built it in anyone's honor but your own."

Time to retreat from the dream. He was faintly conscious of the American photographer upstairs in the house, listening.

"You didn't like it? It didn't—it didn't capture you?" he said in disbelief.

264

"What's it doing here?" she said. "Where no one else can see it? It's only for you, it's like some form of masturbation. It's not for anyone else."

"What's wrong with that?"

She said, "Now that I've seen it, may I go?"

Goddamn you, he thought.

His hand came up and he had slapped her before he could catch himself. The noise reverberated around the clearing.

What have I done, what have I done now. Too late.

His daughter's eyes were expressionless. They looked at him as they must have looked at his shrine, seeing nothing.

—

Uneasy at lunch, apparently not caring this was practically her last meal with her father, she glanced at Simmons from time to time and picked at the spiced lobster salad as if it might be poisoned. Whenever he tried to speak she rebuked him for his slap with stiff silence. He avoided Simmons's eyes, hating the kindness in them. Would it have cost her so much dignity to answer? It wasn't as if she'd have to endure his presence in her life for much longer.

They were finished eating in fifteen minutes. Esther had pushed back her chair, was beginning to collect the plates, when he said, "Leave them, Esther. I want us all to have some brandy together."

"In the middle of the day?" she asked.

"For courage," he murmured.

And here was Scully Moses, bearing three small glasses and a brandy named after another exile. Important to have the bottle with them on the boat in a few nights, to lend strength at the appropriate hour. Nearly the same moment as Thérèse had chosen.

Scully set down the brandy with a bang and said to

Simmons, "You head okay, man? Sure you not rather have a aspirin and rum combination?"

"That's all right."

"You go to a doctor he not give you that kind of treatment, you know."

"I know that," said Simmons.

For an instant Scully regarded Simmons and Esther with a single querying eyebrow, then glanced over at him to be sure he'd caught the dubious Bahamian gesture.

For six years, he thought, this man has been more enduring than the sand beneath my feet, the only thing I had here to depend on, the person who patiently solved every problem of the shrine when I couldn't think of a way. If I hadn't met him by accident, if he hadn't known this island, if he hadn't arranged my drowning and brought me here, I'd never have managed to keep it secret. Never been able to accomplish any of it. If he hadn't found the right protecting agent for the shells they'd have paled to nothing and it would all have been pointless. If he hadn't kept me going I'd never have waited this long for Esther. What a remarkable man this has been to know. If only it had all turned out differently.

He watched Scully lope away with the plates. Simmons poured out three glasses of brandy.

Esther said, "Thomas fixed his engine. He wants to wait and set off early tomorrow morning."

"To give ourselves plenty of time," said Simmons.

Away: we will never come back again. Never again to this place.

He said wearily, "Esther, I have something to tell you. Scully and I are leaving also. I'm not sure when. In a few days, a week. As soon as I organize things."

"Are you joking?"

"I'm telling the truth."

"Where are you going? Hollywood?"

"Up the islands."

She raised her head. "There's no need for you to leave. Thomas won't tell anyone."

"He found his way here. Anyone could. I don't want to be found."

"He was only looking for me," she said. "Where else are you going to go?"

"It doesn't matter. Some empty cay. Perhaps a short trip. A couple of weeks. Perhaps much longer. I haven't decided."

She said, almost gently, "You do need a vacation."

"We could leave sooner. If you both wanted to stay. Pinder can keep you supplied or pick you up when you decide to leave."

She only shook her head.

Words were folded somewhere in his throat. It was difficult to extract them. Treading water, he said, "Esther, there are things from here you'll want to take back with you." All business now. "The two Goyas. The photographs of your mother. Perhaps those drawings in your room. It would be a shame to leave them behind."

"Don't you want them here?"

Only a small surprise at that.

"It's probably safer for you to have them." He felt in his shorts pocket. "I never gave you your Christmas present." Just a few hours more, just a few hours to hold.

He pulled a worn paper bag from his pocket, handed it to her. "So you can't say in years to come that I didn't keep my promises."

She peered into the bag cautiously, as if it might contain a snake. She pulled out a small bundle of blue silk and tentatively unfolded it: a Persian scarf.

"I remember," she said.

"So that you have at least some of the history straight, I bought it for your mother in 1963. In Isfahan."

267

Esther said quietly, "Thank you," and put the scarf back into the paper bag.

"Aren't you going to try it?"

"Later."

Perhaps I won't get to see it later, he thought. Never mind. I'll tell Thérèse you looked lovely in it.

He said, "It's the last of her things I have. Except her ring." I will take that back to her, he thought.

He was already tired of treading water.

She said, "I'm going to take a nap. Thank you for thinking of the scarf."

Is this how it ends? he thought. One word from you could stop me. One word.

God Almighty, he was drowning already. Dipping below the surface and thrashing.

He said, "I wish there were enough left between us to pass the time of a second brandy."

Brandy in his throat, not sea water, made his head whirl. He came up gasping for air and said, "Before you go, listen to me."

She'd pushed back her chair.

"Your mother wasn't half the woman you are, Esther. She didn't have your confidence. She didn't have your courage. She was all instinct. She didn't have your intelligence, she couldn't move independently in the world as you can. She had enormous problems with the idea of my work, with the time it took. She had enormous problems with what to do with herself." The waves closed over him. "She even took a lover, a year before she killed herself."

"I know," said his daughter. "Do you really blame her?"

The betrayed man, the lost man, the guilty man in him said weakly, "How do you know that?"

"I found some letters he wrote her. Hidden away in a cupboard at Nerja. Years and years ago."

Letters? Suddenly it was as if twenty-two years had not passed and the man had written Thérèse that very day.

He managed to stammer, "I thought she took them with her."

"It doesn't matter. He wasn't the problem."

"I want to see them."

"I destroyed them. A long time ago."

"What gave you the right to do that?"

"I didn't think you should see them. I thought you hadn't known."

All these years he thought he'd been protecting her, she'd been protecting him. Thinking she understood why her mother had taken on someone else. Thinking he had not been man enough to hold onto Thérèse. Thinking her mother had not loved him that last year or longer. Understanding nothing.

"But you don't see," he said. "She couldn't bear that I had this other life." Her face was indistinct, merging with another before him in noon glare. "She didn't feel sure in being herself. She couldn't bear being only your mother. Or my wife."

Everything he said, all the words that came unbidden to his lips, was wrong.

"Who made her feel so unsure?" said his daughter. "Who still does his best to make everyone around him feel that way?"

"That's not true."

He caught from the corner of his eye Simmons watching them both with, of all things, skepticism.

Esther was standing. "I'm going up for a rest."

He said, "When your friend is finished photographing here, take a close look at his pictures. Then you can see if what I built for you and your mother looks like masturbation."

She said, "You make it very difficult for someone to feel sorry for you."

"I don't want pity, I want conversation."

At least Simmons had the sense to follow her upstairs.

He waited until they had both vanished. He pushed back his chair, feeling the brandy unreasonable in his knees.

Enjoy the brandy. Enjoy my daughter.

He set off down the obscurity of his path; the palms made way for him. The entire sky was awash with sunlight. It annexed the shadows on the sand into tiny kingdoms through which he passed in safety. He was walking to the barren edge of the world. It was a strange country but he knew the way there, and he was not alone in walking.

In his dream they came to a twisted tree, gnarled and broken. There was no sea here, only a cracked and burnished landscape. He had failed her, but Esther was walking beside him, listening to his final admonition.

My daughter, he was saying, I will show you the last drop of dew as it slides off the last green leaf of the last branch of the last tree on earth.

But when he turned to see her face she was no longer there and he was alone, an old man standing at the edge of the world, talking to himself.

22

IT WILL NOT ALWAYS BE LIKE THIS. IN sunlight I watch you walk in splendor across a dazzling ocean. Only now you are walking toward me, not away. Still your breath is ice.

I never hear you speak, I can barely remember the music of your voice. Sometimes I think I have invented it. I still have all the books you gave me with their careful inscriptions. Each one a contract, keeping me a child and you a loving mother who can never be anything else.

Sometimes I cannot see around you. You are either before me wholly or gone, either in the world with me or vanished entirely, never in the next room over, waiting. It is my father who is there, eavesdropping. You are never with him.

Sometimes I try to imagine you as you might look if it had gone differently. If you had been different, or he. I can't imagine you older, I only see a cartoon of you old, then I see myself at the age you were when you left. Our images turn and change like Renaissance dancers who touch parchment hands, fingertips, and go.

Sometimes I sense you listening. He says he feels you here also but that is his wish, his invention.

You left me here with him, you abandoned me to this place. Because you felt I was stronger even as a child than you could be as a woman. I would have given you all the strength I had, we could have been strong together.

Look at this sea shiver beneath changing light. I would never have imagined the world would give me so little back. That the years would use you up until you were only an indistinct memory of arms holding me, too many places thought about too often, a snapshot montage gone over so many times I can no longer bring myself to look again. I have rationed you out over so many days and nights hungry for the sight of you that now there is little of you left that is not my invention.

My father owns you now. Owns not only my memories of you but all those other thousands that are only his, the rest of you I will never know. One day all this will be lost, then the possibility of you will never come back to me.

I have decided to tell you I cannot speak to you anymore. I cannot think about you anymore. I can feel both of you between me and someone else. Perhaps this man, or anyone. I can no longer walk from here to there without feeling you blocking me and I can't go around you.

It will not always be like this.

I know it isn't you, it's someone I've invented. Not the person who loved me and whom I do remember faintly, beneath all the meanings I have wrapped you in. Behind your utter silence. Some days I hear you speak very faintly and believe it really is you I hear, but then my father joins you and it frightens me to see the two of you together.

Perhaps there will be another day, years from now, when we can speak again. When you will see me and feel proud finally of who your daughter became. When you will regret not having stayed.

Sometimes I imagine you out there, suspended in deep space like a wild unruly star, and I hear you whispering that you wish you hadn't done what you did.

Sometimes I imagine you blaming me, that were it not for me you could have simply walked away from him years before and gone on to someone else. You could've taken me with you, though.

Sometimes I imagine you as a breath that has passed from the planet in silence. Like a wind long since replaced by others. So I am your breeze, left behind.

Sometimes I imagine your body picked at by the ocean, your skin worn away and your white bones gleaming, washed far from that cold shore. Caught on an undersea reef somewhere and encrusted with coral, transformed into something majestic and blooming.

He has these thoughts too. The same thoughts of you. I can hear them in every letter he writes, I feel them around him like a vaporous radiation. He surely feels them coming off me. You have left us with nothing else to think about and this is why we cannot bear each other's sight, why it renders us incapable of human speech, because we cannot talk about how little you left us with and now, twenty-two years on, there is nothing else to say or do.

Because I remember how little he loved you at the end, like a man imprisoned, he makes me wonder if this is what you saw when you looked at me. Is this why you left? Didn't you realize all I would have given you to stay?

It will not always be like this. I cannot keep you any longer, I cannot hold you here with me anymore, I have nothing to hold on to when I think about you. I see the same empty-handedness in his eyes, he must see it in mine. And I realize I have nothing more, after so much time, to say to either one of you.

I used to feel splendor when I thought of us together, I would feel touched by a distant glory when I could look in the mirror and see ever so slightly how I had come to resemble you. I thought this little splendor like a gift from you, a floating enchantment that I might inherit. All these years I depended on it and neglected daring my own. And after so many years wasted, to have to come finally to this remote island to say good-bye. To both of you. I look in the mirror and see no splendor there, only a sullen residue left after all splendor has passed, and the echo of so much withheld.

I can no longer separate the two of you in my thought. When he is dead it will be even worse that way.

I want you to know that even though it frightens me to think of going away without you, without the feeling you might be there beside me again one day, still I know this is what you would want. I know you felt yourself a poison to me, I know this is why you took yourself away from me forever. It has taken me a long time, too long, to understand this, to pull myself away from you.

There will be perhaps some other time when it is safe to feel you near me again.

I have missed you without knowing ever who you really were, this was my lack but you could have chosen to speak to me, to answer, to give me more, to tell me I was wrong in my judgments or right in my instincts or at least how to go about finding my own splendor. Not to rely on something reflected from my idea of you and then to see it vanish, abandoning me here in a place where I don't belong.

And a place that I cannot believe you have ever seen or were ever near. It frightens me to feel this, to say I was really alone all those years I felt certain you were with me, felt your unsure hand brushing mine. I am going to stop wondering about this, very soon.

How long it takes for these afternoons to creep in and settle until the light slips away. Little by little until it is too late. Then there is only starlight on the ocean, glittering, and how little of that light comes from you.

23

THE AFTERNOON WAS WAN WITH MUTED
sunlight. Thomas could just make out the ocean becalmed
beneath a hazed sky. Only a faint line, a lie of perspective, to
show where the world ended.

An hour before, she'd lashed out when he tried to explain
her father's request, for him to seriously photograph the
maze. He had considered keeping it from her until after they
left the island; it had been difficult enough earlier, persuad-
ing her to wait until tomorrow morning to depart. His vague
idea was to return as soon as possible with plenty of film and
equipment. But he'd found himself uncomfortable with the
idea of not telling her, and their ensuing argument ended in
silence. They lay down for a nap, the exhaustion of the day
before still on him, they didn't make love, and she stayed far
outside the reach of his arms on a bed ten miles wide.

When he awoke at the height of afternoon heat she was
already gone. He went searching; she wasn't on the beach.
Having to look for her awakened his old annoyance, his
resolve. Eventually he found her picking her way aimlessly
through the shallow pangola grass, within sight of the sea.

He hadn't brought it up after lunch, but he was certain she
hadn't seen the maze, no matter what she'd told her father—
that much Spanish Thomas could understand. It was her lie,

275

to equal all de la Torre's. Thomas had heard it in her silences, seen it in how she avoided her father's glance at the table.

Now she stood in the pangola grass and watched him come toward her. She obviously wanted only to be left alone: they were back to where they'd been when he'd followed her into the gardens of the ruined hotel.

"I didn't hear you get up," he said. "I was all over looking for you."

He came near but not close enough to touch her.

"I can't believe you're considering this," she said. "Don't you see what he's trying to do?"

"I think he's right. Someone should capture this place while it's still untouched."

"You don't know him. He's simply hoping you'll decide to stay, so I'll have to stay. He'll do anything to get what he wants."

"You didn't have any problem telling him you'd seen what he built."

"What makes you think I haven't?"

He shrugged. "By now I know when you're not telling the truth."

"Listen, you stay here and photograph all you like. I'll take your boat back myself. I'll send Pinder over to pick you up in a week. Be sure to stop off in Geneva on your way to the photo lab."

She set off angrily toward the path. As he caught up with her she said despairingly, "Why couldn't we have met on the way back from here!"

He said levelly, "It would take so little to change things with your father. A few more days—"

"Nothing's going to happen in a few more days. Twenty years haven't changed anything."

He said, "You didn't have to come here, did you?"

"He wrote me he was dying."

"Did you believe him?"

"I wanted to believe him." She nodded as if he had reminded her of something. "I thought it would be worth trying once more."

"You should believe him this time."

She said tightly, "I don't know what that means."

They were on the path now.

"What do you think he's really planning to do?"

"He's run out of strategies, so he says he's leaving. It's another case of cancer to keep us here. Like asking you to do the photographs. He's not going anywhere. Where would he go?"

"There are hundreds of uninhabited cays. That's not—"

"This is the only one that interests him. He's trying to get us to wait around and talk him out of it. To be concerned, to worry, to discuss it, to persuade him not to. All to make us stay here with him."

Thomas said, with a trace of impatience, "It would be a generous gesture, before he leaves. As a last chance."

"What did he tell you?"

"Nothing. Scully told me a little. I'm convinced they are actually leaving."

"Scully says anything my father asks him to. Suppose he is going on vacation, what's wrong with that? I'll help him pack."

He heard for the first time, beneath the pain, the hint of hysteria in her voice.

He tried to speak as calmly as possible. "Esther, you know that if you didn't love him you wouldn't have come here."

"That's not true," she said. "Trust me, nothing's more unbearable than some man giving you a psychological report after one week together."

"Why do you think this can wait? If you didn't love him you'd have gone back to Geneva, no matter how ill he was."

She said with accusation, "You have no idea what I've gone through because of him. I came here because—" She hesitated. "It's what my mother would have wanted me to do."

He said gingerly, "And what will you do when he dies?"

"I won't believe it."

He lost his temper. "You sound just like him. Stop complaining and think for a minute. If you leave, does he have any reason to go on living? He knows what a burden he is to you. He knows how unhappy you are."

"Did he tell you to start making speeches at me?"

"He told me not to waste my time."

"He was right."

"Esther, don't pretend he doesn't understand what you live under."

"I don't think you understand!" she burst out. "And you could have waited to talk about this some other time. He was a burden to my mother, too, look how unhappy he made her."

"Perhaps she felt she was a burden to him," he said. "Perhaps he feels a burden to you the same way."

"You don't know anything about my mother."

He saw she was barely holding herself in check.

"I don't. But I can see that your father hasn't gotten over her death, either." He put out a hand gently; she took two steps away from him, as if retreating from a fire.

She said, "Why should I forgive him? He wouldn't even speak to her the last month. He didn't turn sentimental until it was too late to save her."

"You must have forgiven your mother for not being with you when you were growing up."

She said bitterly, "How could I be angry with her? She was so unhappy she wanted to die. If I were that unhappy, too, I'd—" She swallowed hard, wheezing.

He said, "Esther, both my parents are dead, there's nothing I can say to them. If there's any forgiving to be done, you'd better do it now. Because I don't think he'll bother to live very long otherwise."

Her eyes widened as she realized what he was suggesting.

"What do you think happened back then?" Her voice faltered. "I wasn't responsible before, and I'm not —"

She broke off. Her face contorted and for an instant her whole soul was in her eyes: the Esther who never showed herself or spoke and who was always in hiding, the Esther he had wanted to photograph.

Then she turned and ran, along the palms and up the path, plunging down the branch of it that led to the maze.

For a moment he was so surprised he couldn't move. He called out to her but she didn't turn and then she was gone.

He ran after her. The broken light cast imprisoning shadows on the path. They hadn't been far from the entrance, and as he hurried through the colonnade of palms, he saw her disappear past the wall of rock.

He made the left-hand turn at the path's end into the maze and came upon the first watching man, who seemed to be looking at him strangely—why? Then he saw that one of the eyes was smashed. Several shells lay in the sand, ordinary brown periwinkles now, devoid of intelligence, and he realized he had lost her.

———

She ran through the first corridor of the shrine barely seeing what was on the walls around her, a rock gripped in her hand like some talisman. Around its edges her fingers bled slightly, cut by the shells in her father's eyes. She whacked at a few butterfly shells in the ocean vista as she ran past. By the deformed tree weeping tears of blood rose another tree surrounded by seven girls, her father's wrathful face in the middle of the trunk—she smashed at his face even as she saw him loom large again, beckoning at the end of the corridor.

His eyes dared her to smash them again. He was taller than she and she had to stretch her arm. The rock glanced off his cheek. Behind her Thomas was yelling her name and she ran to another corridor, past many birds limned against black night, feeling a plaintive panic course through her. Now her father was covering his eyes, unable to look at her. She spared him. There was her father's tiny face hiding in a crowd by a medieval harbor—she destroyed it in one blow— here he stood large again, looking weary at all the destruction she'd wrought. She smashed at his false self-pitying mouth.

The maze branched again, trying to confuse her. She knew only that as long as she kept running there were more images of her father to attack. Behind her was someone who would try to prevent her. It was like hurrying through the labyrinthine corridors of her father's brain, glimpsing the images that tormented him over and over, the destruction of the men on the discovered island, the angels roaring down from heaven, the peacock image burning before the dying men. The colors leapt out at her in the garish daylight but she was searching only for her father's face. She was satisfied to see its likeness in one of the disembodied heads hacked by the angels; she left that one alone.

She no longer heard Thomas following. Here was her father naked before her, a young man, her own age. Such a mild face. She slammed the rock into his genitals and then followed a severe corner of night and birds into a great semicircle with a narrow passage at the far end. Around the walls was Havana: plazas, the cathedral, the castle with its old cannon, the baroque streets, and the café that went on and on, face after face. Here was the inflated man with the cigar she remembered, there the grandparents she'd never known, the boyhood house with its courtyard of flowers and statues. Dead friends, an old world crowding her father's mind.

She heard someone wheezing frantically beside her and she realized it was her own asthmatic gasping, a plank of ironwood down her spine. She had enough breath to seek out her father in his café, conveniently seated at eye level as she stood before him. Ignoring the pinpricks of cuts on her hand, she swung the rock again and again at his head.

There he stood once more, at another corner, beckoning her out. Another of him to smash. She was drenched in sweat. She put her hands on her knees and tried to regain the breath to run at him. When she did she faltered and nearly fell. The rock slipped from her hands and glanced off his feet. He stood laughing at her. She went over and attacked him with her fists. The shells bit hungrily at her raw fingers.

She stumbled through shadows and found herself scraping along a narrow walled passage that she had to slip through sideways. Her head was pounding with the effort of breathing and she felt the wooden plank forcing her throat. There were no mosaics on this passage and it went on endlessly; she pulled herself along, using the wall for support. Just as she thought she might faint, the passage opened abruptly on her left and she fell through onto the sand.

Her ankle twisted as she went down. She felt it protest and go every which way as she tried to pick herself up. Heat enveloped her head. When she straightened up an unreal daylight blasted her face, blinding her, and she cried out and put a hand to her eyes. She stood in a vast garden, a huge central chamber of her father's brain. A great mirror covered one entire wall; it seemed to have swallowed her. Peacocks were glowing within its territory and regarding her proudly, like a prize captive. Light came at her from all directions, strengthened in the mirror's depths.

She was going to fall. Sweat was in her eyes, her hair. She reached up to wipe the sweat away and felt blood coursing down her arms in rivulets. All those eyes hemming her in.

Before her in the sand lay several rocks, one as large as her head. She went to it, wrapped her bleeding hands and wrists around its hardness, managed to lift it. As she did so she saw Thomas come from a corner of the mirror. So he was in the mirror with her. But far away: he said something but a fine singing pain was in her ears and she couldn't make out the words. Her breathing, inhumanly loud, had taken over all other sound.

She heaved both arms up. The effort nearly toppled her backward, but she regained her balance. She walked forward and, as she gained momentum, threw herself the last few feet. She felt her entire body catapult the rock toward the mirror, and as it left her hands she felt herself flying right behind it.

Then the heavens came down. Unearthly explosions engulfed her as the vast mirror shattered; they went on for several seconds, all up and down its length, and as shards of glass began to fall she instinctively put up her hands to protect her head. She scrambled back from the avalanche of mirror. It seemed to start for a long time and then gather momentum all over the sky. Sand rose in clouds around her and she couldn't see. She heard glass still falling with heavy plops. As the risen sand drifted the thick air was sweltering and began to choke her.

As if in afterthought, a few pieces of glass tinkled off the rock wall and died in the sand. She pulled herself to her feet.

She stood transfixed, gaping at what she'd done. She felt her mouth loll open. Her legs were trembling. She sensed Thomas approaching her cautiously.

Where the mirror had hung the high wall of rock surged out in full mosaic, a final burst of vibrant color. It was an image not meant to be seen, a hidden signature that stared her down where she stood.

Again it began at the base as a sandy shore that touched blue ocean. In the foreground two peacocks faced each other.

Beyond them, towering, were the detailed images of a man and woman in repose on the sand, hands barely clasped, fingers just touching. They were nude, the man her father in middle-age. The woman was serene, her body brave, raven-haired and as tall as Cristóbal. They were watching, before them, a little girl playing with shells in the sand, playing in the safety of knowing both parents were watching over her from nearby. Her father's other hand stroked the little girl's hair; her mother's free hand lay across the little girl's foot. Behind them lay the blue sea of butterfly shells; above, the sky deepened to a black midnight of many stars and the rolling waves of heaven. Among the waves the destructive angels, benign with folded wings, looked down on the watching man and his wife and daughter and gave blessing, the blessing of possible futures, from the last wall of Eden.

Gazing at her mother, her father, herself between them as she knew they had been once, she heard herself weeping.

She stood hugging herself with both hands on her cheeks, seeing her mother's loveliness, waiting for it to speak and embrace her. She saw her parents' fingers intertwined, saw the living hands grip each other. She saw how stalwart, how free in her play the little girl was between them, with the force of her parents' hands running through her from head to foot.

Blood was trickling down her forearms and her shoulders shook. She let go of herself. She did not seem to hear Thomas come to her, but when he put out his arms she felt herself move into them willingly. Her arms went around him and her hands clasped painfully at his back. Over his shoulder she could still see the mosaic rising above her.

Her face, wet with tears, was against his. He held her and

a moment later she realized that she had shut her eyes; the image still rose before her and when she opened her eyes again it was still there. She whispered, "Why did I make him wait so long?"

24

IN THE HARSH REMAINING SUNLIGHT HE felt like a phantom. He mopped his brow with the edge of the T-shirt. The afternoon was already edging in on him, the end of the day gathering speed like a murderous locomotive.

Before him Scully was fiddling with the sail canvas. In the palm shadows the Bahamian looked eternal, a patient man preparing to set sail. Out to sea a wind was scarring the water, the sun hurrying toward late afternoon, toward dusk, toward nightfall. The sky was widening. Three days ago from out of that sky had come his own attacking angel.

Give Esther what she wants, he thought. Perhaps she will not fail a child of her own as I failed her. Unless, years from now, she comes to feel she failed me, and this is all perpetuated.

How would it be, to have two parents who gave up? Is that what I want to leave her with? Isn't that what I am trying to prevent?

Believe that, try to believe that until one last nightfall.

Lord, I have coveted this island and this time here. But only so I could give it away when I chose. Only out of a deep cherishing. I am sorry to finish so badly but in the end Thérèse and I were right for each other, proven two of a kind.

He felt a breeze rising. The sloop was ready; to linger after

Esther left would be pointless. The tide would turn in another hour. He would depart when it turned four times more, not a day from now. If he stayed awake all tomorrow afternoon, out in the sun on an open boat after little sleep, when night descended he would not have to swim for long. He looked down the generous stretch of beach, past the tip of the island. Soon he would be out there, beneath a white triangle of sail, gathering light on the blue swells, heading—where?

To Thérèse.

"Einstein." Scully had his hands on the gunwale. "You sure you want to leave, man?"

Cristóbal felt his heart stutter. "Try anything," he said.

Scully Moses laughed. "You asking for a bad reputation, you go round say things like that." His eyes measured the slant of the mast. "Maybe it time we get this gal in the water. You feel strong enough?"

"I could do it alone."

For some reason he could not catch his breath. He leaned wearily against the sloop's white hull. He thought: Thank you, island, for giving me this chance to give in return all the beauty I had left in me. I am sorry to leave but I ran out of hope, and you could no longer give me that.

"You all right, Einstein?"

"I'm all right."

Scully squinted down the beach.

"Aha," he said. "You rest, Einstein, we got help on the way. That bastard always turn up when you not expecting him."

Cristóbal whirled. Far down the beach two figures were walking toward them.

"Coming to say bye-bye, Einstein."

Surely they could not be leaving now, not this late in the afternoon, could they really be coming to shove off in their boat? To say their farewell already? He found himself struggling to walk in the hot sand, the sun unforgiving on his face. Couldn't they wait until morning? He could see that Esther had her hands wrapped in some material, and Simmons had his arm around her. He could not yet make out their faces.

He tried to think of something to say to her, tried to prepare himself to speak but his mind was absolutely empty. The sea and sky seemed to upend around him. For a moment he thought numbly he must be having a heart attack. But he was still moving, that couldn't be it, it was fear, blank fear of what she might say to him, fear of her saying good-bye for the last time.

Stand where you are, he thought, don't walk toward her, it will last longer if you stand still.

Yet there would still be good-bye.

He felt his legs quiver and he thought: Look at you, cowardly old man, no wonder she doesn't love you. He felt his chest begin to heave, and sweat run down his legs onto the sand. He thought she looked different, though he could not say how.

Stand up, stand up, don't collapse, he thought.

Then he realized that all this time her eyes had not left his.

Heart, be still.

She left Thomas's side and came forward alone. Her face broke like pure sunlight flashing on open water, and she said in Spanish, quietly, "Father," and when she ran to him across the sand, and flung her arms about his neck, he felt another, more familiar pair of woman's arms receive him again into their softness, finally.

25

ANOTHER AFTERNOON. THOMAS LEFT her asleep in the house and walked down the path to the beach. In the distance the white sail was faint enough to be an imagined thing against the solid blue of the ocean, and he did not watch it for long. He headed down the path to the shrine and walked through, scarcely glancing at the walls. He knew his way around it now.

In the garden of the peacocks his shadow dissipated on the sand. A wind followed him, bearing the afternoon scents of the entire island. With the wind, singly, came the peacocks, expecting the food that the old man always left in the sand. Thomas moved among the living birds, and from a bag he scattered bread, crumbling it as he threw it to them. Their din was tremendous.

The sun descended into the palms beyond the walls of the garden and the shadows lengthened. He found his own shadow revealed to him on the sand by the departing peacocks. He looked around at the faces of the people, the wild animals and birds, the three figures interlocked beneath angels. All the watching eyes regarded him dutifully. They seemed charged with waiting, with the absence of the actual human in this garden of the divine. How much longer to wait, in Eden?

Then Esther entered the garden, and took his hand. One by one the stars came out in their far-flung allegiances, Venus first. As evening deepened into night the stars cast their faint light upon the earth, upon this island. The moon had not yet risen, and with the clouds there was barely enough starlight to see her face. When the wind of nightfall finally came up she led him out of the garden of the peacocks. It was growing cold, and they were alone on the island now, with only each other.

—

Out on the reaching ocean, immersed in night, he looked into the deep sky: black cavern of stars. Eyes watching him, wherever he went. Beside him his companion was silent; soon enough they would reach a larger island, the warm lights of other lives.

He looked back to the low brooding form of Desirada. It lay like a darker mass above the horizon of full dark sea, below the spilling trail of the Milky Way. He could just make out the white roar of reefs before it, subdued, almost voiceless to him now but whose echoes filled his brain, calling to him. He felt their hold on him slipping. When would he be back? Another life, now, as he reckoned time. The sluggish ocean held aloft his hurrying boat as a stiff breeze guided it. He listened harder and heard the waves bravely whisper to him across the reef as they had whispered every night, intimate with shared secrets, trying to pull him back.

And abruptly he realized he was hearing the murmur of other reefs, not his own, and he knew he had missed the last moment of possession. But had that island ever truly been his? He had belonged to it, surely, and now every wave pulled him farther and farther away. He wondered if he could sustain himself without that island.

Then the moon finally rose, and light flashed on the far reefs of Desirada, illuminating a torrent of white water before the departing island. He gave a cry at the sight, and felt the vision break within him. He stood up unsteadily in the boat, the taut wind whipping at his face, and sensed the force that had tied him to the island release him from those bonds. His straggly white hair was blowing wildly about his face, the urgent world turning beneath his feet. Out in the black waters fish were burrowing, life was teeming. The thought gave him strength, and the strange accident of his own life seemed suddenly a charmed thing, out on this sea beneath a night sky extravagant with stars, and he felt a blessing descend on him, as if there were no more tasks required of him by God.

The boat heaved. He lost his footing and nearly fell; only his companion's hand saved him. When he looked again the island was lost to sight.